HER HERE

HER HERE

Amanda Dennis

Bellevue Literary Press
NEW YORK

First published in the United States in 2021 by
Bellevue Literary Press, New York

For information, contact:
Bellevue Literary Press
90 Broad Street
Suite 2100
New York, NY 10004
www.blpress.org

© 2021 by Amanda Dennis

Library of Congress Cataloging-in-Publication Data
Names: Dennis, Amanda, author.
Title: Her here / Amanda Dennis.
Description: First edition. | New York : Bellevue Literary Press, 2021.
Identifiers: LCCN 2020002400 (print) | LCCN 2020002401 (ebook) |
    ISBN 9781942658764 (paperback ; acid-free paper) | ISBN 9781942658771 (ebook)
Classification: LCC PS3604.E58633 H47 2021 (print) | LCC PS3604.E58633 (ebook) |
    DDC 813/.6--dc23
LC record available at https://lccn.loc.gov/2020002400
LC ebook record available at https://lccn.loc.gov/2020002401

Bellevue Literary Press would like to thank all its generous
donors—individuals and foundations—for their support.

This publication is made possible by the New York State
Council on the Arts with the support of Governor Andrew M.
Cuomo and the New York State Legislature.

This project is supported in part by an award from
the National Endowment for the Arts.

Book design and composition by Mulberry Tree Press, Inc.

Bellevue Literary Press is committed to ecological stewardship in our book production practices,
working to reduce our impact on the natural environment.

♾ This book is printed on acid-free paper.

Manufactured in the United States of America
First Edition

1   3   5   7   9   8   6   4   2

paperback ISBN: 978-1-942658-76-4

ebook ISBN: 978-1-942658-77-1

for my parents
and for Laura

Toti se inserens mundo

—Seneca

Our vanity, our passions, our spirit of imitation,
our abstract intelligence, our habits have long
been at work, and it is the task of art to undo
this work of theirs, making us travel back in
the direction from which we have come to the
depths where what has really existed
lies unknown within us.

—Marcel Proust

Contrary to what people say, using the first
person in films is a sign of humility.
All I have to offer is myself.

—Chris Marker

HER HERE

I

The View from Elsewhere

1

I HAVE BEEN UP ALL NIGHT and now the day is gray, the narrow streets slick and silvered outside the taxi window. Sleeplessness gives the city an unreal, varnished air—shops, shutters, pigeons, and trees all flickering and chromed, like movie stills cut together in the old way.

The driver stops alongside stone steps that lead uphill. He tells me again that the street I am looking for does not exist. On the ride from the airport, he spoke of his childhood in Montmartre, of parties in squares strung with lights, where children were allowed to stay up dancing. As he spoke, he looked into the rearview mirror, his gaze warm, soliciting. Sometimes I give the impression of not paying attention, but I'm gleaning all I can from the present, encoding it carefully. It is unlikely that this man, who has lived here all his life, does not know my street. Perhaps he is right. None of it is real: Siobhán, the flat, the missing girl.

I find the place Marcel-Aymé on my GPS and show the driver. His bright laugh fills the car. He swivels into reverse. Maybe I was mispronouncing the name.

On the square, which exists, my eyes travel up the building façade, balcony after balcony, to a dome with a topmost window, which will be mine. Through sheets of cloud, sun strikes the wet brick and stone. Looking up like that gives me vertigo. By the door, which faces the square, a tree sways under its burden of pink, excessive blooms.

At the square's far end, people are gathered. They are looking at something hidden from my view by their windbreakers and backpacks. When the group drifts away, I approach, leaving my suitcase by the door.

The statue is of a man stuck in the wall—or emerging. I can't tell. His face of dark bronze is resigned. His fingers, long and expressive, reach toward me out of the stones, rubbed gold by many eager, living hands. As I move to touch the fingers, a high, shrill voice stops me.

—Isa!

A woman from the tourist group is gazing at me from the street.

—Isa! she says again, and runs down the slope that joins the street to the square.

Embarrassed, I stand still, my legs taking root among the stones. My face is one people think they know, and strangers will often tell me I remind them of someone. When she sees me up close, this woman, too, will find some detail in my face to set her right. She'll apologize, ashamed of her error, but aglow with the memory of whomever she took me for.

Now she runs across the square, her black hair loose behind her, her low heels unsteady on the cobblestones. She reaches me, breathless, and takes my hands, pressing them to her chest. Her forehead is broad, and her eyes are black and wet with tears.

—Isabelle, she says.

Her smile makes me want to smile, too.

—No, I say.

She steps back and studies me, probing my gaze for recognition.

—But Isabelle, it's you. Of course it's you.

She laughs again, but more sadly this time, performing a calculation.

—If it was you, you wouldn't tell me, she says, squeezing my hands.

Her touch is warm, her skin a little dry.

—No, I'm not her. I'm not Isa. My name is Elena. I'm sorry.

I *am* sorry. I've hurt her without meaning to. To appease her, I ask:

—When did you know Isa? Isabelle?

The ground of stones swells up like the sea, and the woman looks at me with such confusion that I turn away, embarrassed, and move quickly with my suitcase into the building.

Leaning against a wall of mirror in the foyer, I watch her retreat across the square. A scene like this shouldn't bother me so much, but the world is strange today. I've been awake all night, crossing the ocean, and now I can't shake her look of need. I'm not Isa, but the time I've lived and don't remember deprives me of certainties. I'm sick of grasping, *still*, for the strong, solid shore where life can begin.

I imagine myself arriving at Ella's door—or finding her on a beach or in a square—and saying, *Ella, Ella! Do you know how long your mother—your real mother—has been looking for you?* I'll bring them together, mother and daughter. I can do nothing for the woman outside, but I can help Siobhán. I believe that Ella is alive and can be found.

I carry my suitcase up seven flights to the flat that is to be mine. My mother was British, and, though my accent is American, she has left me with certain words, ways of saying. Taking the key from under the carpet, I twist it in the lock until the door opens onto a studio with high ceilings and parquet floors, dormer

windows and false balconies, balustrades beyond which the city
flickers under exchanges of sun and cloud. I find Ella's journals
immediately, on a table by the entrance, stacked under a Post-it
with my name on it. Six books, all with hard canvas backings and
each a different color. They seem both childish and prematurely
ancient. I open one. Beige cover. Sharp scent of its paper is full of
elsewhere. The handwriting is neat, round letters anchored to the
lines of every page. Some entries are a paragraph, others much
longer. I turn to a page at random and begin to read:

> *A Lanna house has no borders. Walls are doors, open
> to breezes blown across rice fields, orange orchards, and
> tea plantations. Jasmine is everywhere, on the highway
> with its trucks and motorcycles and at the roadside
> pineapple stands and noodle shops. I first noticed it on
> the tarmac of the tiny airport—its sweet, heavy scent.*

It's ridiculous to feel this frisson and hint of smell from words
alone. A thought flies up, made of sounds: *I'd rather be her than
here.* It doesn't make sense. Ella could be dead. Maybe Siobhán is
deluded to think she can be found. No. Siobhán is strange—secretive and intense—but not deluded. And she has lost a daughter—
twice. Once given up, once taken away by the world.

Flipping through the pages, I feel embarrassed, catching
phrases not meant for my eyes.

Her is Ella. She is so alive in her journals, the way I want to be.
Looking for her feels urgent, a task with clear edges, purpose. She
is someone I might love.

Here is a room with wide windows, a metallic sky rising like
a dome over rooftops and monuments. Far below, in a park,
branches are bone white under veils of leaves. Nothing moves,

and it is cold for early summer. The clean white emptiness of the studio flat makes me think of Irigaray, that feminist philosopher of watery things, who thought women use pronouns differently than men, who cast herself as the marine lover of Nietzsche, and who—a professor once told me this—lived in a white apartment, wore only white, and would not let others touch her. This is what I see. Others might say what a nice flat this is.

Here is also the city I left a month ago. Returning to it now—audaciously, as if the place were a sort of home—I feel its foreignness more acutely. The language still trips my tongue, and I don't know this part of town. I was probably wrong to return.

Today is the sixteenth of June. The date is significant because Ella began the journals on the same day eight years ago. Siobhán must know this, working carefully as she does.

When Ella disappeared more than six years ago, her adoptive parents conducted a search in Thailand. The detective failed to turn up anything—only a few interviews (inconclusive) in the village where she lived. Even so, I'd rather be *him*, too, tracking Ella through jungles. All I have are her words, their rhythms—bodiless and abandoned.

Closing the beige book, I slip out the journal at the bottom of the stack. Green cover. The pages are stiffer, marked by rings of salt and warped by sea air. Her handwriting has changed, black threads of sentences unfurling over ruled paper.

> *I have glimpses into what is real. Can't sustain them. Thresholds vanish as I try to enter. The world I'm writing is already gone.*

I flip back, looking for context. A guesthouse in the hills near Chiang Rai. Teakwood gives the room its odor, rich and sharp.

A breeze touches my face and arms—*her* face and arms, which, as I read, are mine. Someone is packing, suitcase on the bed. His back is turned, and his white shirt stands out against polished wood walls. Behind him, through wall-size doors, hills stretch into Myanmar.

Reading on, I see the brown track of the river, layered green hills going forever. Then a sun flash through the window returns me to myself and to *here,* to this white room in Paris.

2

I FIRST MET SIOBHÁN TWO MONTHS AGO, over coffee in the gardens of the Palais-Royal. It was April, and the long rows of trees were blooming. Raw warmth dug up smells of turned earth and flowers, a too-sweetness that made me think of decomposition.

Siobhán was seated when I arrived, reading a glossy arts magazine. I knew it was her because she stiffened in recognition as I approached, though she'd never seen me before. Her sunglasses showed me a distorted version of myself before she raised them, extending her hand.

—Your mother was a close friend of mine a long time ago. It's a pleasure to meet you.

Siobhán spoke with calibrated calm, with a poise I found contagious.

I don't remember my mother ever mentioning Siobhán. She never liked to speak of the past, of remote people or things. She loved what was immediate, present to the senses. It was my father who had put me in touch with Siobhán. We know someone in Paris, he'd said over the phone. She and your mother were very close. I might have asked how they'd known each other or why I'd never heard of Siobhán, but all I could think of at the time was his way of saying *your mother,* as if she were more my relation than his.

Espressos arrived at our table without our having ordered

them. Unless Siobhán had ordered them before I arrived. Or they reached us by mistake. We sat for a moment, immune to the shouts of children, to the absurdly flowering trees.

Siobhán looked at me evenly, her eyes very blue and calm. Her hair, light gray, was pulled together at the base of her neck. Her skin was smooth. She slipped her magazine into an outer pocket of her briefcase and reached for an espresso.

I was afraid she would tell me I reminded her of my mother, but she said nothing more about it, and we spoke of other things: my doctoral research on the French filmmaker Chris Marker, my reason for being in Paris (a monthlong trip was all I could afford), architecture, which had been Siobhán's profession, and the gallery she'd designed after retiring. I asked to see it, and Siobhán offered to give me a tour.

Siobhán had grown up in Montreal and had an Irish mother, which explained her name and her accent (not quite North American). When she learned that my research trip was nearing its end, she asked if I'd found what I was looking for. I laughed and told her about my plan to teach in the summer and fall to save enough for a longer trip next year. A month was too short. Besides, I'd misspent it, writing a poetic essay about being able to *see* a vibrant world, precisely and with clarity, but not touch it, not feel it living as part of me and me of it. My essay was inspired by the film *Sans Soleil,* but it was too formless and full of feeling for any academic film journal to take seriously. I felt silly after telling her this—it wasn't something I ever talked about.

—You're a writer, Siobhán said.

Her calm, which I had admired earlier, was on full display.

—No, I said, pleased.

There was a long, uncomfortable pause.

—Did my mother exhibit here—with you? I asked.

—No, Siobhán said, looking up, surprised.

She tapped the spoon from her espresso on her cup. It made a small bell-like sound.

—I'm sorry, Elena, she said finally, in a tone that made it clear what she was talking about. Your father was in touch. I wish I could have been there.

—It was a long time ago, I said, meaning she shouldn't worry.

It occurred to me only in retrospect that Siobhán and I might have met already, at the funeral. I was relieved we hadn't.

Siobhán shifted, recrossing her legs.

—I wanted to be there, but I couldn't.

Her gaze drifted above the building tops to a raw patch of sky. Her face was youthful—fine lines, yes, but a fullness of flesh that made her expression innocent, unmarked by life. She wasn't indifferent, just intensely private, and mercurial.

—Ella would be your age now, she said. You're twenty-nine?

I nodded. I didn't want to ask who Ella was. Our intimacy felt strong and comfortable in that moment, because of my mother.

—I don't know why I'm telling you so much, Siobhán said, although she hadn't told me anything. Your mother was there when Ella was born. That must be why.

She looked at her shoes, black heels whitened by the gravel of the gardens. With the napkin from her espresso, she bent down and began to wipe the leather.

—Is Ella your daughter? I asked.

Siobhán sat up and was quiet. When she finally answered, her speech was stilted.

—I gave birth to her. I haven't seen her since she was three months old. She was raised by friends I trusted, in America.

Siobhán looked again at the sky and went on.

—She grew up not knowing. They wanted her, as they put it, to grow up "whole." They waited until she finished university to tell her.

I took a sugar cube and rolled it between my fingers until it was dust.

—Her response was to go live in Asia. If she saw how big the world was, maybe her own crisis would matter less. Or it's just what people will do at that age if they have the means—go live somewhere they can't fathom. London was that for me—it's where I met Ida, as you know.

My mother's name sent a tremor through me. So she and Siobhán had known each other in London, where she'd studied sculpture at the Slade before following my father to the United States. I felt ashamed. It was clear from Siobhán's face that something terrible had happened, and I could think only of myself, of my mother and how much I still needed to learn about her.

It occurred to me to ask why Siobhán had given up her daughter in the first place, but I refrained out of politeness.

Siobhán swallowed hard, then smiled—it was an expression I knew better than my own, tying up pain with terrible lightness. It sucked out my breath, ran gravity through my limbs. Siobhán's own expression returned, but I still wanted to fling my arms around her, a stranger. In the coldness of her face, I wanted to find that smile again. It was my mother's.

—I wish I could help, I said.

My reply was genuine, though I meant it abstractly, the way most people mean *I'm sorry,* which is what I should have said. But Siobhán stared at me strangely, narrowing her eyes as if to take in my whole body.

A WEEK LATER, I STOOD ON THE SIDEWALK in front of the Ormeau Gallery. Having arrived a little early, I peered through the glass front into the space. Siobhán was inside, with her back to me, her phone pressed to her ear. Her movements were bird-like, polished and abrupt. Not at all like my mother. Seeing her end the call, I tried the door. Locked. She turned and crossed the space to let me in.

Inside, daylight intensified. City noise faded.

The gallery was empty except for a few covered sculptures and a spiral staircase, its iron railing too intricate in the bare space.

—We're between shows, Siobhán said. New work goes up the day after tomorrow. But you have a sense of the place. There are two levels.

She gestured to a loft at the top of the spiral stairs, which extended halfway across the gallery, leaving a cathedral ceiling over the rest of the space. That was the tour. Then she invited me to lunch at a nearby café. We had omelettes.

—What interests you about Marker? she asked, after telling me she didn't like to mix egg with cheese, preferring plain omelettes to the version I had ordered.

—He makes what's ordinary *mean* something.

I was thinking of the fictional cameraman in *Sans Soleil*, "tracking banality with the restlessness of a bounty hunter." Instead, I said:

—He takes his cue from Sei Shōnagon's list of "things that quicken the heart." He said it wasn't a bad criterion for making films.

—Filming things that quicken the heart?

—He isn't afraid of emotion.

Siobhán nodded, cutting a neat wedge from her omelette. If I was her daughter's age, she was also about the age my mother would have been, and something about her bodily presence threatened to fill a need I'd thought permanent. The intensity of my reaction embarrassed me, so I hid it behind a mask of competence, describing Marker's idea that memory travels from person to person, his theory that montage produces meaning, and his debt to the Soviet montage theorists: Kuleshov, Vertov, and Eisenstein, who said that narrative always proceeds with an eye toward rhythm.

Siobhán looked intrigued. Perhaps it was this brief show of passionate professionalism that decided for her. I can't imagine why else she'd think me competent for such a task. I'm told I speak well, that I'm articulate. It leads people to believe I'm cleverer than I am.

I returned to the gallery the following day at Siobhán's request and was shown the journals.

Heels clicking over the hardwood floor, she led me through to the gallery's narrow back room. Walls extended to a skylight, which revealed clouds and the edges of buildings. She knelt beside a low bookshelf and gestured to a set of notebooks, ragged and multicolored, their broken spines pressed between elegant art books.

She picked one out—blue cover—and turned it over in her hands.

—It was too much to go into the other day, she said. Ella is missing. It has been six years. She was twenty-three when she disappeared.

My breath caught. My imagination ran wild: cults, sex trafficking, drugs.

—I was the first to know, Siobhán said. A package arrived for me from the south of Thailand a month after its postmark. There was a letter and Ella's green journal, her most recent. She must have hated me, or the idea of me, to send that. Monstrous.

Siobhán laughed bitterly, then composed herself.

—It worried me. I called her adoptive parents. We hadn't spoken in twenty years. Ella had asked them for space, and they were trying to respect this, but they'd had no news and were frantic. We flew to Thailand. Police. Detectives. We went first to the south, then to the north—she was teaching English near Chiang Rai. The university where she worked told us nothing. Only that she'd gone to the south because she needed rest.

Siobhán stood and began pacing the narrow space.

—In Chiang Rai, we found her things. Ella's adoptive mother kept her clothes, in case she returns. After reading the first pages, she wanted nothing to do with the journals. The detective dismissed them. Girlish and irrelevant, he said. So they're here, all six books. When a year went by and we hadn't found her, I sold my firm. I built this, Siobhán said, indicating the gallery.

I stared at the blue book in Siobhán's hands. Its physicality made Ella more real.

—You've read them? I asked, turning my gaze to the others, in a row on the shelf.

—It doesn't help. I don't understand them the way I would like to.

Siobhán opened the blue journal and handed it to me.

I made a show of turning pages, squinting at lines of script: *jasmine, gray eyes, lights in the river.* I couldn't focus on sentences. But the language was clear, logical.

—Once, Siobhán said, I hired someone to translate them into French. I thought—I still think—there must be something in them, a clue. I thought I might access them better in another voice.

I felt my muscles stiffen.

—And did you?

—It was too much the same, just in French, Siobhán said, shaking her head. It was clear from the sample. I canceled the contract.

Siobhán was looking at me expectantly. She wanted me to offer—she wanted *something*. Wary of her intensity, I said that my flight back to the States was in three days. It was true.

Siobhán took a slip of paper from the top of a filing cabinet and handed it to me. It was more like a poem than a contract, words islanded by white space, winnowed to essentials.

> *Accommodation: private studio flat, eighteenth arrondissement.*
> *Airfare: paid by reimbursement*
> *Living Expenses: paid by stipend, six hundred euros/month*
> *Project: length negotiable, unified story*
> *Duration: one year*

I looked up, unable to hide my shock. Siobhán gazed back at me, composed.

—I have a studio I'm not renting. Seventh floor, no elevator. The stipend is not a lot, but it would enable you to begin your dissertation research right away. You wouldn't have to teach and save. In exchange, you would work on the journals.

I pointed to the line that said "project."

Siobhán nodded, as if expecting this.

—You would rewrite the journals as an account of what happened.

—A report? I asked.

—A narrative. A *story*.

Siobhán's face was impassive. I asked myself why she would want this. I could understand her asking me to analyze the journals; I was good at analysis. But a *story?* And why me, whom Siobhán hardly knew? Emotionally, something clicked into place. I felt satisfied.

—Is Ella alive? I asked.

Siobhán's gaze settled on me. Fine lines seemed to deepen and extend around her eyes.

—Ella is an American citizen, she said. According to American law, a missing person is declared dead after seven years. By law, she's alive until January.

Siobhán sat down at the table, her forearms resting on the contract.

I could feel the breath in my lungs. From their shelves, the journals seemed to peer out, as if to impress upon me how long they'd waited, asking patiently, urgently, for something Siobhán could neither ignore nor understand.

—I've never been to Thailand, I said. I know nothing—

—We won't find her by going to Thailand, Siobhán said wearily. We tried that.

She put her fingers to her lips, as if deciding whether to go on.

—You know, she said finally, I used to think one day you and Ella would meet. You were born only months apart. You might have been great friends, like your mothers. When I saw you yesterday, I thought you were a ghost. You look just like Ida.

—People say that.

She rose from the table, composed and certain. Watching her move was like watching an infinitely protean form, her scarf, her belt, her jewelry keeping her in flux.

—Don't answer now, she said. Take some time. Think about it while you're in the States.

PHILADELPHIA WAS A RELIEF. There was the familiarity of my apartment with all my things, closer contact with Z by phone, beers with friends from graduate school, and the light humidity of early summer on the East Coast. No more sullen sky and heaviness of gray buildings, just cheery bright brick and right-size coffees. I could imagine I'd never met Siobhán, never seen the gallery, knew nothing about Ella or her journals. And Siobhán's proposal had exposed Paris as an *ideal*. Now that living there was possible, it became less desirable, less necessary. At this early stage, much of what I needed could be found through the university library. What would I do now with rare footage, letters, notebooks, and typescripts?

I even thought of other places I might go. In Berlin, for instance, I could research Weimar cinema or UFA in the era of silent film. But it wasn't the origins of cinema that interested me; in Paris, I cared little for the Lumière brothers. We never fully know the reasons for our obsessions; such knowledge would cure or quell them. I worked in a fever dream the months after my field exams, rewatching films, teaching myself the language and political history of France, Cuba, and Vietnam, sifting through Marker's many pseudonyms, until this man, lover of cats and owls, began to define me: a scholar of Marker in training.

Around this time, a professor recommended an essay of mine for a prize. I was flattered at first, but actually winning provoked a bizarre sort of crisis. I found myself telling the second-place essayist seated next to me at the prize dinner that Marker was a distant relation of mine, the great-uncle of a third cousin, as if to explain why I could write about him with any authority. When, later, she mentioned she'd grown up in Moscow, I told everyone at the table I'd valiantly tried to learn Russian for years but found it too difficult. (It felt true. I was sure this would happen were I to try. Russian has seven cases.) I thought a lot about the fairy tale Rumpelstiltskin in those days, the bewildered and desperate miller's daughter. But, unlike her, I was unable to guess the dwarf's name, break the spell, and claim any power as my own.

When I first arrived in Paris, I took notes diligently on the books I'd brought, but couldn't keep to any schedule. I would write something one day, only to delete it the next because it was no longer true. I would walk back and forth along the canal, unable to decide where to go: to the *cinémathèque,* to a library, to a café. In *one* of these places (only *one*), a change would come, and ideas would flow. But if I chose the wrong place, I'd remain who I was, and the possibility of a release from myself—a plunge into something other—would be forever foreclosed.

So, holding all options open, I'd walk between the parc de la Villette and the place where the canal flows underground to reach the Seine, following my reflection in the windows of restaurants, surprised at the length of my arms and speed of my legs. Nights I spent in a rented room on the rue Bichat with the same film on my laptop: the narrator on the runway, seeing himself from the future, watching himself dying. I played it again and again, hoping its images would wake in me what I must have felt once.

Ella might have gone to Thailand for the usual reasons: to teach English, to see the world. Or she went east because it's where *all* lost travelers go. I read once that orientation literally means east-facing. Those who go west (the pioneers) already know what they want—no need to go searching for the heart of things.

My spell of contentment in Philadelphia lasted a week; then I was restless again. The soft humidity turned to poisonous vapor, and I felt stuck in my old ruts and routes. I called Siobhán to test (so I told myself) whether the proposition was real. The first stipend arrived in my bank account three days later with instructions to forward airline receipts. Things were in motion. After that, it was easy to tie up affairs; a medical student agreed to sublet my apartment, my teaching jobs went to other graduate students in need of funding, and my professors approved further research abroad. To avoid fees, I withdrew temporarily from my doctoral program.

Z used his vacation days as soon as he could and drove down from Boston. He moved there in January for a job that will devour him, and he wants me to move with him. I haven't forgiven him for leaving Philadelphia, which he knows. Still, we've been together nine years and have known each other ten. We don't lie to each other. So I surprised myself by telling him that research was going *so* well that I couldn't turn down the opportunity to spend a full year in Paris. Even if I didn't go, I reasoned, we wouldn't be in the same city. Z dodged my provocation with a sigh, reaching for my waist to pull me close and beginning to unfasten the buttons of my shirt. Z, even more than most people, likes things to make sense. And what I still can't explain—especially not to Z, whose mind is so elegantly logical—is the way Ella's story splashes color across a landscape of dull forms, the colors of life I can't remember.

Z sensed the truth, of course, and asked what was *really*

drawing me back to France. He waited until the next morning, then wrote his concerns on a paper napkin at the breakfast table:

> *a). How is copying diary entries supposed to locate a missing person?*
> *b). Why are you looking in Paris and not in Thailand?*
> *c). Are you avoiding the Ph.D.? You can still change your mind and reregister for fall.*

Z began a financial consulting job this year—(1) to raise the material means for his philosophy Ph.D. and (2) because he thought it necessary to flirt with the mundane before conscripting himself to the esoteric. Those are his words, but if he were telling you this, he would letter his points rather than number them. Letters remind him of logic proofs. It might be for similar reasons that he prefers letters to full names. He's been Z and not Zachariah for as long as I've known him and gives the same silly grin whenever he's asked.

Z never told me not to go—he is too kind, too shrewd for that—but, mixing his yogurt very vigorously, he pressed me about it over breakfast. He wanted to understand.

—Why? One good reason.

His voice cracked.

—The dissertation is going nowhere, I said.

—It will only go nowhere if you don't work on it. You might work better here, where you have all your books.

Z pressed his lips together and looked up, waiting for me to agree.

—Reasons don't exist, I said.

—They do! You're just not good at using them.

—We make up reasons *after* the act. To understand what we've done. Reasons are just impulses woven into narrative.

For the first time with Z, I thought I'd had the last word. But after several seconds, he said:

—You can do almost anything well, but you stop just before the finish line. It's as if you're afraid of finding out what you really can do and what you can't.

He was looking at me seriously.

—I'm not *stopping* the dissertation, I said. It's possible I'll finish faster this way.

My words sounded hollow.

—Just think it through. What is your connection to this woman? Asking you to write a story to find a missing person is worse than illogical. And why you? She hasn't seen your writing. Why not hire a professional? Money doesn't seem to be a concern for her.

—Siobhán was a close friend of my mother's, I said, pausing to make sure Z absorbed this. They lost touch. And I'm American, like her daughter—a similar age. I'm in a position to *understand* the journals. . . .

I stopped because Z was shaking his head.

—What's in it for you? he asked. What do *you* get out of this?

The directness of his look told me not to bother mentioning stipends or research.

—There's a chance I'll come closer to knowing her, I said.

—Your mother.

I nodded, hating the sadness, the pity in his look.

—What could she possibly tell you that would help?

—It's intuitive, I said. Not everything is calculated. Getting to know Siobhán might help me understand. Then maybe I can move on. Nothing matters now as much as it should.

I looked down, embarrassed by the bitterness in my voice.

Z sighed, running a hand through his hair. He didn't want me to go.

—Intuition cheats, he said, leaving me to fill in the rest.

It was an old joke between us: Intuition cheats by discrediting argument.

—Please be careful, he said, pulling me to him, resting his chin on the crown of my head.

All that remained was to tell my father, who, like Z, made a case for my finishing my degree on "terra firma," as he put it. I reminded him that he, too, had done his doctorate abroad and look what happened. He laughed and relented—not that I needed his permission. But the concern didn't leave his face.

Ella went missing six years ago. Her case can't be solved, only *resolved*: sutured with a sturdy narrative. For years I've felt disconnected from the places my body occupies. The difference now is *purpose*—one to string itself through my days, adding tautness, definition, orienting them on an axis of someone else. In practical terms, I have a nicer flat, a small income, and a *task* that's an emblem of what I'd be doing anyway: finding anodyne escapes from the life that's mine.

3

Here IS A NEW MORNING, new country. Fresh grounds in the coffee press. Water heating. Sensibilities sluggish, dampened, as if by the middle pedal on a piano.

The water boils and I pour it over the grounds.

From the window, the panorama of the city is a still photograph. Its colors have faded. Tints. Washes. Perceptions are not film images. Still, the world looks like a giant backdrop—a set I could push over with the tip of my index finger, revealing the bright lights and the actors' changing rooms.

A sound shrills in the empty space. A black telephone rattles the table by the door.

—Elena?

—Yes.

—Will the flat be okay for you?

Siobhán's accent is full of odd inflections.

—Yes, it's . . . spacious.

The studio is large enough to fit four small rooms. There's a corner for the bed, nooks for writing and reading by two dormer windows, and an open kitchen bordered by a long bar.

—Friends who stay there like the views. It's close to shops. I put the journals on the table. Did you find them?

—Yes.

I glance at them, stacked together in their faded colors.

—Good.

A pause.

—Listen, I have documents to help you. It's best if I come up. Ten minutes.

Soft click.

I take a shower in the European style, hovering close to the bottom of the tub, then dress and do jumping jacks in the center of the room. I make the bed and straighten the pillows. The green journal is on the nightstand, its pages stiff and rippled. I flip it open.

Monsoons. Everything damp. Memories a scourge.
I outrun them in waking life. But certain ones remain
quiet for only so long.

Closing the book, I take it to the writing table to be with the others. I unlatch the window, and a wet breeze blows through the space. Treetops in the park below, dusted with white blooms, are like graying heads of hair.

Last night I dreamed of a guesthouse in the hills—a scene from the journals—and woke thinking of my mother. (A whiff of perfume, the air you feel when someone leaves a space.) *Is* there an art that recovers what's lost—people, the past? I push the press down over the grounds. The coffee gurgles. I pour it into two cups.

Siobhán kisses me on both cheeks, her skin cool and fresh from the summer morning. She transfers a gray folder from her briefcase to the writing table. *AFFAIRE CLASSÉE* is stamped over the first page. I look at her in confusion.

—It's a French translation of the Thai police report, she says. They closed the case as soon as it opened. They never took

it seriously. Ella disappeared the month of the Boxing Day tsunami—do you remember it?

I shake my head. It happened during my missing months.
Learning about it later isn't the same as remembering.

—More than two hundred thousand dead or missing, Siob-
hán says. A month before it hit, Ella's journal transited through
Krabi, which means she sent it from one of the islands in the
Andaman Sea. For the police, there was no question. But she
was seen in the northeast, the Isan region, *after* the tsunami.
A foreigner with her description asked for a job at Khon Kaen
University, then vanished again.

—She wasn't kidnapped? I ask, to rule out my worst fears.

—If she'd been abducted, she wouldn't have reappeared in
Isan—at least it's unlikely.

Siobhán pauses.

—I think she was troubled, she says, her gaze refusing to meet
mine.

She takes from the folder a wallet-size photograph of a girl, a
young woman, dimpled and smiling, her hair blond and to the
shoulders, eyes looking straight at the camera, fearless, full of that
inner smile native to children. She looks anything but troubled.

—She's twenty-one here, Siobhán says. It was taken before her
university graduation.

Siobhán's hair is pulled back neatly with a clip. Her coloring
is similar to the girl's—something else, too, maybe the shape of
their eyes. But their expressions are different. Siobhán is tight-
lipped, serious.

—Hold on to it until you finish, Siobhán says, handing me
the picture.

I want her to correct herself: *Until you find her.*

—You have the Thai police report, Siobhán is saying, pulling a different file from her briefcase. This is the report from the detective we hired. There are transcripts of the interviews he conducted in Chiang Rai—Ella's friends, people she worked with, administrators at the university. All in English. He tried tracking those who had left, but there was one he couldn't find, a young man rumored to have moved to Japan or India. There are verbal descriptions but no photographs. These are the people she mentions in the journals.

I nod, paging through the report, trying to find some meaning in its official language.

—Keep it, Siobhán says. It's a copy.

Siobhán has to get back to the gallery, but she asks if I'm free tomorrow for dinner.

I smile, wishing we could meet again earlier.

—Oh, she says from the hallway. Please translate a sample, any section of the journal, into a story. It doesn't have to be long, just to give us a starting point. So that we can talk. Bring it tomorrow night.

Before I can ask how many pages, she is gone.

I go back to the table, drink Siobhán's untouched coffee, and read the report. Physical descriptions precede the transcripts: Muay, a politics professor, round cheeks and glasses. Ella was so curious, learning the Thai language. Aurelia, Ella's American roommate, insisting that Ella was fine. Someone had seen her in Isan. Ella was *frail but full of love.* Lek, a photographer, saying she was nice, liked whiskey. Soraya, who had just joined an order of *bhikkhuni,* Buddhist nuns, had a shaved head and nodded yes or no to questions, keeping her vow of silence. The vice president of the university saying what a splendid teacher Ella was, mounting an encomium. Anthony, who had taught with Ella before retiring to Bangkok, saying how delightful he found her, quick of wit. Only one person seemed concerned about Ella's state, a friend and neighbor in the village, a Frenchwoman, Béa. Ella seemed burdened before she left. One man was missing, Sebastian.

OUTSIDE, THE AIR IS DAMP. Stone steps lead from a small plaza to a road rounded like a crescent. Most shops are shut and there are few people in the streets. A man looks at the sky while his dachshund shits lengthily in front of an empty café. The sun shudders onto the pavement, then disappears. More stairs lead up to a smaller plaza, where the beige of buildings colors the city differently. The air is thick with coming storms. A red geranium hangs over a balcony.

A calico with black and tan spots over its eyes stretches on the stone, belly up in a patch of sun. It stops mid-stretch, feeling my gaze, caught in a moment of pure freedom, pleasure— rough stones pulling gently at the hairs of its back as it watches the clouds. I've ruined, with my gaze, the for-itself of the cat. Now, it will be for-another, self-conscious and watchful.

Back in front of my building, on the place Marcel-Aymé, a man is leaning against the wall, looking intently at the cigarette between his fingers. Black hair, dark eyes, black eyebrows. He looks up when I pass. I look back. He doesn't look down, so we stare.

Inside the building, I meet an older woman moving slowly down the narrow stairs. I flatten myself against the wall and wait for her to pass.

—*Bonjour,* she says liltingly.

I reply, botching the cadence.

—*Vous êtes la jeune fille qui habite l'appartement de Siobhán, c'est ça?* She says this very slowly, enjoying each syllable. She looks at me a long time.

I find myself nodding as if to say, Yes, I'm the girl who lives in Siobhán's apartment. It feels good to remind myself who I am, where I am, and why.

—*À tout à l'heure,* she sings, and leaves.

Through the door, open onto the square, I hear her sigh.

—*Ah, Jérémie!*

Back in the flat, there is relief. Empty space. There is so little furniture: the bed, the writing table by one dormer window, a reading chair by the other, two stools by the kitchen bar. I stare at the journals. Open one. Close it. Sit on the bed. Get up. Open the windows. There is discomfort, difficult to explain, as if the journals and I cannot exist together easily in the same space.

Finally, when the clock by the bed reads 5:00 P.M., I spread all six journals chronologically across the parquet floor. The colors of their covers:

> beige
> baby blue
> mustard yellow
> bright red
> black
> green

I open the beige journal. First page: *June 16.* I close it.

I open the blue journal. The letters are neat and round, as in the first journal:

> *Laughter is a discipline. I'm learning it. Elsewhere*
> *is just deferral. Stupid to believe in what is "to come." It*

never arrives. Desire = this love of the impossible. When you look for me (you will), it will be too late. I'll be gone. I'll be laughing. I'll have learned to laugh like the Chinese Buddhas in the spare bedroom with their enormous bellies.

When you look for me? These words will make sense differently in context, fit into Ella's story. But now, shorn of time and place, they address me personally. I know I can't be the "you" she describes, but why not imagine Ella guessing there would be, far in the future, someone like me? Someone somewhere—or always elsewhere—looking for her.

I read passages in the journals, haphazardly, listening to the soft sound of the rain outside, until it occurs to me that I'm searching for something in particular: a teakwood bungalow in the hills, a man in a white shirt with his back turned, the scene from the journals that captured my attention when I arrived. It was the same scene, again, in my dream.

It's nearly ten in the evening when I break, with a feeling of having returned from somewhere—deep in Ella's world (though no sign of the teakwood bungalow). Sharp hunger nudges me out into the summer evening, long in light. On the place Marcel-Aymé, the rain has stopped. The air is warm. I turn down a tiny street that leads to Abbesses, and Ella's early impressions of Chiang Rai flit by: visions of temples and moon gates replaced by motorbikes, telephone poles, and Pizza Huts. When I first heard the name Abbesses, similarly, I imagined stone cloisters, abbots and abbesses lost in thought, not these crowded *terrasses* and buskers.

The restaurants are all alike, tables on sidewalks. A vendor spreads crêpe mixture on a black griddle and cracks an egg in the center. I eat my crepe—egg, salty ham, hot cheese—on a bench in the darkening plaza in the glow of the carousel lights. From here, I can watch conversations in restaurants, leanings toward and away, drinks sipped and poured, and the moon rising over the uneven tops of buildings.

A woman with an orange scarf in her hair ducks into an alcove. I get up and cross the square after her, walking quickly. When I reach the alcove, there is no one. She may have passed through a door. But in that case, I would have seen it open. My breath quickens, and I lean against the building. An elderly couple passes on the sidewalk. Their pace slows as they notice me. They wonder what I'm staring at. Nothing. My heart pounds in my ears. Siobhán's words return: *She was troubled.* Am I safe, reading Ella?

Back in the apartment, city lights make the dark uneasy. A square of paper, blue in the dim light, has fallen to the floor. I pick it up, my hands shaking, though nothing has happened, nothing is wrong. It's a napkin, stiff and pressed with age, Singapore Airways logo. The underside is crawling with ants. The ants become words, tight black letters:

> *Forward forces. Ladders out of ~~the~~ this horror. Body a swamp, where dead things. Inner storms swell. ~~Swollen oceans seethe, spit and cataract, tides pulling, terrible parasites.~~ No words make sense now. Can't struggle against anything but mySELF. String Time on a line or it will eat me, or I will eat it, Time, until I burst. Dead possibles. Devastated Time.*

I turn on all the lights. The green journal is facedown on a chair. It must have fallen from the table when I opened the door.

The napkin must have been inside. I pick up the book to its open page. Same tiny script:

> *I am too much a god taking life. It will be okay if I write again. Words. On the first flight (she tried to keep me) screaming. Then ghosts of people never born. No, just one. She has dirty knees. And she wants. Plane is metal and high up, so I see skin-flesh ripped away. Nothing more attaches. No earth. The day is black. Home is where I'll never see again. Never knew fear really until now.*

The beating of my blood pounds loudly in the room. City noise fades, far below. These passages are dark, different from the others. What happened to change her? The entry has no date, but others nearby, more coherent, suggest that Ella wrote the lines in late July, five months before she disappeared. She doesn't mention travel, but she describes returning to her village and finding it a ghost town, empty. She must have gone somewhere, but where? Why?

I turn to the last page of the green journal, looking for some indication of a plan—a destination. To my surprise, fat, neat letters on the inside back cover spell out Siobhán's address in Paris. Ella must have written the address earlier, since the rest of the page is filled with tiny, cramped letters, dizzying. It makes me almost physically sick to look at them. There is a ragged edge where the last page of the journal has been torn out. I feel a flash of anger at Siobhán. Had Ella lost her mind? Of course, it's my mother who drew me in—her knowing Siobhán. Z saw it—a way to shirk my dissertation, which, once finished, might open onto a life of my own. Sabotage. Since she died, everything has been about that—her dying. The things I've done have all grown out of opposing drives to discover and escape what happened to her. A sky-wide task narrows back to my obsession, and the world closes up again. The symmetry strikes hard and hurts the way it does when you discover you've been looking away from what's in front of you: Siobhán solving the mystery of her daughter's disappearance, me wanting to know more about my mother. Only Siobhán doesn't seem stymied or stuck. She has a plan, strange as it is, to recover her lost daughter. But I have no power. The room is too warm with the windows closed, and I can't stop shivering.

4

B RIGHT SUN IN THE APARTMENT when I wake. I know without checking that it's late, past eleven. The journals scattered
over the writing table make the walls feel close. I push open all the
windows, and the city glitters in the light.

Before searching for a plane ticket home, I should at least ask
Siobhán what she knows, gather all the facts. It's possible I'm
projecting my own terrors. I'll buy groceries, test the neighborhood's cafés, visit the cinema Cocteau designed. It's supposed to
be close to here.

Feeling better, I take my wallet and keys from the counter
and a canvas shopping bag from the kitchen. From its perch on
the writing table, the beige journal—patient, almost animate—
reminds me that I must produce a "translation" by this evening.
I add it to the empty shopping bag.

Outside, the sky is an arresting blue. It swoops down to meet
the cobblestones in narrow strips between the buildings. I stop at a
kiosk for *Le Monde, Libération,* and my chest tightens; my mouth
goes dry. I look around, searching the innocent shop fronts,
gleaming café tables, and faces of pedestrians for a reason. But fear
isn't reasonable. It springs up at odd times, in plain day, in the sun.

At an outdoor table on the rue des Abbesses, I order a *café crème*
and a croissant. People pass with bags of fruit and newly bought

clothes. Snippets of conversation float toward me and away. I lean back in my chair, sun warm on my skin. The fear fades.

The woman next to me dips her croissant in her coffee. I do the same. She, too, wears a scarf in her hair. A man sits beside her. They share a cigarette, then leave. I think I see my mother in the street sometimes. It no longer happens in cities I know well. But in Paris, where women wear scarves the way she did, I sometimes see her in the crowd. I follow. I always follow until I can see the woman's face, until I can know for sure it isn't her. I know it can't be, but there were the colored scarves she'd weave through her hair, darker than mine. I can still see the flash of her eyes, the curve of her nose. And just as the double turns around, my breath quickens. Then shame.

She died six years and six months ago. My memory from that time is also gone. It's staggering to think there are months in which I was there but remember nothing. Some reflex of my body lowered a floodgate. I remember scraps of a train journey in December, going home, then a field in June the following year, nothing in between. Diagnosis: shock. There was neuroanalysis, psychoanalysis, hypnosis. Nothing. Forgetting is how the body keeps itself sane.

No one said anything—not my father, not the doctors, not Z—but I understood that I needed to stop what I'd been doing. I was working as an apprentice to a photographer in New York, writing stories and painting on photographs on my own time. I felt the world fueled, flowing with colors no form could contain. The photographer agreed to take me back once I'd recovered, but I knew my only chance was to step softly over surfaces, not to plunge deep. If I didn't draw attention to myself, whatever spirit possessed her might pass over me in silence. I got a job as a fact checker for an arts magazine.

One of my first assignments was an article on the history of the film essay. I discovered Marker, intrigued by his ability to turn the failure of a movement he cared about into something playful. Global socialism—the revolution—was the Cheshire cat's grin, a promising smile with no body, no cat. I watched *Sans Soleil, La Jetée, ¡Cuba Si!,* and *Le Mystère,* then Varda and Jean Rouch, then Godard and Truffaut, then Hitchcock, Tarkovsky, and Medvedkin because Marker loved them. In the dark with my lit screen, I was both solitary and connected. I applied to graduate school to keep watching—film studies.

I try not to think about that time, before Marker. There may always be a sealed door in one corridor of memory. But it is that door and no other that would have opened onto life. For the past six years, I've known that *this*—where I am—is the wrong world, a somber imitation of a life I failed to seize. Only in films, the old ones (Maya Deren), does living become vivid again: A woman splits in two; her avatar moves along a shore, gathering pebbles in the folds of her dress, face to the wind. I feel her thrill and her longing—maybe this is what Ella wants; maybe she's tempting me aground like a Siren, leading me to give up my degree, ruin things with Z, and shirk the steady work of rebuilding a life after the world lost its taste.

The coffee has gone lukewarm. In the crowd of pedestrians walking toward me, there is the black-eyed man from yesterday. For a second time, there is the oddness of our mutual stare. He slows and looks for a moment as if he might speak. A feather peeks out from a pocket of his trench coat.

I thrust my gaze to the canvas shopping bag and rifle through, pretending to look for something other than the journal, which I finish by retrieving. When I look up again, the man is gone, disappeared into the crowd flowing toward the place de Clichy.

Now that it's no longer possible, I wish I'd talked to him. If he were a key to a more vivid world—in films, alluring strangers often are—then I missed it, sealing myself more tightly in this one. I run a hand over the beige cover of the journal and open it to the first entry, the beginning:

June 16, 2003

Blood so little of me, what I am. Pure world.

Resolve. It's transmitted less by her words than by the thick strokes denting the page, bold black ink. She must have just learned about the adoption.

Ella. I imagine her sizing me up with Siobhán's sharp eyes, shaking her head and telling me firmly but gently that I'm not living well enough. Every day, not enough. I haven't looked long at the sky, smelled the skins of fruit, touched the wood of tabletops and trees. In another life inside this one, no less concrete than Abbesses with its cafés and crowds, Ella precedes me along a strip of shore, dough-colored sand stretched between two islands. She asks me what day it is and what I've done with it. Keep up, Elena, she calls, and slips from view. To find her, I need only step into that space, that slippage.

June 17

Chipped paint on the bathroom ceiling. All my pillows are in the bathtub. It's the only room in the house with a lock. They're at the door, trying to break it. They can't believe the way I'm acting. I'm not myself. (Are we ever who they think we are?) I am

*no one. A surface of sensations. Sent away across the
ocean, planted here so I'd think I was made of this
soil. Native nowhere. Belong to no one. I will be I no
more. I will be whatever is written here. The rest of
me, body-self, vanish it, only lies.*

Her emotion is too much—histrionics of the kind you have
to shed when you get older. The next entries are even worse:
rants against Siobhán, the mother Ella didn't know and didn't
want to know. They go on, much the same. I skip ahead, eager
for Thailand.

September 30

*Flights tomorrow (four!): Newark–LA–Seoul–
Bangkok–Chiang Rai. Outside my window, a trace
moves across the sky. White cuts through sharp blue. A
solid line at first. It frays. The sky takes it, unravels it.
Then as before, unbroken blue.*

*My room is still my childhood room. It's a palimp-
sest of past selves. To cut through the layers to a younger
self, all I have to do is stare into the beady eyes of the
clown doll hanging from the rim of my closet—those
eyes gave me nightmares when I was little. Photos,
newspaper clippings tacked to corkboards, posters taped
to walls, old perfume bottles from which the perfume
has evaporated. Packing boxes that came back with me
from college. Feet dangle out the window—pachysan-
dra visible in the spaces between my toes. Stare at empty
sky. I'll bring nothing with me. As little as possible.*

October 1

> *Paths dissolve in flight. Is this "letting go"? Is this what that means? Leave behind what you once were. Set out. Be larger. Be the air, the walls of the airplane cabin. The man next to me is asleep. Too dark-electric for sleep. Dad drove me to the airport. Purple evening sky. I am too much. He said nothing. I wanted to tell him that I wished I could rest from being. . . . Awake now over the Pacific. I know why I need to go. Relief from the excess of who I am.*

Between the airplane cabin and her second night: nothing. No record of her arrival, no account of what she felt, stepping off the plane.

October 3

> *Second night and I don't know how to live here. Is this adventure? This not knowing, this release of control, loosening the bolts that keep things in place? On the surface everything is okay.*
>
> *Today, with Muay (pronounced "Moy") I traveled to Chiang Khong, a village near the tip of the Golden Triangle. There is nothing for me to do yet at the university, so we went with some of Muay's colleagues. At lunch, they pointed out Laos across the wide brown river, and I watched the Mekong's slowness as conversation flowed in rapid Thai. Then visits to houses with looms, where women were weaving. I tried on traditional northern Thai—Lanna—dresses made on the looms. Long narrow skirts like mermaid tails, glittery*

*threads in strong sunlight. There's a trick to walking
in them. Muay said you have to waddle, but you get
used to it. She volunteers for an organization that gives
advice to the villages, so they can sell crafts directly to
tourists, without third-party vendors. Poverty is a big
problem in the region. Muay's English is excellent. She
spent a year studying in Minneapolis. She offered to
take me to Big C. Flashes of rice paddies, palm trees,
colorful fabrics, mountains.*

Bravo, Ella. *Poverty is a big problem!* What was I hoping for—
the wisdom of a young sage? As I go to close the notebook, an
addendum to the entry stops me:

*(later, 4:39 A.M.) I can't sleep. My heart is racing.
What can I write that will make it better? My legs itch,
mosquito bites. I should have taken doxycycline. Why
didn't I? It's too late now if I've been infected. Even
Larium nightmares would have been better than this.
Symptoms of malaria . . . Insomnia? Fatigue? Sweating, chills? I'm scared. Try to sleep—*

With more sympathy, I read on.

October 4

Muay wants me to call her pi-Muay, *like an older
sister. She teaches me about Thailand. She doesn't like
to find exact equivalents for things and doesn't like it
when I do, either.* Kuay teow *is not "noodle soup," but
a snack with noodles and broth; Ban Du is not a "sub-
urb," but a village outside the city. She describes things*

carefully in a way I can understand mentally. But the thing keeps a little mystery until I actually experience it. Big C for example: it's a must-have for Chiang Rai expats craving peanut butter and sliced bread, things you can't get at the market. But Muay's students go on Saturdays and spend all day there. I was so confused that Muay went against her anticomparative principles and said it was like an American mall. We're going tomorrow because Muay thinks I need things for my suite at the university. I'll find out.

October 5

Today was the first Sunday after the rainy season, and the sky is the bluest it will be the whole year, according to Muay. Fresh-washed. Its color reminds me of October orchard trips when I was little—apple picking under a sky the blue of potter's glaze. We'd arrive home with too many bags and make pies, our fingers interlacing to scallop the dough around the pie pan, my prints smaller than theirs. They don't grow apples here. Instead, there are pineapple fields and dark green orchards with tangerines winking out like precious stones. There are tea plantations in the hills run by Chinese families. Muay told me her family is Chinese but they came here so long ago no one remembers the language.

Today, on the drive to Big C, Muay stopped the car by the side of the road so I could see what a pineapple plant looked like: pale purple leaves, fruit budding in the center like the eye of a flower. They come in two varieties: one small and sweeter, native to here, and the other saltier, its seed brought from Phuket, a region by the sea. Saparot. *Pineapple*

สับปะรด

Muay teaches me words for things. I want her to teach me writing, too. If I ask her, she'll write words in Thai script so I can practice copying them:

สับปะรด
สับปะรด
สับปะรด

With effort, I can make my characters as neat as hers, but they still look labored. They don't mean anything to me yet, just curves and squiggly lines.

The landscape, its villages, and the university are all more beautiful than I'd hoped. I almost want to call home and tell them about the bands of copper curving over the hills and the purple mists rolling in over the valleys at night. But the things Muay loves best—Chiang Rai, Big C—are ugly and depressing. A road called the "superhighway" connects Chiang Rai to the university and dead-ends in the northern border town of Mae Sai (Tachileik on the Myanmar side). To get to Big C, we drove south through Chiang Rai, which I'd been dying to see. I'd imagined glittering temples, polished stone streets, gurgling brooks, and moon gates. When I saw the city, I thought, I would feel like I'd really arrived.

In the car, Muay told me there was another new English teacher, about my age. She said he was a foreigner, both American and not American. She laughed. I never know if Muay is joking, because she's always laughing. Then she asked if I liked rambutan. When I didn't know what it was, she laughed harder. Then she pulled the car over in front of a busy market sprawling inward from the superhighway. Under a corrugated metal roof, small peppers, curiously shaped eggplants, curries in aluminum trays, bags of cooked rice, chicken legs (both crispy and not yet plucked) lined long tables, along with silver-sequined shoes, handbags, dresses, cooking supplies, and bottles of fish sauce. The woman at a fruit stall let us taste green-skinned mandarins the size of limes, sweet and sour. Muay showed me a pomelo, which was the size of an infant's head and tasted like grapefruit, only sweeter. So many fruits I'd never known existed! Muay was right: rambutan was the best. Under magenta skin with rubbery green spines, there's a globe of translucent flesh, perfectly round, flavored like a lychee but with a firmer texture, less juice dripping, more rugged.

Blurs of rice fields through the windows again as we drove over a bridge and Muay pointed out a statue of King Mengrai, a fourteenth-century ruler of the Lanna Kingdom. Then there were busy streets, nondescript shops, a Pizza Hut, Swenson's Ice Cream, dingy balconies, trucks, lane markings, telephone wires, and traffic lights. Before I realized we were in Chiang Rai, we were through it, and billboards ushered us on to Big C.

We collected a ticket from a guard in a red plastic booth. The parking lot was crowded with families,

teenagers, and motorbikes. Inside the building, we
passed stands selling fried rice balls, books, cell phones,
and beauty products before an escalator took us to Big
C itself: a row of checkout counters under fluorescent
lights. Big C lost its exotic charge: it was like a Walmart.
  I wasn't thinking about garbage bags or anything
practical, but I did need them. We picked out a tea-
kettle I could take with me when I moved to a more
permanent place. As we were waiting to pay, Muay
grabbed my arm and pointed beyond the checkout
lines. It was the new teacher, about my age. I looked
in time to see a white T-shirt and green Big C bag
disappear down the escalator.

On the terrace of the café, tables have been set for lunch. Paper
napkins stick out of wineglasses. This world—Abbesses—jars
after Big C and the countryside. I know how I'll render Ella: passionate spectator, delighted by newness, idealizer of place names.
The innocent banality of the journals makes last night's suspicions
seem like my own paranoia.

  —*Ça va, mademoiselle?*

  A waiter hovers, his head backlit by the sun. What must he see?
A girl with clenched hands spread across a dirty book. I look up at
him, embarrassed.

  —*Désirez-vous autre chose?* he asks.

  My table is the only one not set for lunch. He wants me to go.
I'm in a strange mood. I order an espresso to keep thinking. A few
pages give me the texture of a country to which I've never traveled.
And Ella's mystery is starting to feel . . . *interesting*, as if solving
her case might bring some clarity to something now muddled. I

don't have to find her *today*. All I have to do *now* is choose a passage to translate as best I can, transferring the taste of rambutan,
which I've never experienced, to the page. I stare into the space
vacated by the waiter, enjoying the way my imagination, long dor-
mant, stirs in the wake of her words.

A scene struggles into view: I see Muay. Her shiny black hair
swings to just below her chin. She wears an ill-fitting skirt suit
and speaks with great energy. I hear her voice—her way of phrase
making in English. I open my notebook, writing only what I hear
and see (no invention):

—There is *another* one—a foreign teacher. About your age.

Muay studied the steering wheel, her cheeks dropping down
with her gaze, then looked up, full of energy, her eyes magnified
behind thick lenses.

—American but not American.

—Is that a *koan?* Ella teased, as if she didn't care.

But she did care. She wanted to know more, and the force
of wanting made her coy.

Muay's whole body laughed.

Ella frowned.

—How old is he?

—Twenty-four, twenty-five. Not old.

—How old do you think *I* am?

—You? *Yee seep song.* Twenty-two. We know. The vice president told us.

—Wrong! I'm twenty-one. I'll be twenty-two in two weeks.

—*Ahh,* Muay said, her voice rising, then falling like a song,
her head nodding the way the toy cat with a bobbling neck was
nodding on her dashboard among other trinkets and amulets.

As they passed a temple, Muay took her hands off the steering wheel to *wai*.

She's not religious, I hear her say to Ella, not very much. . . .
As if emerging from the neat, childish script, Muay appears in focus. She is pleased to have a charge, someone to look after, but she worries that Ella is so young. No older than the students. Ella is fuzzed out, a blurry animation of the photograph Siobhán gave me. It's harder to hear her voice. I flip to the next entry, hoping to find something that will coax her into definition.

October 10

 Khantoke, *Muay told me, is a "footed tray" made of wicker, and food is served from these little trays on the floor. There are containers for sticky rice, pork, chicken, and vegetables. At the Welcome Dinner for New Faculty, we sat on mats on the floor while the vice president made a speech about the university, which was built into a hillside to honor nature—folded into the land. Its buildings are earth-colored because the university is part of the earth, a gem in the hills. Jasmine necklaces smelled like the honeysuckle in our backyard at home. The other Western teachers were there—all except the one supposed to be my age. I like Anthony best. We had Thai iced tea after work, waiting for the event to start. I have the feeling I know him from somewhere, which is impossible. He's from a town I've never heard of in England! He polemicizes against the university—calls it a "superface" with no depth. I'm tired of depth. Sometimes, with others, I'm a comedy of myself— here in this book is the only place I can live honestly,*

not performing. Quick, don't think, don't feel. Only
describe as much as possible. Fade out in pure world.

The sun is directly overhead. No shadows. Light prisms the
water carafe. An espresso is next to it. It's hard not to read Ella
from the point of view of the future, every line full of her fate.
The desire to fade out, disappear—it's just one of those things
people say . . . *I'd rather be her than here.* I would know. I want
to hold this thought, turn it over in my mind and examine it
from all angles. But a landscape is already appearing, faint at
first, then gaining solidity. I wait, totally still, not wanting to
interrupt it. Abbesses fades. The other world springs up: a university with covered walkways and taupe-colored buildings. Ella,
uncomfortable in an A-line skirt, sits on a low wall. She's eating
wasabi peas from a bag, slowly. Parts of her are in focus: wisps
of blondish hair, loose to frame the face, forehead drawn in concentration. She notices Anthony, a foreigner like her, neat white
hair and collared pink shirt. He is gesturing, bending toward the
vice president as they walk.

Ella stood up and straightened her skirt as they approached.

—Anthony, have you met our *youngest* member of the faculty? the vice president asked. Ella joins us from a *prestigious*
university in the U.S.

Anthony switched his briefcase to his left hand to offer Ella
his right. He had thin, luminous skin through which the faint
tracing of veins was visible. He looked to be in his early sixties.

—Enchanted, he said. Prestige is very welcome here. It
reigns above all else.

Anthony's thin lips overenunciated, even as he smiled.

The vice president looked at the sky and sighed, then said

he looked forward to seeing them again soon at the Welcome Dinner for New Faculty. He *wai*'ed and left them.

—*Mai bpen rai, mai bpen rai,* muttered Anthony.

—Let it go, Ella said.

She knew the expression, having read a Thai phrase book from cover to cover. Twice.

—Yes, Anthony said. But there's a problem when it's *always mai bpen rai. Nothing* is serious. *Serious* is the *worst* adjective you can have attached to you. Always *sanuk maak* . . . The vice president has vetoed my course on environmental planning because it makes the government *look bad.* But *mai bpen rai!* God forbid anything should be *serious.*

Ella smiled to herself. She liked intensity in others. It made her feel less strange.

—Don't misunderstand me, he was saying. It's nothing against the Thais. I *adore* the Thais. As long as things *appear* well, it can go to hell on the inside. Shall we have an iced tea?

Coppery light streaked the tables in the refectory pavilion as they entered, and Anthony informed Ella that the farthest booth had the best selection of drinks.

—Have you sampled the staple beverage of Thailand? he asked.

—Singha?

—Thai iced tea, he said, overenunciating. It's too sweet. Terrible stuff. We'll have two, he told the shopkeeper, pointing to a milky orange drink displayed on the counter.

—*Ao song, ka,* Ella repeated, embarrassed by the impudence of Anthony's English.

—Yes, but they know what you mean. *Kap khun krap.* Thank you.

He carried the drinks to a nearby table.

Across the terrace, crowded now for lunch, float smells of roast chicken, potatoes, and quail. I set coins on the table, take the still-empty shopping bag, and start up the hill.

It's hot inside the flat. I open the long windows and sit at the writing table in front of my computer. Clicking open the browser, I find the road Ella calls the "superhighway," Phahonyothin Road, listed on the map as Highway 1. It snakes up the screen, connecting the city of Chiang Rai to Thailand's border with Myanmar. It passes a university. Another search shows that pineapples are native neither to Chiang Rai nor to Thailand. Europeans brought them, having discovered them in South America. The plants grew well in the tropical climate.

I should type up what I've written, but the two flimsy scenes don't feel like enough. There needs to be more Ella: something she wants, something she's running from.

Delaying, I take the beige book to the window. With the summer air—skin temperature on my face, I read that every office in the Faculty of Arts and Letters has its own large window. Ella's looks out over hills and pineapple fields, while Muay's faces an inner courtyard, with views across into other offices, even on floors above and below. Sitting again at the writing table, I draw a line under the scene with Anthony in my notebook and write:

Ella unwrapped a piece of candied ginger from a jar on Muay's desk. Slowly.

—Every Thai nickname means something, Muay was explaining. *Lek* means "small," *Yai* means "fat," *Gai* means "chicken," *Mu* means "pig." If you look like something, you get the name. Or it's your personality. Like if you love to eat, you're called Yai.

—But nicknames are given to babies. How can you know what they'll look like or what their personalities will be?

—The personality grows up to suit the name? Maybe it's that way, Muay said, squinting at the large computer screen in front of her, which lit up the lenses of her glasses.

—What does your name mean? Ella asked.

—Ah! It means "woman of Chinese descent."

—But that's not a personality—

—No, it's my beauty!

Muay laughed, squishing up her eyes. Large dimples flowered on her cheeks.

—Chinese origin means light skin. It's why women from the north are famous for beauty.

Ella knew how little cultural obsessions with beauty mattered to Muay, whose doctorate in political science had earned her a professorship before she turned thirty, who valued wit above all.

—What could *my* nickname be? Ella asked.

Muay adjusted her glasses and peered through them at Ella.

—I've got it, she said: A.

—Okay. What does A mean?

—No meaning. The letter A maybe?

Ella was about to protest, when one of Muay's students came into the office. He *wai*'ed deeply. Muay returned the bow. As Ella turned to go, Muay called after her.

—Don't forget! Smoothies at the market after work. I'll come get you.

What isn't there—the space between words—gives me an image of Ella walking back to her office through big open rooms, sitting down at her desk, and staring at her reflection in the black computer monitor. Then she takes out her journal—the same book I'm holding open next to my notebook—and writes:

October 15

> *Two hours until Muay will come with her bottomless cheer and we'll go to a market that has smoothies,* arroy mak maak. *Delicious. Muay is thoughtful. She gave me a collection of short stories in English she'd found at a traveler's bookshop in Chiang Rai (Hemingway disproportionately represented, as if he were the god of all literature). I told her I didn't know what to teach, but that's not the problem. I don't know* how *to teach. I can't say that! I should turn on the computer but don't want to because there will be messages. The monitor is a black mirror. It shows me how my hair sticks out of my ponytail. My eyes look wild, dark. Better look at the hills. The view will never get old. It will mend the spirit and make it wise.*
>
> *I'll keep this book open when I turn on the computer, for strength, because these pages are the best of me. Five e-mails from her. Her justifications: blood not mattering, nothing changed, not lying, but obeying the truth of feeling. Truth of feeling! In her heart I am her daughter. They are worried. They want to know I'm okay. No apology—no acknowledgment that I'm right to be angry. My whole life until they told me was a mirage. Now the ground of the world is gone. Nothing is real. Was I an object to give and receive? How could they look at me every day of my life and lie? Breathe,*

look at the hills, little gold patches now, lighting slopes
of green. Thai alphabet. Letters, squiggles, lines.

The next three and a half pages are all squiggles that struggle
toward characters, some more successfully than others. The Thai
alphabet. Ella copied each letter again and again until she got it
right. She probably did this until Muay rapped on her office parti-
tion, miming a steering wheel with her hands, lifting Ella's mood.
I skip a line in my notebook:

~~Muay appeared at six, full of good cheer, and Ella was saved~~
~~from the whir of her own mind, from thoughts of too many~~
~~mothers—~~

No. Ella and Muay in the car, in motion. There is dirt and
dust, and sun lighting the land as it sinks toward the hills. The
journals give me the scene. All I have to do is copy what I see:

Ella rolled down the passenger window as Muay drove the
stretch of road connecting the university to the superhighway.
October sky, few clouds. Curves of hills becoming familiar, like
the Thai pop music on the radio, like Muay's hand tapping the
steering wheel, out of time.

Ahead, cut out against the landscape, was the back of someone walking, sandals kicking up dust, white shirt billowing against
the blue sky like a sail. He wore cotton trousers folded at the
waist in the Thai style, but his hair, or something about his walk,
betrayed him as a foreigner.

—Is that *him*? Ella asked as they drove past.

—Who?

The car swerved as Muay turned to look.

—The new teacher, the one my age, Ella said.

—I don't know.

The car found its lane again.

—But you pointed him out at Big C!

—I was only guessing. You met him already?

—No. He wasn't at the Welcome Dinner. But . . . there aren't many *falang* here, so . . . Turning the air-conditioning vent toward her, Ella observed how odd it was that he should be walking.

—We should give him a ride, Muay said.

Ella felt a prick of shame. The heat must be stifling. It hadn't occurred to her to offer a lift. Brakes screeched, throwing her forward. The car reversed a hundred meters.

—Ask him, Muay said.

Ella got out of the car, struck by the heat of the afternoon. She called to the man ahead, who turned. His hand, visored against the sun, set his eyes in shadow.

—It's hot, she said. Do you want a ride?

The man moved closer.

—Absolutely, yeah, he said, reaching out his hand. I'm Sebastian.

He had delicate facial features, high cheekbones that didn't match his tanned skin or his stubble beard. His parts didn't seem like they should fit together, but they did. He eased himself into the backseat and greeted Muay, who asked:

—*Bai nai?* Where are you going?

—Just to the main road there. I'll catch a *songteow* to town.

His shirt was sticking to his sides.

Muay asked Ella:

—Do you know what a *songteow* is? A truck with two—*song*—benches. You pay twenty baht.

—They come every ten minutes or so, Sebastian said. You hail it like a taxi.

He had a formal way of speaking.

—Sometimes they don't stop, and it can take forever to get anywhere. I'm going to town now, actually, to pick up my motorbike. You have more freedom that way.

—*Ahhh,* Muay said. Where do you live?

—*Ban Du,* Seb replied, inflecting Thai like a native.

—Be careful, Muay said, regarding him in the rearview mirror. Get a helmet.

She pulled over at the turnoff to the superhighway, and Seb thanked her in Thai.

—Handsome! Muay said to Ella, grinning.

Seb was hardly out of the car.

October 16

> *Each day, topography of mind is different from the day before. Filmstrips flash before the eyes at night. Damp soil under my fingernails, so the smell of my hands is orchids and warm rain and rice fields and mountains. I love drives with Muay. I love the bumps of dirt roads in the villages and the children staring. I am alive, want to be deluged with it all. I want the texture of petals on the tips of my fingers, more touch, skin on skin. Yesterday we met Sebastian. He was walking the university road like a beggar-saint. In the car, he was polite, soft-spoken. Muay thought he was handsome, but he looked so lost walking like that. Today he came by my desk in a bright blue shirt and was cleanly shaven. He asked if I would begin with the*

hero's journey. He's teaching a literature class, too. He seemed like a different person, so I asked if he'd gotten his motorbike, and he said he had.

I know already I never want to leave this place. I never want to feel indifferent to things again, not living fully—as intensely as possible. Here I'm alive, flooded by sensations, suspended over anger and uncertainty. I am whoever I want to be, finally content, finally free.

5

Our table is tucked away, far from the picture windows with their heavy drapes. The tabletops are mosaic suns, candles at their centers. Siobhán stands to kiss me on both cheeks, filling the space with a light musk, oddly familiar.

—You do eat meat, don't you? I've ordered us wine and prosciutto to start.

Her manner is formal. I am nervous. I sit across from her, hands in my lap, wondering if her face holds clues to Ella's future: skin creased around the mouth and eyes, tautness giving way in her cheeks. She is all refinement, nothing raw or spontaneous. She wears a charcoal blazer. A necklace of silver triangles nets her collarbone in lines of light.

I take the sample from my bag and hand it to her, hoping she'll read it immediately. She canceled a French translator's contract at this stage. I want assurance I'll fare better.

She sets it on the table between us.

Linguistic translation would be easier. Narrative is too much responsibility. I might have brought a foreign flavor to a French version of the journals, rendering them not quite native and a little strange. Already Ella is making *my* language strange. My thoughts, no longer tired, snuffed out at their ends, unfurl along the contours of her syntax, in the style of the beige journal.

—I don't know if there's a thread yet, I say. I'm making up a lot.

Siobhán says nothing.

—I think it would be more accurate to transcribe the journals. She writes well. There's freshness.

Siobhán looks down, tapping her long fingers on the table. I go on, wanting to make myself clear.

—A story could complicate things. It might bury her, make it harder—

Siobhán interrupts with a wave of her hand. She says:

—If the journals said where she was, we would have found her already. The information we need is not in the journals—not in what they say. Do you understand?

I stare at her. Not in what they *say*? Then *where*? Having moved across the ocean at her request, I need to believe that Siobhán knows what she is doing.

—I see Thailand, I say. Ella describes the colors and smells. It feels like I'm there.

Siobhán inclines her head, pleased, then tenses under the pressure of some thought.

—You've read the green journal? she asks.

—Parts, I say, ashamed at my overreaction to its intensities, an effect of too much solitude in this still-strange city.

—If you've read some, she says, setting down her fork, then you know Ella was troubled.

Remembering Ella's writing on the napkin, I stare at Siobhán in horror. Can she know about my mother? Does she realize what she's asking? Tracking madness would plunge me down a path I'd spent the last six years—if not my whole life—so carefully avoiding.

My mother was institutionalized twice for "nervous paranoia." It happened the first time when I was eleven, the second time when I was eighteen. She cut off all her hair—that most visual part has stayed with me. She had it styled in a boyish cut and was home in time for my high school graduation. But she was thin, with dark circles and skin so pale, it made her lips too red in contrast. Her death was long after her last episode, tragic in the way accidents are, seeding desire for worlds in which it hadn't happened. I like to think that my memory isn't there the months after her death because I was living elsewhere, in counterfactuals. But the terror is that I'm marked for what happened to her, the nervous paranoia. My father is afraid, too. I feel it. Most terrible were the times I lost her without losing her, when her thoughts dipped and lost coherence—when she was there in body but reacting to a world only she could see, one that she, somehow, had created. Both times she was gone for two months and then returned to us, frail. In time, her fun side would flower again. My father didn't talk about the episodes, and not even our extended family knew. My mother had a small reputation in the sculpture world, a part-time teaching appointment at MICA. She didn't want others to know, so it was kept private, secret.

—You should have mentioned it earlier, I say.

—I did, Siobhán says, her surprise genuine. What does it change for you?

I look at her, searching. Her manner is so innocent. She can't possibly know my mother's history. The condition came on late, after I was born, after she and Siobhán had lost touch. Siobhán hands me a menu.

—Better have a look. I always get the duck, but the mussels are also very nice.

She looks at me strangely as I try to read the menu.

The woman in the alcove last night—had I imagined her? I try not to think about it.

—Elena, you're an artist on commission. Read the journals, first to last, then tell me if you still want to accept.

I nod, suddenly afraid that she'll rescind if I hesitate too much.

—A journal can mean a lot of things, she says. It's the patch of land traveled in a day. It's the record an *I* makes of itself as it passes into things.

She turns to the waiter.

—*C'est bon, merci.*

He fills our glasses. Light through the wine casts ruby patterns on the table. Siobhán holds my gaze a moment. I look down. *Passes into things?* I must have misheard her.

—You knew my mother in London? I ask.

—Yes. Your mother was there when Ella was born.

I look up, very still.

—It was a long time ago, she says, picking up her glass. I love this wine.

It tastes of pomegranates. When I imagine her and my mother together, Siobhán grows younger. She might tell me about that time. There may be more to my mother than I know, an alternative she missed that I might take—one that doesn't lead where she went. Siobhán and I might help each other.

Suddenly, as if just remembering they're there, Siobhán takes the pages I've written. She reads in silence.

I wait, swirl my wine in the glass the way she did, smell it. At another table, a man leans in, candlelight on his lips and teeth as he talks, gesturing with his arms, fingers splayed, telling a story.

—No, Siobhán says, setting down her wineglass. Not like that. No.

—What? I ask, alarm spreading.

—I can't find Ella here. I don't know what she's feeling. There has to be . . . more feeling.

I look at Siobhán in confusion. The scenes *do* have feeling. I remember my thrill at seeing the *place* arise from the journals, its colors and smells.

A plate of prosciutto arrives with a basket of bread and miniature pickles.

—Do you know where Ella is? I ask, sensing I've asked this before.

There's too much urgency in my voice; I need to know I'm on the trail of someone living.

Siobhán's eyes catch the lights, flashing anger in the dim room.

—If I did . . .

Her face falls. Her loss of composure disarms me. We sit in silence, not touching our food. My words come on their own, out of instinct to quell Siobhán's distress, to comfort her.

—What can I do?

Siobhán looks at the pages still in her hands, mouths some of the words, then turns to me.

—The journals say "I." You say "she." Maybe you would capture more if you—

—You want me to write in the first person?

Siobhán hands me back the pages. I scan them. It's a strange request, but it makes sense. Siobhán wants to find her daughter. If I write from Ella's perspective, if I say "I" and not "she," I'll feel her feelings as my own. I'll be with her at every juncture, making her choices, going over her steps to find her way. Siobhán looks so inconsolable that I push away my suspicions.

The waiter approaches, clean and professional. When he has taken our order and gone, Siobhán requests five new pages from Ella's perspective. I should deliver them to her at the Ormeau Gallery at noon. Tomorrow.

II

Loi Krathong

6

S IOBHÁN SOFTENED. She gave me three days to write the new
pages—three days, ample and round, like peaches ripening
in the summer markets. But the visions do not return. Now that
I must be an actor, involved in the scene, the journals withhold
their magic. I'm left cold. No vision, no spark.

Since I cannot write, I follow the black-eyed man. He lives in
a timber-frame house up the road (there are a few in Montmartre; they must be expensive), above a café with a glass front. The
smell of roasting coffee beans draws me inside. No one is behind
the bar, so I sit for a while. The blue journal is with me, but there
is the tug of the world and the fear that if I open it, the smell of
coffee, the warm wood of the table and dust in the sun might
slide away. Irrecoverable.

The black-eyed man appears behind the bar. I open the book,
so that I'll seem busy.

> *She is forty-two and needs to be reborn. Soraya.*
> *On the full moon, we'll strip off our memories, wash*
> *them in the river, and put them back on, purified,*
> *like clean clothes.*

The blue book is easier to read. The beige book was terrible—
a summer of malaise with one mother too close and Ella plotting

her escape in desperate fury. Rage at the other mother—Siobhán—who had given her up. The blue book begins in Thailand with Ella's ersatz family, with Soraya, her chosen mother.

I'm deep in Ella's descriptions when I notice the black-eyed man beside me, his eyes soft, almost brown, in the afternoon sun. He speaks French at first, then English. He asks what I want to order, says he named the café the Cave and does this sound good in English and have I ever seen a coffee plant and do I know the fruit is red? He tells me his name, Jérémie. He asks about the journal. I tell him it's a story I don't know how to begin.

—Beginnings are the best, he says with a lightness I don't expect, given the sullen dreaminess, the airy gazes riveted to his cigarette I noticed before.

—Why?

—You do just what you want. Everything is possible.

He moves like a cat, nervy and exact, long, thin limbs given to sudden gestures. He seems both very young and very old.

His words about beginnings stick. What do I like best? *On the full moon, we'll strip off our memories . . .* a ritual about sending the self away in tiny boats: *Loi Krathong.* In the café, I make a draft of a scene.

I'm supposed to inhabit her, like an actor accepting a role, but I'm reluctant to lend my *I* to Ella. If I change body-minds for a time, mine might slip away forever, leaving me *I*-less, one of Marker's haunted watchers.

As I walk the city, taking a detour back to the flat, I follow Marker's example, stitching together what's disparate in my field of view: oddities like the discarded braids and clouds of fake hair on the rue Poulet and the goat heads at the *boucheries* at the market at Château Rouge. All these impossible things make up a city—a very large man carrying a puppy beneath his coat, sheltering it in a cloudburst.

When I reach the flat, I reread the scene I wrote in the café, hoping to find some life in it. It's stilted. Ella's not breathing; it's still my air. Under my pen, she dies a little. A different example shows how absolutely my words bury her impressions. Ella's entry versus my translation.

Transcription:

> *Paths dissolve in flight. Is this "letting go"? Is this*
> *what that means? Leave behind what you once were.*
> *Set out. Be larger. Be the air, the walls of the airplane*
> *cabin. The man next to me is asleep. Too dark-electric*
> *for sleep. . . .*

Translation:

I was twenty-one when I flew west to go east, which, if you never return, adds time to your life. From the airplane window, interstate-rivers of light. Leaving tugged like a tide as the city receded, its people invisible, slower than cars. Time spooled around the earth curve.

On my first night in Thailand—everything new, tiny hammers to the senses—I crept out of bed and carved my name in blue inside the kitchen cabinet. It was out of desire or terror or premonition that the raging world would swallow me whole, spit out my bones, dissolve me into *things*. I was afraid if I slept of becoming a *thing*. Wouldn't see wouldn't hear wouldn't touch. Osmotic skin. Place would grow into me. To stay conscious, thinking, I'd need tactics. The groove would be there tomorrow. I'd know I carved it. Mark of my passage.

Transcription. Translation. Ella's round letters press into me the dark quiet of the airplane cabin. But even the journals are not *what happened*. They're only glimpses. Stills. Incomplete. Not even a camera the size of a pinhead, recording from Ella's eye, would allow me to move with the weight of her body, or see Chiang Rai vectored by her interests (her frustrated love or her penchant for jasmine). Then there's what her perspective obscures: Orchids bloomed behind her back and seeds of rice were sown in the ground while she gazed at the sky. Am I meant to expose *more* than her words reveal—or cast form upon her living, the way the Gregorians reordered the past according to their calendar? Thoughts like small screws spinning in the darkening room.

THE NEXT MORNING, I WALK FORTY MINUTES to the Ormeau. It's not a pleasant walk, most of it along the busy boulevard Magenta. The quiet, narrow streets south of République are a welcome contrast. Siobhán and I sit in a bright café, speaking of things other than the project: the new show in her gallery, work by a Franco-Portuguese artist whom Siobhán refers to affectionately by her first name, Zoë.

As we walk along the cobblestones, I admire the large formats through the gallery front, stalling because I have nothing to show her.

In the skylighted back room, Siobhán pours fizzing water into tall glasses and tells me that Ormeau is the name of the road where her mother had lived as a child. Her mother is a poet, not one I've heard of. She asks about the pages.

—I don't understand your strategy, I say.

It's a poor excuse, but I can't describe what comes over me as I write, a feeling of dissolving Ella and of being dissolved.

—My strategy? Siobhán asks, surprised.

—When I write over her, she becomes more shadowy. I don't want to bury her.

Siobhán loosens the scarf around her neck and selects a group of folders from a filing cabinet. She pages through them, squinting at photographs of artworks. Next to her is a large graph-paper notebook with the names of people she must call.

I sit in silence, wondering if she's ignoring me or merely concentrating on what I've said. I should have brought *something*—even a page might have spared me Siobhán's chilly anger. Her position isn't hard to understand. The journals are the messy notes of a daughter she couldn't know and wants to love. My job is to make them into something she can access. And it's not impossible that something in the journals—overlooked until now—might lead us to Ella.

—Your question, Siobhán says. Does a kind of writing bury a person? Maybe. But the opposite is also true. It can also bring life.

She goes back to sorting the portfolios, moistening her index finger with the tip of her tongue. Her words are eerie but not absurd—at least not here in this room with the sun showering down from the skylight. Composed, calm, Siobhán exudes certainty.

—*All* writing is translation, she says. Experience is just darkness until it's lit from behind. Like a negative.

Siobhán is bizarre—elegant, but bizarre. Ella's journals have to be illuminated by some other mind—mine? Vague nausea tells me I cannot continue. If Siobhán looks up, I'll tell her—

—Tomorrow, Siobhán says, her eyes never leaving her work, please bring the pages.

Bells from a nearby church chime noon. As I cross the gallery, a painting gives me pause. Part paint, part photograph. A tree seen from below. Stopping in front of it, I let myself be drawn in by its bright leaves, which, frozen in eternal sun, seem more real than the branches outside the glass front of the gallery. Caught between two versions of the same space, the same leaves, I find the painting's title: *Nulle part ailleurs.* Nowhere else.

I turn around, wanting more of the sensation—pleasure in art that makes the trees outside seem fake, their power to seduce weak because they can't flaunt their reality. The other large formats fade around a wooden sculpture on a high white table on the other side of the gallery. Making sure the door to the back room is closed, I move closer. Its smooth forms seem to be hugging, fit together like an egg to its shell. Wood so polished it looks like skin, so familiar that it's terrible to think I didn't notice it before. It's not part of the exhibit. I know who made it. I touch the surface, smooth wood I half-expect to be warm. Most of my mother's work was destroyed.

On the street outside, I decide: no more doubt. I seal a pact with myself to develop Ella's impressions. Her words will disclose a world inside of this one. *Nowhere else.* I have the sense that what the journals hold isn't irrelevant to me, to what I'm looking for. I'll transcribe each entry. Save file. Rewrite. I'll weave her fragments into a story. It's okay that in my own experience, none of it has happened—unless it *has*, in other ways, involving other characters on other streets in other cities. This way, I have the means to understand, to live something other as if it were my own.

7

Here, with the palms and banana trees and the airport tarmac
as my witness, I vow to dissolve my Self in pure world. After
more than a day in the air and layovers (three), I came to Chiang
Rai's little airport. On the air was the smell of a sweet flower.
The sun was high and there were green hills . . .

Immediacy cannot happen immediately. Get inside her, Siobhán would say. It takes work. Closing my eyes, I lay my head on
the writing table and see the evening sky over Philadelphia—a
skyline I know. *Adventure or escape,* Ella's thinking. She's sitting
in the passenger's seat. Her father is driving her to the airport (in
my mind, he looks like my own father). *Adventure, escape, or a
third term,* she thinks. *It's living. Just life. Succession of flights: run-
ways, cities fading into cloud, ocean's tug at the belly of the plane,
pacifying Pacific,* Ella thinks, and the distance from home—its
illusions—calms her until the unknown catches on and pulls her
forward. Excitement. Bangkok airport, then the last leg, a short
flight to Chiang Rai, a northern city. Arrival:

All at once there was the place. I held up the line coming out
of the plane because of the air. It carried flavor and living. On the
breeze was a sticky-sweet smell I'd come to know. All at once
there were palms, banana trees, and tea plantations stretched

across the bellies of hills. Pausing to take it all in, I vowed that in a struggle between my Self and the world, I'd back the world, which bursts in anyway sooner or later.

The walk across the tarmac made me aware of my clothes, loose sport pants that dragged on the ground and a long-sleeved shirt, cotton sticking to my arms and stomach in the heat. My carry-on was overfull and bulked against my hip. None of it mattered. Living green hills cupped the airport in their valleys.

Arrivals was a single room with linoleum flooring. Signs with names disappeared one by one, and the crowd thinned to a single woman cleaning the floor in circular strokes. The heat and the smell of the cleaning fluid made me dizzy, so I sat with my bags facing the glass doors, one of which stood open. Someone from the university had been supposed to meet me. My heart began to race. Then a wave of thirst and fatigue swept in.

When I woke, a woman was leaning over me, eyes like fish swimming behind thick lenses.

—Ella, Ella.

Startled, sweating, I gathered myself and made a bow.

The woman erupted in laughter, full-bellied and real. She *wai*'ed in return.

—Oh, she said, it's perfect. Come. This way.

Later I'd learn that Muay had been mortified to find me dozing and dressed the way I was, hair stuck to my face. Her laughter covered embarrassment. I'd been in the air for days, I told her later. What did *she* wear on the airplane?

—Not pajamas, she said.

Now, she led me out of the glass doors to the parking lot, and we loaded my bags into her car, which bore decals of tender-faced anime creatures and the logo of the university, where she was a professor of political science. She said that the vice president had asked her to take me under her wing, since I was young and new to the country, and she knew something about where I was from, having studied in Minnesota.

—Why did you choose a place so cold? I asked, knowing nothing about Minnesota.

—*Choose?* she said, laughing. I hardly choose anything. But I learned that snow disappears in your hands. I was amazed, like a kid—you know, snow is exotic to Thai people.

—You didn't want to stay?

—Sure, she said, starting the engine. But, again, I don't choose.

She had dimples, many of them, and hair cut straight, chin-length. Her blue blazer was too tight in the arms. She must have been hot.

—Why don't you choose? I asked.

—My family needs me close by. The United States is too far. You know, in Thailand family is so important. I wanted to stay longer, but not forever.

—Would you go back?

Muay shrugged.

—I'm happy here, lots of friends, good job.

She smiled, showing her dimples.

—And my family wants me to find a husband. That's harder in America.

—Your family, I said. Do *you* want a husband?

—Do *you?* Muay asked me, mocking.

—I want lovers first, I said without thinking.

Marriage belonged to a different phase of life, but love had no phase. I was open to love.

—*Do* I want a husband? Muay repeated, amused. I don't know. Sometimes I think I have better things to do. But don't tell anyone—at least my family—just don't tell my family.

I promised, and we laughed.

—Call me Muay, she said, or *pi*-Muay. You know *pi?*

I shook my head.

—*Awww*, she said, her voice rising and falling, *pi* means older sister, but here we say it all the time. With friends.

We gained speed along a straight road—Airport Road—which cut south of Ban Du village to the superhighway. All this would become part of my intimate geography, but at the time I was just drinking colors: cerulean sky, yellow pineapples in roadside carts, rice fields glowing green.

—Was your plane late? Muay asked.

I shook my head. Four flights. All perfect. On-time arrivals were validations of my direction, while delays meant that my strong will had run afoul of the fates. It was a ridiculous superstition I took seriously.

—The driver from the university came to look for you, Muay said, merging onto the superhighway. He didn't find you.

—I was there! I said, not liking things to escape me.

—Yes, you seemed wide-awake.

Muay looked at me sideways, chin tipped up in amusement, until I laughed. We laughed at nothing, at my indignance, at the driver I failed to notice, at my ability to sleep anywhere, at family, at being far from home.

—It's no problem, but there is one problem.

We laughed again, at contradictions.

—I'm sorry, she said: your clothes. You have a meeting with

the vice president. The driver would have taken you first to your room, but now there is no time.

I glanced at my sneakers and Adidas pants.

Muay explained that the vice president of the university would leave in a few hours for Yunnan, China, to manage a partnership between universities of the Greater Mekong Subregion. He had to meet me before I could sign my contract.

—He approves all faculty, Muay said.

Bright banners and a flowering meridian announced the university, a uniform village of taupe-colored buildings and covered walkways cut into a hillside. Muay gunned the car uphill, gears changing under us. At the summit, we pulled into a circular drive outside a building with palatial doors. Getting out of the car, I was all dread.

—Why did no one tell me, I asked, about the interview?

Muay shrugged, as if to suggest that a foreign teacher's arrival was not foremost in the administration's mind. She looked at her phone.

—Five minutes. Anything near the top of the suitcase? she asked.

I shook my head helplessly.

She kept studying me as we approached the doors, her expression troubled.

—Is the job really important for you? she asked.

I nodded.

She bit her lip and took my elbow. We crossed the black marble floors of the empty lobby to the women's restroom. Muay locked the door and put a finger to her lips.

—Don't *ever* tell *anyone*, she said, full of the bright energy I'd seen earlier.

I was so grateful I didn't know what to say, but she was already in a stall, tossing her blouse over the top. I changed quickly.

The full-length mirror returned to me a girl playing dress-up in a navy skirt suit. It made my body look boxy, prematurely aged. But Muay's shoes fit perfectly.

—Better too big than too tight, Muay said, peering out from the stall. Now go! Second door on the right; ask for the vice president.

Full of verve, I unlocked the bathroom door.

—Hey, she said.

I turned.

—Don't forget me here. And good luck.

8

THE SKY OUTSIDE IS A TIN BOWL, humid and uninviting, different from yesterday's heat and sun. Siobhán has invited me to her flat for tea, which she serves from a Chinese clay pot decorated with frogs and lizards. In the flat are white couches, Oriental rugs, and high French windows (and a white rug in the bathroom that I stepped around for fear of getting dirt on it).

As Siobhán reads my pages, I sit on her white couch and study the geraniums, oddly humanoid, in flower boxes outside her window. She will love the pages or hate them, or she will say nothing. Whatever happens, I'll continue. This time, writing *I* to mean *she*, I was more than myself, Ella leading me into a world of edgeless spaces and vivid colors.

Siobhán is so finely polished that it's hard to imagine her close to my mother, who hated things too rigidly in place. But the wood sculpture in the gallery is proof of their friendship—and precious, since so little of her work survives. She wanted it all destroyed. My father hesitated. Then fate decided for him: an electrical fire in her studio, where we never went, three months after she died. Old wiring, yes, but what is errant electricity if not the work of ghosts? Apart from the pieces in galleries or private collections, nothing is left. She worked in wood early on, then plaster and metal, returning to wood at the end. She must have given the sculpture to Siobhán, but when?

Siobhán sets the pages on the table between us.

—The story is fine, she says.

She sits rigidly on the edge of her chair, her spine very straight. I stare at the Oriental rug, wishing she had a small dog, something I could hug or pet.

—So much detail, she says. How did you do it?

I tell her about the virtual tour, the campus map and faculty profiles I found on the university's website (which, fully updated two years ago, had no record of Ella). Nicknames weren't listed, so I went through the profiles of all the female professors of political science—there were only four—and found a picture that fit Muay's description in the journals. I checked for Minnesota on her CV and even ordered her book from the library: *The Thai Government's Position on Ethnic Minorities,* translated by Muay herself and published four years ago in English. This is what I tell Siobhán, but it isn't the truth. The truth is that the journals carry a sort of magic. They speak. How else could I feel the breeze on Ella's arms, her easy laughter with Muay on their drive from the airport? It may not have happened that way—the level of detail means it almost certainly couldn't have—and yet it's true.

—You're thorough, Siobhán says.

—I'm obsessive, I say, and try to smile.

We sit in silence. A minute hand is ticking, but I can't find the clock.

—My mother's sculpture in the gallery, where did you get it? I ask, Ella's voice making me bold.

Siobhán inclines her head, pleased.

—Ida sent it to me. It was the last sculpture she made before leaving to join your father in the United States. She was pregnant with you. A good-bye gift.

—Were you studying curation at the Slade? I ask.

Siobhán's laugh is terse and dry.

—I was painting. But I wasn't sure of it, not the way Ida was. She is quiet a moment, then energized.

—Ida and I shared a studio. We used to sing. Ida could harmonize to anything. When Ella was born—it was difficult—I hid away from everyone. Ida found me. Here, in France.

Siobhán smiles, then stumbles—a dry root in the path of memory. Her face loses expression. The past closes up.

—The pages are fine, she says. Be in touch in two weeks. We'll keep track of your progress.

On the walk home, I wonder how I violated one of Siobhán's boundaries in air.

In the flat, to distract myself from thinking about my mother and Siobhán, I open the blue journal. Scenes gather against the dull afternoon: Soraya, Anthony, Sebastian, a young man called Mr. Koi, a Frenchwoman in a batik dress. The scenes are there, and I've only to hang on, taking minutes like a scribe, reconstructing without knowing (like Ella) how it's going to end.

9

LULL, THEN RUSH. RHYTHM OF THINGS. In the lull, Muay took me to her tailor in a nearby village to have a suit made. I chose a smart gray fabric that looked great on the roll but felt scratchy against my skin. The suit had been made to measure but fit me poorly, too square.

—You'll have to square yourself to fill it, Muay said.

I was thinking of this, of squaring myself into suits, and into the terra-cotta tiles of the walkway as I waited for the Welcome Dinner for New Faculty to begin. I had so little to do that I'd begun arriving early to things, a parody of a professor in my square skirt suit.

Ahead on the walkway, the vice president appeared with a Western man with shock white hair making animated gestures. It felt good to see someone who looked like me—not a feeling I was proud of, but I'd been Muay's constant companion since I arrived, and was beginning to feel like her like her indolent pet—mute, save for when a friend of hers would trot out his rusty English, out of pity, since I couldn't speak his language.

Anthony, from England, had been in Thailand fifteen years, mostly Bang*kok*, which he pronounced with the stress on the second syllable. With him, I didn't have to be ashamed or apologetic or grateful. He proposed refreshment to bide our time,

time that felt heavy. For the first time in my life, there was too much of it.

In the refectory pavilion, over Thai iced tea—which Anthony drank with relish—I learned about cow and chicken traffic in Ban Du village and *the bloody cocks crowing at all hours.* My suite at the university felt sterile by comparison (plastic wrap still in the creases of the sofa). When Anthony asked why I'd come to Thailand, the story of my adoption seemed far away, almost unimportant, so I said adventure.

—Alas, said Anthony, sighing dramatically, most English faculty here are like myself, archaic. You'll be petrified with boredom until you meet Sebastian. He'll return from his travels soon.

Then Anthony remembered he was supposed to be interviewed for Thai television, *of all the abject horrors,* so we returned to the banquet hall, where guests were milling by the bar or sitting on tatami mats. By the entrance, a woman was pacing in little circles, agitated, her hair twisted in a braid around her head, her Lanna dress, teal and silver, wrapping like a mermaid's tail. She hurried toward us, encumbered by her dress. She was even more elegant up close, mouth drawn in, cheeks dark and smooth. It seemed only natural that she should be trailed by TV cameras, though Muay told me later she'd contracted them herself to cover the event. Laying a jasmine necklace around my shoulders, she asked if I would like to be on Bangkok TV. She would interview Anthony first; then it would be my turn. Her name was Soraya.

The next day, I asked Muay about her, and my friend's mouth twisted as if she'd tasted something sour.

—In Bangkok, Muay said, pausing for effect, Soraya lives

with her husband and *children*. In Chiang Rai, she lives with the administrator from the university.

She left the room to retrieve a handout from the printer.

—No story is too small for Soraya, Muay continued, pausing in the doorway. Student buys fruit drink at campus store. *Ooooh,* Muay touched the back of her hand to her forehead, It's local Chiang Rai *saparot*—let's go interview the pineapple growers! She thinks she's so important with her camera going everywhere. It's not important. She should just go back to Bangkok.

—Also, Muay said spitefully, Soraya gave herself that nickname. Goddess-empress or something. It's not even Thai. She thinks *falang* will like it. She is always with *falang*.

—Why is she always with *falang*?

—Thinks they are better, can help her more. It's how she is.

At the Welcome Dinner, Soraya *had* seemed more comfortable with Westerners, choosing to sit with me, Anthony, and the other English faculty rather than with the Thai professors. She'd drawn me out with her questions, both attentive and distracted, stealing glances at the administrators' table.

AFTER THE WELCOME DINNER, the rush began. The new semester was so hectic that I didn't pay much attention when both Muay and Anthony announced the arrival of Sebastian, back from his travels. Did they think I needed a companion, because I was young, female, and alone? I was not vulnerable, so I resented Sebastian steadily for trotting in like my savior in the imaginations of others.

Teaching was a minor disaster. Sensing my inexperience, my students informed me that speaking practice would help them more than reading literature, so the readings on the syllabus could be simply optional. Incensed, I launched into a monologue about the value of literature, about the need to escape the strangleholds of our own experience. The students listened in silence, patient and polite but shaking their heads as they left.

I was at my desk digesting the debacle when Sebastian came by to ask how it went. I told him I'd been a parody, and he laughed.

—The authority role takes getting used to, he said kindly. It did for me at least.

He said there would be a dinner in his village to celebrate the first day of classes. If I wanted to come, Anthony could give me a ride in his truck. Seb, of course, would follow on his motorbike.

I recognized Ban Du Market from outings with Muay, but it seemed tired and dusty so late in the day. Anthony swerved onto a dirt road, waving to villagers selling candy and tires by the roadside, then pulled into a quiet drive lined with bougainvillea next to a yard with papaya trees. Men's dress shirts ballooned on clotheslines at the end of the drive.

We entered through the kitchen, and Anthony set about fixing gin and tonics. A young man, statuelike, watched us from an alcove, then stretched his arms and yawned.

—Mr. Koi! Exhausted after a day of napping, I presume? Anthony said.

Koi made a few flicks of his wrist, gesturing to the shirts drying.

—Thank you, Koi. I saw.

Later, Seb whispered that Anthony employed Koi as live-in

help. Seb himself could never do such a thing, having been a Marxist in his late teens.

We took our drinks to the veranda. Anthony offered more gin to keep the mosquitoes away.

—Not many mosquitoes, Koi called disdainfully from the kitchen.

We were joined by a Frenchwoman who lived across the street, Béa. I admired her dress—it was batik and colorful. She said they were fifty baht at the night bazaar in town. She'd show me. Béa was only six years older than I was, but she seemed so at home in her world—full of humor and practical wisdom.

Anthony tilted his head toward the kitchen, listening.

—Koi? Are you *eating*?

—Pork sticky rice.

—We're going for dinner, he called. *Moo Kata* in the village.

Moo Kata: metal domes over hot coals where slivers of raw meat cook, dripping juices to make a flavorful broth. Rounds of Singhas came in buckets of ice. We talked, laughed. Béa described a dessert from the Basque country, where she was from: cherry jam and cheese. Seb stuck out his tongue in disgust. She spoke Basque, to our applause. During that first dinner in the village, I felt scooped out of my troubles, held together by bands of light. In a strange country, in motley company, I felt utterly, entirely at home.

After dinner, Seb offered to drive me back to the university. It was a nice night, he said, and he was still breaking in the new motorbike. He didn't seem affected by the rounds of Singha with our meal or the gin and tonics at Anthony's, but I was light-headed, drinking drafts of jasmine, mouthfuls of mist as we drove. We sat for a moment on the sidewalk in front of my apartment, blood returning to our cheeks, cold from the wind on the ride.

We sat close, our shoulders touching.

—Hey, Seb said, getting up from the curb, want to see how to drive?

—Now? I asked, feeling drunk.

—It's pretty easy.

He started the engine and showed me where the kick-start was. He told me to watch the muffler; a lot of girls had scars from where they'd burned bare calves. He held the handlebars, bending close as I practiced steering, until I sped off, unsteady, then gaining momentum. I circled the parking lot, once, twice, exhilarated by the night air.

I sat down on the curb again, breathless, hoping Seb would join me. But he was leaning against the motorbike, letting its engine idle. He told me he had plans to rent a car and drive to X, where he lived last year. To pick up his stuff. There would be a costume party. Halloween. I'd meet younger expats, more our age, different from those in Chiang Rai. His smell: cloves, hints of sweat.

His taillights grew smaller, until the landscape swallowed them. Inside, I put on music, letting impressions from the day filter down. Songs swelled, and I had the urge to compose something, a story or a poem. But I was too much in the valleys. Instead, I opened the book I was reading and copied a line from it into my journal.

October 20

"down the hill amid the tumult of suddenrisen vapours of wounded pride and fallen hope and baffled

desire. They streamed upwards . . . in dense and mad-
dening fumes and passed away . . . until at last the
air was clear and cold again." Resist self-portraiture.
Unless ironic. Beyond the parking lot, dark hills are
sine curves. Night mist settles on the rice fields, clamp-
ing the earth. Music plays. Hands in the dim. Can't
write anything but this. Am too much in the valleys.
Tangled desire in the dark. Now, just happening. Liv-
ing is enough. Some other my-self will give an account,
from a peak above mind-maddening mists where all is
clear and cold. Words like amber to trap sensations, so
they'll live again in a body other than my own.

10

NOTES COVER THE WRITING DESK, character notes for Seb half-mooned by coffee stains. Idealization. It smells the way jasmine must smell in the heat, cloying. Saint Seb.

What would a *writer* do with a saint? To be fair, Ella resists idolatry at first, insisting that Seb is a friend, a big brother figure, *pi*-Seb. He is three years older than Ella, twenty-four when the story begins. He doesn't talk much, but he thinks deeply, and he writes. Ella sees his leather-bound journals in their regular haunts and when they travel. Is she tempted to read them?

If the lives of saints are told in passionaries, accounts of their sufferings on Earth, why not have a little fun? A passionary—a *Sebastianaria*—will reveal the true Seb, not the animal AntiChrist he was in his own eyes, nor the saint-idol he became in hers, but an ordinary blend of animal desire and the sentient divine.

Sebastianaria

Born and raised in Halifax, Nova Scotia, and educated in progressive Toronto, Seb strives to be unpredictable, pathless, beyond good and evil, with a disdain for bourgeois morality that he views as ideologically constructed. Antibourgeois sentiment means that he relishes shocks to the expectations. Terrified of boredom, he reroutes the ruts of habit. Is this what Ella loves, craves?

An avid sensualist, Seb loves bodies freed from gravity's vice-grip by movement (travel), sex, and drugs. His passionary, therefore, will be in motion, in cars he rents with Ella to explore some bit of nature: a waterfall, the brown expanse of the Mekong, the poppy fields of the Golden Triangle, or the tea plantations that terrace the hills and the Chinese villages at their summits. As for Ella, she was always willing to travel. It was all so new.

With Seb driving, in cars or on the motorbike, shielded by his body from the wind, she could slip from the heat of her center and become more free.

Their tradition of motion began just after the first day of classes, when Seb took Ella to the elephant sanctuary where he'd volunteered when he first arrived in Thailand. It was a hospice for elephants who were no longer useful because they'd been injured in logging accidents or were old. Seb had bandaged their wounds and watched their unhurried gaits. The mahouts recognized Seb and spoke to him in Thai. Seb let Ella hold sugarcane and bananas so that the elephants could swoop them up in their trunks. On the drive home:

> Seb *(making up lyrics to a Thai pop song on the radio)*:
> Bella Ella cerebella.
> Ella *(cautious)*: I don't get it.
> Seb: No ground to be found, Ella cerebella, darling.

Darling is what Seb calls nearly everyone. Ella knows this but can't help heat spreading though her body at the word. But she interprets the rhyme based on what she knows about Seb's view of intelligence—corporeal—and is insulted. More reason in your body than your best wisdom, he would say. For Seb, intelligence is moving into turns as he steers around bends.

I GET UP. POUR A THIRD CUP OF COFFEE. Sun flashes. Gray settles again.

ELLA AND SEB ROUND A BEND. Mountains come into view.

Seb: What do animals have that humans don't?
Ella: Sharper instincts.
Seb *(nodding)*: Smells so strong, they rip you open, and they can move without maps—
Ella: They can still sense the magnetism of the Earth.
Seb: In human animals, instincts are weakened. Through disuse. *(Grinning, he leans into a turn: Ella knocks against the side of the car.)* The human eats away the animal in us. But we still have it. . . . It's like (*He looks at Ella, his eyes almost white in the sun*) . . . fucking someone in a rainstorm, where you feel the electricity, just bodies and nothing but . . . sensation. Wait for the monsoons. (*He rocks into a turn, a switchback down the hillside.*)

She felt his presence even in his absence, she wrote, the way the rocking of a boat at sea recurs in the body hours after you've been on solid ground.

November 4

Traces in the sky seem like slits in atmosphere. Like you can look through them to another world. Wait ten minutes. The traces fray, the passageway is gone.

One night, when the little group had gathered over market dishes on Anthony's veranda, Seb tucked chopsticks from a noodle vendor into his upper lip and became a walrus, clapping his arms together. It went on for several minutes. Later, Ella asked him why he'd come to Thailand.

—I'm molting, he said. I was tired of the old ways. You?

—I'm destroying myself, she said, giving her most charming smile.

—Good luck. Let me know if I can help.

A ROUTINE HAS GROWN AROUND ME IN PARIS. Mornings I work on the journals. The hours fly. Afternoons I spend in the national library, and in the coolness of its space I think of Ella. There are doctoral students who stay in the library all day, busy. Sometimes, after closing, we go for drinks on one of the *péniches*. When they hear I am taking time off, they grow uncomfortable. They tell me to be careful. I'll lose momentum. Soon they'll go home and begin teaching, as I would have, too.

Today, I leave the library early and bike along the river to one of the small cinemas by Saint-Michel. It is one of the hottest days of summer. I'm almost to Île de la Cité when I see him, a man with hints of copper in his hair and a way of dressing and walking that is Seb's. I stop. He passes. I park the bike and follow him on foot.

He crosses the river and turns right, continuing along the lower quai. Then he sits on the stones and takes out a leather-bound notebook. I watch him a moment, sweating in the meager shade, then ask:

—Sebastian?

It's so hot, I can't think. It can't be Sebastian. It's too unlikely.

But if it *were* him and I missed it, I wouldn't forgive myself. Sometimes, as a reward for being on the right path, uncanny luck will strike.

—No. Sorry, he says, turning toward me.

He tells me a name that isn't Sebastian. I stare at the river, green in the sun.

—I thought you were someone I'm looking for.

—Sorry, I'm not him.

His answer unnerves me. I sit apart, pretending to wait for someone. Even his accent is Seb's—soft, polite, faintly British. I ask what he's doing.

—Sketching, he says. I do it to relax. Reminds me to be in my body. Otherwise, you're in your head all the time.

He speaks matter-of-factly, the way Seb would. With a slow thrill, I tell myself it doesn't matter whether this man is or isn't the Seb Ella knew. He'll be a prototype: Seb and not Seb. The city seems to waver in the heat. Trees dip their long boughs along the quai.

—Are you on vacation? he asks, jerking me out of my thoughts.

—No. I'm a student. I study French cinema.

He goes on to tell me, softly, in few words, about the travel-adventure company he's starting with a Parisian friend he met in India. They're pitching to investors this week. He draws a business card from his leather notebook, and I move next to him to accept it. We sit close together despite the heat. The card has images of kayaks, palm trees, a shadow doing yoga.

—Travel gets you into the world, he says. We're about that. You're only in the world through your body, you know, the way it interacts with different places and with people.

—You're not from Nova Scotia? I ask.

He shakes his head, unsurprised to be asked this.

—I grew up in New Zealand, England for school, then India the last six years. I have an odd accent. I know.

I observe the rhythm of his gestures. He exudes ease, comfort with his body despite the heat. He wears a faded red T-shirt that looks soft. We are still talking as the sun begins to set over the river island and people crowd down to the quais with picnics and music. The man who isn't Seb buys beers from a man selling Heinekens, who knows Hindi and is amused to speak it with the man who isn't Seb. We go on talking. I learn about his love affair this way. His first month in India, he met a girl from America. She was learning Ayurvedic medicine in Varkala. She wanted to be a doctor. It was years ago, but he describes her vividly, talks of the way some people burrow inside you and won't let you forget them. He didn't realize. All that mattered to him at the time was freedom, the ability to follow his instinct in any direction, unfettered.

—And now?

—Yeah, he says, you can go too far with it, like anything. Go too far with freedom and it shuts itself off. I lost her. She must have married, changed her name. I can't find her.

This isn't the Seb of Ella's time. He is reflective. He feels regret. Yet such sensitivity may have been exactly what Ella found in Seb. With a start, I realize how close I'm sitting, the way my face is tipped to his, my eagerness for his soft, slow words, for the texture of his voice and breathy silences. And him? He is pushing the girl, the lost love, between us. I have slipped into Ella, become too much. And this is the point.

Nevertheless, I try to recover myself, to return to researcher mode.

—So you did love her. You just didn't realize it at the time.

He makes a joke and dismisses the subject. Later, his friend meets us on the quai and invites me to dinner. The friend's flirtation only exacerbates Seb's disinterest. I leave them, pondering in the harsh light of the Métro tunnel how this encounter will feed the development of Seb. This man lost all contact with his Varkala love, as Seb had with Ella. He grew sad when speaking of her years later. Is Seb similar? What, if anything, did he feel? He and Ella spent so much time together. Is he haunted, wherever he is, by the Ella who, according to the journals, he couldn't love?

11

THE SUN ON THE ROAD TO X burned down into rock valleys dotted with shrubs and pines. The road tacked at hard angles. I'd asked polite questions when we rented the car and bought green mango strips with chili at the market. How long was the drive? How often would Seb return to X now that he lived in Chiang Rai? He was laconic. I almost regretted coming. Then he said something weird:

—I think you'll like the people in X. It's like . . . they're *playing* at being.

His body leaned toward me into a turn, brushing my shoulder.

—Isn't *everyone,* I asked, playing at being?

—No, he said, smiling at the road. I'm different.

—Why?

—Take you, for example. You've come here, you'll find yourself or whatever, and you'll go home. This isn't a phase for me, he said, gesturing to the countryside around us, wild and mountainous. I'll do this for the rest of my life. I've given up home.

He spoke gently, but his words reproached me for clinging to a home that had never been real. Brief flash of us traveling together, nomadic around the world. I asked where he'd go next.

Seb slid his hands around the steering wheel.

—Korea or Saudi, maybe . . . supposed to pay well there.

Silence settled again as Seb eased around the switchbacks, controlling the descent of the car. Muay had been scandalized when I told her about my trip. *Alone? With someone you don't know?* I'd told her I trusted Seb, which was shorthand for the grounding I felt when he was there.

—In X, they're *fun,* Seb was saying. Nothing is *serious.* When the house flooded during the monsoons, we bought beer and Super Soakers and shot the floodwater out the windows.

—Why did you move?

—Oh, you can't stay in X. You'll see. And . . .

His expression hovered between a smile and a wince.

—*And?*

—There was a girl.

—In Chiang Rai? I asked, feeling my stomach tighten.

—In X, he said. With some Thai girls, it's . . . It can be too much.

Seb's laughter, raw and nervous, made me feel an immediate sympathy for the girl.

—X is a strange place, he said. It's like time doesn't move there. I knew if I stayed, I'd wake up really old and not know how it happened.

Whenever Seb said something serious, his vowels changed, became almost British. In another tone, practical, logical, he said:

—Now *this* is what I'll never understand. Different vendors selling exactly the same thing at exactly the same price right next to one another. How does that *work?*

Along the road, pineapple carts were spaced at intervals,

then tamarind sellers, pomelos like bowling balls, then carts filled with baskets of a small brown fruit I thought was longyan.

—Think of the opportunity, I said. You could sell guavas, condoms, *anything* different and make a killing.

—Ay, capitalism, Seb said. Can't take the American out of the girl.

—You could sell haircuts.

—Or stereo equipment.

—Or motorcycle tires.

We descended this way, the sun burnt orange, moon rising low in the sky. The highway smoothed and flattened, and there were lane markings, billboards, and traffic lights. In Chiang Mai, we stopped at a riverside restaurant Seb knew before pressing on to X to eat the lotus and forget the pull of home.

THE PATIO WAS LIT WITH TORCHES and thronged with zombies, chests painted white, flappers budding out of red feather boas, Batman and Superwoman straining a hammock, wine-stained Bacchae, Hansel and Gretel smeared in icing, human-size insects, antennae bobbing, faces distorted by carnival masks. Electronica buzzed in my bones. Seb's friends were dressed as butterflies. They gave me satin, wings, and glitter. Seb persisted in his white T-shirt, refusing offers of rapiers, wigs, and lederhosen. We left our bags in the car. I wondered where we would sleep.

At the edge of the lawn, fire sticks burst into flame. A crowd gathered to watch as a man swung the chains in simple circles. He stopped. A girl was crossing the lawn, silver bangles reflecting the torchlight, wings slipping from her shoulders. Her hair in dreads made a sort of crown. A murmur moved over the patio as she took the fire sticks. Ribbons of light unwound from her arms, fire scripts spinning in air.

—She's good, Seb said under his breath.

Another butterfly girl, beside us, heard him.

—Nunchucks, she said. You need them if you want to get good. She practices every day.

The arcs soared higher, energetic. Seb turned to her.

—I'll leave you my pair, darling. I can't use them in the north. No parties like this.

The girl looked me over; then Seb squeezed her shoulder as she wandered off. Her brash British accent remained in my ears, unsettling.

Around me, everyone was *falang* and young—though costumes made it hard to know for sure. In a corner of the patio, a man was crouching with a fancy camera, tucking it close to his abdomen for different angles on the dancing flames.

—These people, What do they *do*? I asked Seb.

—English teachers, mostly. She's in massage school, he said, gesturing to a girl making grass angels on the lawn. Some on gap years . . .

I liked how he would say something, then let it settle, feel its weight. He took a fresh beer from the cooler and opened it against the ledge. The fire dancer had stopped to talk to someone. Seb took a swig of his Chang. The flame dangled like a listless pendulum from her wrist.

I asked Seb about the other girl's accent. Something off about it, British but too strong.

—She picked it up from Tatiana and the others, he said. American as you when I met her. She's from Ohio.

Across the patio, a Thai woman, uncostumed in a white tunic

and jeans, was looking around her, amused, twisting her long black hair around her wrist. It made me feel sane to see someone else registering how senseless all this seemed. Feeling my stare, she smiled.

—Are you from here? I asked, moving toward her.

—Not far, she said. Chiang Mai.

—How do you know these people?

—They're friends, she said with a hint of suspicion.

I wanted to tell her that I was more out of place than she, that I'd asked out of solidarity. But I looked just like everyone else with my glittered face and butterfly wings.

—They can be silly, she said, but it's different, and I like variety. See you again soon, she said politely, moving past me.

Seb, who had been talking to someone, noticed us and leaped after her, taking her hand. They hugged a long time. I felt a noble bruising. He loved her. How could he not? She was *herself* amid this lurching sea of travesty. If I were him, I'd love her, too. Alone in the crowd on the patio, I was too much, out of place, angry at myself and at Seb.

On the lawn, a man in a sailor suit was singing and stumbling away from a flapper trying to calm him. Giving up, she sat on the grass and smoked, while the sailor bared his chest to sing to the moon.

—He's singing Icelandic folk songs, Seb said, beside me again. Out of control.

Seb reached as if to put a hand on the small of my back but stopped, thinking better of it. Next to us, a group opened a Styrofoam box of *pad thai* and began to eat with their hands.

—Sing the one about the lovesick goat man!

The sailor's movements grew wilder, more exaggerated.

—His ex used to live in the house, Seb said. From Norway or Sweden. Incredibly sexy.

I shot him a glance. Was I his confidante, a drinking buddy?

The sailor set off toward the driveway, the fire dancers nowhere in sight. Dunking the sticks in kerosene, he blew tongues of fire.

—He's going to kill himself.

—He'll burn.

Laughter. The voices were high-pitched and overly clear, as if telling stories to children.

—Burning bodies.

—Smell bad. *Putrid.*

—Charred skin.

—A roast, Seb said under his breath.

A group assembled in front of the sailor, lurching right, then left, mirroring his rocking. I expected Seb to help, but he just leaned his elbows on the ledge, shaking his head.

The man began to dance more vigorously. Towering over those trying to calm him, he sloughed them off like insects, his face waxen in the firelight.

A splash extinguished the flames. I looked up in time to see the female fire dancer set a bucket on the pavement. Someone caught the sailor's arm, but he wrenched himself free, wiping his face and then fleeing beyond the hedges and into the street. The pursuit continued.

—He's going right for the monkey, Seb said. They keep a wild monkey in a cage. It screams at you with a human scream. Tear your face off if it ever got out.

Soon there were strains of a victory song from the street:

—*What shall we do with a drunken sailor? What shall we do with a drunken sailor? What shall we do with a drunken sailor?. . . Ear-ly in the morning.*

The rescue party appeared on the lawn, carrying the subdued man by his wrists and ankles.

—Put him in the brig!

—Not yet. Rusty razor first!

The music had stopped. The man lay limp on the lawn, a plaything for the revelers, who appeared to be shaving the soft hair on his stomach. I turned to Seb in disgust, but he was no longer there.

I was independent, of course, and didn't need to be hitched to his side all night. But his absence made me anxious. Why couldn't he have said where he was going or that he'd be right back? Hoping to find him, I moved into the house, feeling suddenly the effects of all our drinks. Masked creatures brushed my body as they passed.

Sinking down against the wall of a corridor, I breathed patchouli and sandalwood, smells that signified a world without weight. Low light turned faces alien blue, drunk on our elsewhere Orient. The Thailand of X is not a place on any map, but a made-up country, a land of grown–up children who've stopped clocks to live in a world projected onto living space. X is a playground with motorbikes and monkeys, where everyone is young, glittered, and feathered. X is not a place, but the negative of place, latter-day colonialism of the existential kind.

I got to my feet and walked on, jostled by masked inebriates. Time stood still. If I couldn't find Seb, I'd be stuck here. I'd wake up in this corridor, an old woman with butterfly wings.

Pressing on a half-open door, I found myself in a room full of butterfly girls, chatting and draped over triangle cushions and bamboo mats in a circle. Pictures of Hepburn-looking women were taped to the walls, along with cutouts of collaged red lips and Louis Vuitton handbags.

—Sit down, someone said, and tell us who you are.

I recognized the faux-British accent.

—Seb's friend from Chiang Rai, I said.

—We didn't think he was fucking non-Thais, she said, laying out tarot cards. That's his rule, anyway, what he *says*.

I didn't correct her. The fire dancer, hiding a smile, rose from her seat and took my hand, leading me to a free cushion. There was a teapot in the center of the circle, a clay pipe streamed white smoke, and fat bundles of incense burned in coffee mugs throughout the room.

—Have some tea. Lapsang souchong.

—Smoky.

—Poppy.

—No, that's opium. *Idiot.*

—No judgment.

Someone handed me a cup. Tea leaves drifted lazily to the top. Lapsang souchong had the taste of smoke, of ashes.

—Tell us *all* about yourself, someone said. Can we not interest you in a smoke? How long have you been in Thailand?

—A month, I said.

—You're a baby! You'll stay on. You'll love it. None of us ever wants to leave!

—You can't get a closet in London for what we pay here, said the faux-British girl.

—She's American. You'd never guess, would you?

—She'll never tell you. You'd have to beat it out of her.

—We did! Have a listen.

Laughter.

—It's sad with Seb gone, she said, shifting subjects. We miss him. And Fah was lovely.

—She's not dead, is she? Just have her over! I'm sure she'll tell you all the luscious bits, what he's *like,* all you want to know.

More laughter.

—Separate beds, the fire dancer told her, gesturing at me, rolling her eyes.

The faux-British girl reshuffled her tarot deck. She warmed to me after that. We talked. Stubborn Americanisms stuck out under her polished vowels and ascending interrogatives. I wondered if it was a conscious effort. When I grew tired and tried to leave, she held me back.

—Your tea leaves! Tatiana reads them! she said, gesturing to the fire dancer.

—I should be *first*, said another girl.

—Come here, the fire dancer said calmly, brushing away the other cup.

There was a huskiness to her voice I found agreeable. But I didn't want my tea leaves read. I'm superstitious and don't like these things. I hate the tarot, for instance. But Tatiana was staring at me. It's rare for someone to really look at you. I know it's silly, but it made me feel close to her. Adjusting my wings, I moved next to her, holding my cup to my chest. She smiled, taking it from me. Her arms were covered with tattoos, a snake eating its tail at her wrist.

She stared up at me from the teacup, then put a finger inside to adjust something.

—Now you won't die, she said, putting the finger in her mouth.

When I laughed, she narrowed her eyes at me.

—I may have saved your life, but there will still be a break. Nothing I can do about that.

My instincts said to bolt, but as I scooted backward, she grabbed my elbow.

—Look, she said, tilting the cup so I could see. It's better to know.

I looked, but the leaves made no shape.

—The pattern means a break, she said. See?

She pointed, but the clusters of leaves and stained ceramic meant nothing to me.

—Most of the patterns are about challenging times, she said, periods of change, moves, even war, conflict. Most people think that if the leaves break here, it's a bad sign. You become someone else. Or something else. But it can also mean opportunity.

She looked at me carefully with something like pity. I felt anger rising. I wanted her to laugh so that I could laugh and then leave this ridiculous room.

She traced circles with her finger on the soft part of my wrist.

—Has it happened already? I asked, thinking of the adoption.

—No, she said, dropping my hand to take a joint from a girl next to her. Maybe. I don't know. It's not exact science.

She flung the leaves from my cup into an ashtray.

Outside, the patio was nearly empty. I made a tour of the perimeter, scanning the lawn. As my eyes adjusted to the darkness, shadows appeared, people under trees. I made out Seb's white shirt, purple in the blackness. Relieved, I ran toward him, then stopped. He was bending toward someone, her face tipped toward him in the darkness. Long black hair. I retreated to the patio amid the cloying incense, kerosene vapors, and jasmine.

As I stood, confused, sorting hot feelings, the screen door banged. Then a click. The photographer I'd seen earlier stood in the doorway, his camera pointed at me.

—Sorry, he said. Do you want to see it?

He showed me my image in the display: my profile shadowed by butterfly wings. I'd forgotten I was wearing them. He clicked through other images. In all of them, orange bled into the night. Faces and limbs became stretched patches of flesh.

—What happened? I asked.

—You were moving here, see?

I looked. My arm was a blurred patch in an otherwise-focused photograph.

—I like getting people when they don't know they're being watched. It's the only way to get people looking natural. It changes everything when they know they're in the picture.

—I take a lot of pictures, he went on. I was in India two months, three hundred and eighty-nine rolls of film, and that's not counting digital images. I upload when I can, but it's so slow that I mostly copy files to drives and send them home. I'll send you these if you want.

—You're from the United States? I asked.

—More native than you. Native American. An eighth Athapaskan. It might not be true, but it's what my family says. They were nomads—the Athapaskans. I'm interested in native-ness. Native populations—it's the name of my series. Most of the pictures are from India.

I was suddenly exhausted.

—This is my third-to-last stop if I go to China. I end in Mongolia. You know the *takhi*?

I shook my head.

—Wild horses in Mongolia—ponies, actually. I'll photograph them and live in a *ger* with nomads. You know, you can take the *ger* with you when you move—I mean, *I* can't, but they can.

I started to say something, but he cut me off.

—Do you know the Przewalski horse? It's another name for the *takhi*, after a Russian scientist who rediscovered them in the nineteenth century. They think the ponies were common in Europe during the Stone Age because they look like the horses in cave paintings.

He shrugged.

—Their lifestyle is incredible. Kids learn to ride before they can walk, and the ponies just stay, without fences or anything.

He paused for air and then went on, speaking uncommonly fast.

—They drafted a global management plan to stop extinction. It's a good cause, but if I'm trying to *do* something, I can't capture as much. You start worrying about the UN or whatever instead of the image in front of you—you know, things like color.

He grew thoughtful for a moment.

—If I see a scene, I capture it and take the consequences later, rather than trying to re-create something lost because of politeness. I'll send you the photos—good ones of you watching the fire spinning.

He showed me more images in the display: Seb laughing while I gestured with ghostly hands, a second photo, then a third of us entranced by blurry flames.

—The moving fire makes it hard, he said. People move, too.

I tried different lenses, but it didn't stop the blurring. If you jack up the ISO, it gets grainy. Slow shutter, *everything* shows.

He took my e-mail address.

—You live here? he asked.

—No, in Chiang Rai.

—North, right? You like it? Good place to decamp for a while, earn money?

—I think so. But I just got there.

He said he'd send the pictures, and I turned to go.

—I'll see about a job in the north, he called after me, since you recommend it.

From the lawn, I saw him change lenses and go back into the house. After a lap around the lawn, I caught sight of Seb. This time he was alone in the driveway, swinging chains with coals extinguished above his head and across his body, the way the fire dancers had done. Roosters crowed in the neighbor's yard, and I watched him duck swiftly as the chains veered out of the orbit he controlled.

12

THE WEATHER HAS TURNED, but I cross the city to the Seine. The pleasure of watching the water—gray-green under a changing sky—propels me down along the quais. I step up to the boulevards when they dead-end and rejoin them when they begin again beneath me. Collars are turned up. Trench coats, scarves. Walking keeps me warm. Bridges go by. In a café, outdoors under heat lamps, I sit close to the woman at the next table. She wears a fur coat.

Two hours later, I reach the allée des Cygnes. There are other walkers. We move back and forth along the alley of the island like weights on a pendulum: an elderly man and a child, two men speaking seriously, two women, hands entwined. We pass one another twice, three times. At the pont de Grenelle, I leave the island and walk up to the Bois de Boulogne. A museum is open. My fingers have grown cold. Inside, there are textures: paint, flowers, ponds. A thin man with a dark beard is painting in one of the galleries. I sit on a bench and watch his wrist flicking and dabbing, his gaze lost inside the image he's copying.

Ella. A still point, my doppelgänger, myself in a twisted mirror; she'll show me what I'm missing, what I've yet to understand: how to live. Find her.

At porte Dauphine, I catch the Métro. Lights glow on in a

hundred city windows before the train sinks underground. This must be the opposite of lonely: a body flowing through the city, drawing closer to the quiet and the dark.

13

A FEW DAYS AFTER MY RETURN FROM X, Soraya called to ask if I'd like to visit the mineral baths of Chiang Rai. I looked forward to the outing. X left me craving a wholesomeness that everything about Chiang Rai represented by comparison, and I was in a phase of wanting to turn myself inside out and rub into the country, every sight, smell, and taste of it.

For all her glamour, Soraya had a childlike, fragile side that didn't emerge until we'd spent time together, just the two of us. The mineral baths were one of the great benefits of the region, she assured me—the sort of thing she used to do with her daughters, but they were in school in Bangkok and didn't have time anymore.

At the baths, Soraya showed me where to store my things, and an attendant escorted us to a row of individual clay pits, corked at the bottom, with spigots for hot and cold water. The hot water smelled of sulfur. I watched Soraya's pool fill. She had brought a terry-cloth headband to keep her hair out of her face and dabbed sweet-smelling liquid from a vial onto her temples.

—It's peppermint and lavender, she said, handing me the vial. It helps you relax.

Soraya's eyes closed, and her skin began to sweat from the

heat of the pool. I dabbed the fragrant oil under each nostril and filled my pool, adopting her pose of relaxation.

After the baths, we had massages with two sisters Soraya promised were the best outside of Bangkok. The sisters served us tea and *kanom*. Soraya spoke to them in Thai.

—I tell them you're my "Western daughter," she said, patting my arm. They ask what kind of pressure you like for the massage.

I discovered muscles I didn't realize I had—the muscles in my big toes, for instance, which, like every other muscle in my body, were kneaded and stretched to release the tension of years. Remolded like clay, twisted and re-formed.

Colors seemed brighter, smells stronger as we walked back to the bath complex's wooden terrace overlooking the hills. There were other bathers on the chaise longues, sitting and talking. Soraya ordered *nam duk crai*, juice made from lemongrass stalk, and explained its cleansing, detoxifying properties.

—But you don't need to detoxify. You are young. Still a baby! Too much of a baby to leave home! Why have you come so far?

—I came to study meditation, I said, and believed it.

My reason for having come seemed to find a new form every time I was asked.

—You know, my elder daughter—probably your age—she is in her last year at university. After her studies, she wants to become a *bikkhuni*, a Buddhist nun. She goes every night to meditation at the temple. Everyone meditates together three hours by candlelight. When I am in Bangkok, sometimes I go with her. Have you been to a temple before?

I shook my head.

—We must go! She clapped her hands. There is a beautiful

temple near Mae Sai! The nuns wear white. There are candles. You will like it.

Our drinks arrived in bamboo cups. The juice tasted like earth and flowers.

—My younger daughter is in high school in Bangkok. Both girls live with their father.

Soraya shook her head, to dispel the bitterness. But her features darkened. Mother moods did that, changed suddenly like storms.

—They hate me, she said, her eyes lit with new intensity. Yes, they hate me.

Soraya focused on a point ahead of her, staring without seeing. Then she turned back to me, childlike again.

—My husband made me lie to them. They hate me, but they are right. I don't blame them, you see. I cannot.

There was pain and rage beneath Soraya's innocence. Still, she had lied to her daughters. I could think only of that.

—He *made* you lie? I asked, bitter, mocking. How?

Soraya fell out of her reverie, surprised. She'd counted on my sympathy. She considered me a moment.

—He didn't want them to know why I left, she said slowly. I left because I caught him. Everyone said I should stay, that it wasn't so unusual. But I *saw* him! I couldn't stay after that. He didn't want to lose face in front of his girls—he wanted them to think it was my fault, that I was tired of our family. I was allowed to leave, but I lost everything that mattered. I lost the trust of my daughters.

Soraya dabbed her eyes quickly with the edge of her sarong and looked out at the hills. Chastened, full of sympathy, I asked how her daughters had learned the truth. It felt important.

—Oh, no, they don't know, Soraya said airily, her gaze lost in the landscape.

—They still think you left for no reason, that you left *them* as much as *him?* Indignation rose within me. The solution to Soraya's trouble was unbearably simple. The misunderstanding had only to be cleared. Her daughters would understand.

—I don't know what he tells them, Soraya said.

She pulled her gaze from the hills to look at me, her face all lines and tiredness. Then she laughed, buoyant again, in good humor, her eyes alive with unearthly charisma.

—It wouldn't be good for them! They should believe their father is a good man.

I stared at her helplessly, wanting to tell her how I hated lies, how I'd grown up not knowing who I was. *You can't lie out of love. You only lie out of fear.* I was thinking of my own mother saying she'd lied to protect me, a justification I didn't believe.

—My mother lied to me, too, I said finally.

—*Jing law?* Soraya broke into Thai from surprise.

As I spoke, the present shrank around me and the past welled up—not only the recent past—conversations on the porch in June, silence rising like smoke through the house after I'd gone upstairs—but the distant past I hadn't lived, the world my mother tried to conjure for me: her closest friends, like sisters, the three of them in London, beginning art school the same year. My *biological* mother was the youngest of the three.

—When I finished university, they told me they weren't . . . that they weren't actually my parents. They lied my whole life— out of *love*, I said bitterly.

Soraya patted my shoulder, drew in breath and let it out in a long sigh.

—Your *birth* mother, did she never try to get in touch with you? she asked.

—They asked her not to when I was growing up. They thought it would be hard for me. It was hardest learning later. They say I can call her. She has an Irish name that isn't spelled like it sounds. She lives in France.

—You should call her! You should call your mother. That bond— Soraya's voice broke off abruptly. She must want to see you!

Her concern irritated me. I stared into the gaps between the planking of the terrace, bits of earth, grass, and rocks below us.

—I never knew my father, either, Soraya said after a while.

She blinked at me, as if I should notice something.

—Green eyes! she said. Western father. That's why I've had such an easy time with English. For TV, it has to be perfect. I have a bilingual show. Sometimes I think English is more natural to me than Thai. But still, she murmured. How strange for you. All the more reason for you to be my daughter, she said warmly—my Western daughter.

Soraya's stare caught the light, gold outlines of hills. I felt warmed by it, late sun in the deep calm of early evening.

—Life is sad, you know, Soraya said with a laugh. Thai people, we never say that. We say it is beautiful. It is also true. It is beautiful, yes, and sad, both at once.

Not knowing what to say, I followed Soraya's gaze into the distance, where the sun was sinking down among the hills.

14

SORAYA HAS MY MOTHER'S GREEN EYES. Why shouldn't she? I made her. The still air ripples. I'm with Soraya on the terrace by the mineral baths, skin slick with oil from the massage, taste of *nam duk crai* on my tongue. Lingering in her presence is satisfying, as if what's lost moves in her, animating her speech and gestures—her solicitude for Ella, whose role I play.

There comes a time when a writer must see the whole. Gone are the days of god's-eye omniscience, so I'm told, but a daughter and her substitute mother by the mineral baths, what is it driving toward? What torque does it give to plot, to the story of a girl who disappeared?

If I'm to use the mechanism of plot to my advantage—to the advantage of my story—it is necessary to know how it ends. Meanings are in endings.

So far, I've been "translating" as I read to put myself in Ella's body-mind. But now I need to see ahead, to gain narrative distance. I can't go becoming my character, can I?

Yesterday, I finished reading the journals from cover to cover.

They are so far from recounting what happened as it happened that Siobhán's request for a narrative makes sense. There is a sharp decline in decipherability in the last three journals, making the lucidity of the early ones eerie and portentous. I tried making a transcript, thinking it would free me of her disturbed penman-ship, the verbiage that magnetizes my own, causing a swerve. But I got only as far as the third book.

Only when I'm writing do I begin to understand. Only when I'm writing the story of Ella's life do the journals make sense. There is no *outside* the project, no outline; it's *here*, growing out of each scene I write.

I want to call Siobhán to tell her how terrifying it is to have this kind of power. She'll tell me it's only a story, that whatever happened to Ella has already happened. I don't have to save her, just find her.

Did she know the journals would remind me of my mother's most terrifying moments? Or, even worse, that I'd recognize *myself* in Ella—a seed of who I might become if I'm not careful? I'm moved by passages that were nonsense to me a month ago. I see connections others can't. But I find myself holding fast to furni-ture, edges and corners, because of how solid they are. Is this all part of Siobhán's plan, her "process"?

SIOBHÁN HAS INVITED ME TO DINNER with her brother and his partner, in town from London. In the small, crowded restaurant, we sit close to one another. Siobhán's brother seems surprised when he sees me, about to say something, the way people do when they think they know you from somewhere. But he says nothing about it, and the strange look fades.

Aidan is garrulous, full of jokes and warmth, with none of Siobhán's reserve. He's been in London over thirty years, he says. His partner speaks little. I don't know whether he is a business partner or a lover. Probably the latter. The lover is decades younger, closer to my age than to Aidan's. He is good-looking and seems almost apologetic about it.

After ordering our third bottle of wine, Aidan leans across the table. His neat white hair in the low light lends drama to his gestures. Raising his voice over the buzz of the small restaurant, he says:

—She's lost her mind, my sister. And we've abetted. We've spent the entire day disassembling a press—an 1847 *Albion*, mind you—and putting it together again three feet nearer the stairs. You can't move the thing without taking it apart. It's too delicate.

He appeals to me:

—*Why*, for a week, has she spoken of nothing but presses? And then why *purchase* one—terrible whim—and call me down to help with delivery, tempting me with opera—it always works— and making us labor for hours to reposition it? *Why?*

—For pleasure? I suggest, playing along.

Siobhán leans back in her chair with an inscrutable expression.

— Oh, the old aesthetic pleasure argument! Aidan says. Reaching back to her Slade days! Do you sculpt?

At Aidan's mention of the Slade, a pulse in my ears cancels all noise. Aidan knew my mother, too. I cock my head, acknowledging this.

—Don't be an idiot, Aidan dear, Siobhán says. Elena is a film scholar. She doesn't do everything her mother did.

Aidan apologizes, murmuring something about the byways of associative thinking under the influence of Côtes du Rhône.

—Siobhán simply didn't tell me, you see. I didn't know about the funeral—

—It was a long time ago, I say.

—It was impossible! Siobhán says sharply. We were looking for Ella.

Of course, they don't know—my father had no reason to mention it—that if they had been at the funeral, I wouldn't have remembered.

—What a time, Aidan says. Let's switch the subject, shall we? The press. You have to understand—my sister does nothing if not impeccably. Excellent architect, like our father. She retires early, builds a gallery. I had my doubts, but she pulls it off, yes, impeccably. Gorgeous space. But the press—at least she went with the antique. If you spend ten thousand on a whim, you must at least get the original, not the "modern" Albion some nice obsessive is re-creating in Utah. Still, it's a baseless expense.

Siobhán looks annoyed. There is no safe subject upon which we can land.

—You knew my mother in London? I ask Aidan.

He bows his head, smiling.

—She wasn't the kind of person you forget.

Full of courage, I turn to Siobhán.

—When was the last time you spoke to her?

I meant the question to sound casual, not accusing, but even Aidan's partner, silent for most of the dinner, looks surprised. My hands start to tremble, and I stick them under the table.

—I'm not sure I know, Siobhán says, frowning. It was hard to stay close after she left—after we both left London. We spoke by phone. . . . I wrote her letters.

—Was she *well*? I ask, aware that what I'm saying doesn't make sense, that she and Aidan may not even know about my mother's illness, let alone think of it constantly, as I do.

—What do you mean, Elena?

At her concern, so distant and clean, my anger boils over.

—Did you know my mother was institutionalized twice? Did

you know before giving me those journals? I ask, my jaw clenched, my hands shaking uncontrollably.

Aidan looks down at his plate. Siobhán stares at me in confusion. I hold her gaze.

—Are you putting me through it on purpose? I whisper, my mouth close to her ear.

Siobhán's face drains of color. In the silence that follows, she gets up from the table. With no excuse, no hint of anger, she pays our bill at the bar, then walks out of the restaurant.

I look at Aidan, half-hoping he'll give some other reason why she had to leave so abruptly. But of course, she feels accused—after she has done so much for me.

Aidan's partner looks amused.

—If we all did just what we wanted, it would be a beautiful world.

Aidan starts to say something and then stops.

—The journals, he says finally, shaking his head. Still so sensitive. It has been six years.

He lifts his head to look at me, sizing me up.

—Ella'd be about your age now. How old are you?—no, don't answer. I'm being rude.

—I'm twenty-nine, I say. I don't think it's rude.

He cups his face in his hands.

—You do look just like her, he says.

I blink.

—Like your mother, he adds.

I was sure he would say Ella.

—A press is such an odd choice, he says disjointedly. She could've acquired a dozen paintings for the price.

15

PAIN BEHIND THE EYES, sheets clinging like a second skin. The space around me came alive, vaguely familiar. Sunlight clamored against the shutters, leaving strips of light on the floor.

Surge of nausea as I sat up, looking around wildly, trying to work out where I was: brown couch where I'd slept, sheets, a pillow. Dressed in a T-shirt. Not mine. Underwear. Mine.

Panic surged, shadows settled into patterns, and the room came into focus: Seb's living room. Fresh wave of nausea. How had I gotten here? I crossed the carpet to open the shutters, then the window. Sky blue, scooped clean of clouds. Too-bright sun.

Seb was reading in his hammock in the shade. He was the last person I wanted to see.

—How're you feeling? Okay, yeah?

I fought the urge to vomit.

—Just some water and I'll be great, I said, making my voice cheery.

—There's some cold in the fridge, he said.

His voice was untroubled. If something had happened between us, this wouldn't be so. Fury at myself for drinking too much. My mind lurched through what I could remember:

At the discotheque, I kept falling. It's a forty-five-minute drive to the university. Seb was fucked up, too, and probably didn't want to risk driving so far. More logical to bring me here. Did I try something? Did he? Nothing is more terrifying than a loss of memory—the texture of reality gapes and the self in rags is reduced to nothing. I wanted back every lost minute, to be sure of myself and how I got here. I drank from the chilled bottle in the mini-fridge. Cold water buzzed through my brain.

—I'll go to Anthony's soon, Seb said through the window. You still coming?

Anthony was cooking Sunday brunch. There were plans for Scrabble. We'd agreed—early in the night—to meet at noon. Bad as I felt, I wanted to go. The thought of a *songteow* ride home and then stewing alone all day in embarrassment seemed terrible.

—Yes, I said. Give me a sec.

It was 12:15. Seb had set a towel for me on the coffee table. I took a cold shower, brushed my teeth—after some hesitation—with Seb's toothbrush, and joined him outside.

He rolled out of his hammock into a patch of sun. He was reading Emerson.

—You okay? He asked again, solicitous, too polite.

If he mocked me, things would feel normal, intimate. His hair was wet. He had shaved and looked more boyish than usual.

I nodded, aggravating the pain in my head.

—One too many whiskeys, I said, trying to draw from him a sense of how embarrassed I should be.

—We were all stupid. You were charming. I'm glad you're feeling okay, he said, as if he didn't quite believe me.

Whole chunks of the night couldn't be lost entirely. Effort would coax them back. I closed my eyes and saw dancing, colored lights, images out of focus.

—I had to put you to bed, he said.

His expression was overly kind. He was holding nothing over me, just exonerating himself: a nice guy who'd put my blackout-drunk body to bed. Building my truth on Seb's story made me feel out of control. I wanted to *remember,* to know for sure.

—Thank you, I said, looking away. Shall we go?

There were two routes through the village to Anthony's, and we went by way of the rice fields. The tips of the crops were green, fields verdant in the sun. A cow poked its white head out of its pen. A man with a leathery face passed, grinning with few teeth. A motorbike sped by. Bougainvillea splashed hot color, and the smell of frying eggs and bacon reached us in the street.

Beyond a screen of papaya trees, the long table on Anthony's veranda was set for brunch. Anthony, in his apron, was bringing out plates from the house.

—If it isn't the revelers. You're awake before Mr. Koi. I can't rouse him. I've been at it for the last hour, HAVEN'T I, KOI? he called into the house.

We removed our shoes. There were people in the kitchen, a friend of Anthony's I recognized from the university with his girlfriend, a Thai woman who was toying with the handle of a coffee press. Béa kissed me hello, tucking a stray hair behind my ear. She put a hand to my cheek. Was it obvious— my barely being able to stand?

We sat down at the table. The Thai woman offered me

tamarinds, miming how to spit out the seeds. The sourness made black dots squirm before my eyes. She told me she didn't speak English. I asked how she talked with her boyfriend, who didn't speak Thai. She laughed, as if I were a fool. We surveyed the spread: steaming brown eggs—Anthony had fried them in bacon grease—browned bacon, pieces of toast beside a tub of butter. Next to the foreign food, papaya and dragon fruit looked like a color-enhanced photograph.

—You must eat *something*, Anthony chided her as he began serving.

—*Im laao*, she replied, putting a hand to her thin stomach.

Anthony served her anyway, distracted, and began talking about how much it would add to the veranda at night to hang Chinese lanterns.

—We should hang those lovely paper lanterns we saw, SHOULDN'T WE, KOI? Anthony yelled into the house.

Koi, fully awake, was watching us, a pale shadow behind the glass door.

—What rough beast is this? Anthony asked, turning.

Koi drew up next to him, blinking in the sun, his hip against Anthony's shoulder. He *wai*'ed to us, smiling easily at the Thai woman. As Anthony twisted to keep Koi in sight, the muscles of his face slackened around the mouth. Then the expression, a momentary weakness, vanished, and Anthony said in his stage voice:

—After centuries of stony sleep . . . you must be ravenous! Come, Koi, eat.

He opened his arms, and Koi settled on his knee. Anthony's gaze softened again and settled, vacant, on the bougainvillea. From those shirts drying in the breeze on the day I met Koi,

I'd built a narrative that wouldn't complicate my impression of Anthony as a proper gentleman. *Mr.* Koi, the young man from Bangkok, dancing last night with such abandon, was hired help. All the signs I ignored: tenderness in Anthony's gaze, the way he spoke of Koi when he wasn't around. Everything fit effortlessly. Anthony. What could I call him, now that I knew? Gustav von Aschenbach to Koi's Tadzio? Socrates to Alcibiades? Was Koi a kept man? No label seemed to fit their bond, which was just itself, entirely particular.

Was it *good*? Koi was my age, legal age, Anthony four decades older. He had money. What of Koi's household chores? Were they performed for wages—to make it clear that any funds passed to Koi were for laundry, cleaning, shopping, or watering the garden only? There was clearly strong feeling between them. My Manichean order began to jitter and sway.

A shade fell from the veranda, sun shooting pain through my body. Koi squinted, raising a hand to block the glare. Seb got up to fix the shade.

—Best leave it off, Anthony said. The eyes will adjust, and it's nicer with the light.

—*Too* bright, Koi said.

—Oh, but you've been in your cave for twelve hours!

—Six! Koi cut him off. You make me look lazy. It's not true.

Anthony looked questioningly at Seb.

—We left around five, Seb said. He was still there.

Koi pointed at me, laughing.

—I can't believe I see you now. You were falling all the time.

I took a slow sip of orange juice, saw the black walls of the club, dancers on stage, high tables with buckets of ice, soda water, and whiskey.

—Well, 100 Pipers takes getting used to, Béa said kindly.

—Did I do anything awful? I asked, looking at Seb.

Something had passed between us. He was being too polite—or was I imagining things, half-mad with frustration and shame?

—Do you remember falling off the motorbike? he asked.

Flash of sensation memory: leather seat, concrete, bushes.

—It was in the parking lot, Seb said to ease Béa's alarm. She was like a rag doll, kept falling and laughing, so we couldn't get her to stay on the bike.

Anthony steered the conversation away from my embarrassment.

—Koi, we have eggs and bacon. . . .

Koi grimaced and said something in Thai. The Thai woman's eyes brightened, and they drove off a moment later on Koi's motorbike.

—They've gone to the market, insulting my cooking! Anthony said. Ella, will you fetch the board? And get yourself a glass of water, my dear. You're looking pale.

Inside the house, it was dark and cool. The game was on a shelf next to Anthony's books: practical solutions for waste management in developing countries next to Wilde, Genet, Yeats . . .

—From another of my nine lives, Anthony said, glancing over my shoulder.

His hands were full of dirty plates. He was carrying them through to the kitchen.

—I went in for the glamour of a law degree. My wife was a doctor. I had to keep up.

—Your wife? I asked.

—She kept the children. I'm so unsuitable, he said, squishing his eyes together as he smiled.

Behind his exaggeration, he was probing my reaction. He cared what I thought. I was moved. He went on:

—But the lap of luxury begins to sag, to reek of fish. So I became a doctor of philosophy in shit, with a minor in trash, servant of the Queen Mother's institution of higher learning, and your humble host.

A pang of affection welled in my chest for Anthony, who could transform pain to humor at a moment's notice.

—Sorry for the delay, Anthony announced when we reached the veranda, We were speaking of my past. It always takes up so much *time*, the past.

We drew letters. Anthony sighed, complained, then spelled JINN on the board.

Seb challenged and had to read from a frayed dictionary:

—In Muslim demonology, spirits who appear in human and animal forms to exercise supernatural influence.

—Your turn skipped! Now, Ella, you're next. Don't take forever.

Time weighed nothing that sleepy Sunday in the village. The sun drifted down through the sky as letters filled the board. I played on, the odor of whiskey in my sweat making me nauseous, dragging back scenes from the night before. One, buried and important, trembled at the edge of awareness. Anthony made a show of looking at his watch. I was taking too long with my turn.

—The strongest lack the power of their convictions, he told me.

—Don't listen. He's trying to rattle you, Seb said.

Rattle you. Seb's voice tipped an image into focus: bodies on the dance floor, pulled by the attractions certain bodies have for one another. I was standing at a table and leaning on my elbows, hair falling into my drink, when I looked up to find Seb's face so close that I could feel his breath. In his gaze was a mixture of weakness and something like anger. His eyes were devoid of their usual sarcasm, naked. *Your eyes are naked,* I told him. He squinted at me as if I were ridiculous. His look made me flesh, solid—a thing seen. Something shifted in me, opened. In all my dealings with Seb, part of me was always seeking that look. I don't know where it came from, the pull of that look and my need to have it again.

The letter bag was empty. Anthony tallied our scores, moving his mouth as he added. Koi and the Thai woman, having returned from the market, sat on the steps, sharing pork and sticky rice. Gloating, Anthony announced his victory. I joined Koi on the steps.

—Good for a hangover, he said, handing me a piece of sticky rice.

The Thai woman patted my leg. We smiled. I asked Koi if he'd had fun last night.

—Okay, he said, but it's not like Bangkok.

He glanced over at Anthony, who was still gloating about his victory.

—Here is okay, but not forever, Koi said, casting away a feeling with a flick of his wrist.

Béa came over to say good-bye. A moment later, I felt Seb's hand on my shoulder.

—We'll get him next time, he said, nodding at Anthony. Take care of yourself.

He didn't ask if I wanted a ride—or look back as he walked down the drive.

I helped with the dishes. From Anthony's sink, I made my way back to the table at the club, where Seb and I leaned toward each other, our words barely audible over the beat of the music. Broken chips of phrases. I said, *Despite all odds, I*—He cut me off: *You just want someone. You'll forget this by morning. God, if I kissed you, you'd break*—*Try me*, I said. His face was still. Lemony dish soap brought back the present, comforting. I washed; Anthony dried. As I put on my shoes— Anthony would drive me home—we began discussing whether Thai divinities could appear as animals, Koi yelling that Buddha was *not* an animal as we set out in Anthony's truck toward the university.

16

AWAKE BEFORE DAWN, I pass time mulling over Ella's Singapore Airways flight in July. It's the longest stretch without an entry, a gap, after which coherence vanishes. Where she went then seems key to where she is now. She wrote, *I've come back empty, scraped clean of futures.*

At nine, I walk to the gallery. Outside, the air is crisp, leaves yellowing, earth growing old. I love the smell of death in autumn. At home, we would smoke it out, building wood fires in my mother's studio as I watched her work, a child with my little crayons and watercolors.

It's urgent that I speak to Siobhán. I shouldn't have said what I did at dinner, in front of her brother. Privately, I'll ask what she knows. A laugh escapes me on the street. People turn. If her plan was to drive me mad in pursuit of Ella, would she tell me? When we're face-to-face, I'll sense if I can trust her. To fight the cold, I run to the gallery.

The door to the Ormeau is open. Inside, a woman my age is measuring the walls and making notes. She is absorbed in what she is doing. I go to the back room, locked.

I turn to the woman and ask if she has seen Siobhán. Her nails are painted candy pink.

—Siobhán left this morning, she says.

—Left Paris? Where did she go?

The woman shrugs.

I replay last night's dinner, trying to push away the uncomfortable thought that Siobhán left because of me.

The gallery feels different—empty of artwork, yes, but I've seen it this way before. It's the press by the spiral staircase that makes the difference. It sits like a thing alive, a fat spider in the eye of its web. Its parts are jarringly intricate in the bare space. I'm surprised I didn't notice it immediately.

—Impressive, no?

The woman's English isn't native. I can't place her accent.

—Does it work? I ask, running a hand along its parts.

—I hope so—most artists here hate it, think it's kitsch.

I stand between her and the press, defensive.

—Are you an artist or a friend of Siobhán's? I've seen you here before.

—A friend, I say.

I'm sorry not to recognize her. Interns and artists are often passing through the gallery. I haven't paid enough attention.

—Would you help me? she asks, tearing tape with her teeth and giving me two large cardboard cutouts. Just hold these against the wall so I can see.

Taking them, I go to the wall.

—Together like that, she says, backing up to the other end of the gallery.

—You're showing your work? I ask her.

—My first ever solo show was here this summer. I was so fucking nervous. She laughs. It must have been okay, because Siobhán asked me to curate a group show. I'm Zoë.

I remember Siobhán's description of Zoë, Franco-Portuguese,

very promising. I tell I her I loved her painted photograph of the tree, gesturing to the patch of wall where it hung in summer, now bare.

—*Nulle part ailleurs*, she says excitedly. I made it as an experiment with this space.

She invites me to the vernissage, the show's opening. Before going, I touch the wood of my mother's sculpture, as I always do. Zoë looks at me curiously.

FEELING AT LOOSE ENDS, I GO TO A LECTURE. Bergson's writings on cinema. Now, afterward, rain comes in fat, cold sheets, chopping at the surface of the Seine. I cross the pont des Arts, and it comes down harder, soaking the thin fabric of my coat. Ahead are the high, flat walls of the Louvre. The lecture was a mistake. Months ago, I would have hung on every word, but all I took from today is the vague notion that Bergson found cinema inferior to photography. I don't know why. The audience asked questions, the theorist held forth, and the "dialogue" had been going for hours when I left, not wanting to run into people I knew, to have to say what I was or wasn't doing. All that feels like a former life.

On a wide street, arcing away from the river, people are clustered under a brown café awning, sheltered from the rain. The café looks inviting. Inside, it is warm, windows fogged, couples nuzzling. There's a feeling, sudden and strong, of missing Z. I push it away and return to the journals. If Z were here, he would ask questions, prodding me toward accuracy:

How many journals are there?

Six.

Is that all?

There is probably one more.

Have you seen it?

No.

What makes you think it exists?

In the green journal Ella mentions it. If it does exist, it's with her, wherever she is.

The journals, what colors are they?

Beige. Baby blue. Mustard yellow. Red. Black. Green.

What dates do they cover?

June sixteenth to late November of the following year. Seventeen months.

And the color of the one you don't have?

Green, like the one before it—no, I'm imagining. I don't know.

   —*Un café. Un double. Merci.*

What are you doing? the voice asks, ingenuous, like the real Z.

Thinking.

And?

Perceiving.

Perceiving what? (He wouldn't say this. It has been too long. I'm forgetting him, my old life. I answer anyway, since we're both in my head.)

Sound of autumn rain falling outside the picture windows, smell of espresso and perfume, wet wood, old books.

What are you thinking about?

A conversation with Siobhán. (Aidan told me that she wasn't angry, just troubled by the seriousness of my mother's illness. Her trip away from Paris had nothing to do with me. She'd gone to meet a Swiss video artist in Basel.) She said, Commit, Elena. Don't be equivocal. Accuracy is an ideal. If you hold out for perfection, you won't notice that what's *true* isn't immutable. It isn't constant, but slips in among colors and smells; it is accessible from anywhere except from above. Decide on details. Make it real. *Live* in that world. It is how stories get written, how anything at all gets made. The town of X? Use a map, Elena, my God, you're not Balzac!

Siobhán said this?

A version of it.

Then what?

Further discussion.

About what?

A tablecloth: whether or not the table on Anthony's veranda had a tablecloth the day Ella played Scrabble, in her words, *over eggs, real toast! I write "real toast" as if this were a country where you couldn't just buy bread if you looked for it. Nothing is ever exotic enough.*

Feeling warmer now in the café, I peel off my wet coat and flip through the blue journal. I know these entries. I consulted them as I wrote about the Scrabble brunch, as I considered, in the role of Ella, how desire changes people. We studied Anthony. We asked, Is he good?

My throat is suddenly sore, my head throbbing. I'll be more

comfortable in her body, in the sun, as Ella finds her routine in Ban Du.

> *Anthony cooked eggs, won at Scrabble. Seb stranded me after saying I had nothing to be embarrassed about. My head was a bowling ball stuffed with humid cotton, neurons unwinding in the heat. Memory jack-in-the-box. Seb's rattle her rattle her rattle her rattle her. Discotheque. I woke up on his couch in his clothes. Koi is Anthony's lover—Anthony, who says the day breaks "shiny as an egg" over Ban Du, and keeps scraps of Yeats to "buffer inclement weather," despite the sky's unchanging blue.*

> *I hate rice porridge for breakfast. Scallions in the morning are a sin. At work, I have a coconut yogurt and a giant mug of instant coffee with powdered cream and six packets of sugar. Today I discovered the perfect breakfast!* So-La-Pow *(not sure about spelling). Sold in a snack cart on my way to class. Steaming hot. Must be eaten immediately. Filled with yellow bean or red bean or pork (barbecue pork at the Ban Du 7-Eleven). Sol-apow! Want to sing Thai tones to the page. Song words.*

Maybe fabricating detail—extraneously—is a way of reinjecting the music. She wrote:

> *Script where a world was. Sound sense doesn't last forever, so life lives longer when it's written. Does it grow richer, being read?*

Let's talk about the details: the tablecloth. When you picture the scene at Anthony's, is it there?

Yes, English lace, with coffee stains. But it's unlikely there was a tablecloth.

Why unlikely?

Tablecloths are a pain to wash.

So are dishes.

Fine, there was a tablecloth. The details are unimportant. They can't tell us where Ella is.

What did Siobhàn say?

She's reading Balzac. She believes (now) in realism, in textures woven from details, but she also said not to fear ellipses—they can speak, too, if you're careful not to gag them.

(The Z in my head finds this interesting.) What else?

She spoke of Balzac's tablecloth, white as a layer of fresh-fallen snow, upon which place settings rose symmetrically, crowned with blond rolls. All through my youth, Cézanne said, I wanted to paint that tablecloth of fresh-fallen snow. Now I know that one must only want to paint "rose symmetrically, the place setting," and "blond rolls." If I paint "crowned," I'm done for, you understand? But if I really balance and shade my place settings and rolls as they are in nature, you can be sure the "crowned," the "snow," the whole shebang, will be there.

What does she mean?

That you can't write anything more than what you taste, hear, see, smell, touch, and it's only in the *arrangement*—if it breaks new form—that shadows wake to life.

Of course, there are dangers—doubt, uncertainty, solitude, madness—when you imagine to yourself a world that doesn't exist, and then it does.

I didn't ask about her plan. I don't need to. Siobhán wants, consciously or unconsciously, for me to *become* her daughter as I write, to assume Ella's shape and feelings. Temporarily. Quick, describe what's here, what's real, what I see and sense as *me*, Elena: a metal bucket of umbrellas by the door. Drops of water slide down sheaths buckled and snapped.

I drop sugar into my coffee.

The sugar is brown, a rough lump. Imagine it cubed if you prefer (neat edges or white sugar rather than brown), or if you pictured a white sugar cube before I could stop you. If you ignored the word *drop* and imagined loose sugar of either color from a packet or a bowl, keep it that way. Or not. Espresso, double shot, crema broken at the top, by the sugar. Tiny spoon. The espresso cup is red. The saucer is red. It is still raining. The woman next to me is drinking wine the color of pale straw. The glass has fogged from the coolness of the wine and the humidity in the café.

This world won't fade. I won't lose it. When I come back from being Ella, I'll be stronger. Yes, I must see and feel as Ella, detach from the present a while longer. Earlier today, the lecturing phi-losopher said that when we try to recover something—a memory, but it applies to Ella, too—we must place ourselves in a region of the past and adjust our position, as if focusing a camera. What we're trying to recapture comes into view like a condensing cloud, passing from virtual to actual.

17

I T WAS SORAYA WHO TOLD ME about *Loi Krathong*, on the night she hosted a small gathering at the plantation home of her lover. When we arrived, she presented us with jasmine necklaces (to Seb's chagrin), showed us the peach orchards and pineapple fields, then led us to a deck that the administrator had built from local teakwood. It overlooked a small pond in which tea lights and torches doubled themselves, flickering.

A table was spread with spring rolls, satays, and other Thai delicacies. Soraya showed me and Anthony how to assemble dried shrimps, peanuts, herbs, and chilies in a waxy green leaf.

Anthony puckered.

—*Yes*, you eat the leaf, she said, swallowing.

From the pond came the sound of small splashes, concentrated and rhythmic.

—Piranhas, said the administrator.

He was smoking at the edge of the deck, paying us little attention.

—Oh, yes, Soraya said, it's why he built the deck so high.

Her laugh was like glass breaking,

Koi assembled a leaf and gave it to me. It was delicious, mineral, like eating the earth.

—My Western daughter, Soraya said proudly, seeing me eat the leaf.

Then she asked about my plans for *Loi Krathong* night. Aghast when I didn't know what it was, she sat next to me and explained that *loi* means to float, as on a river, and a *krathong* is made of banana wood, leaves, orchids, marigolds, and candles. The *krathong* is the self, the river the world.

Soraya whispered, her green eyes full of intensity in the candlelight, that most people neglect the most important part of the ritual:

—*Loi Krathong* is about love.

—Aligned with Christian baptism, Anthony argued. It's about the forgiveness of sins.

—*Not* Christianity! Koi said. You compare too much.

Seb pointed out that the ancient Sukhothais had devised a way to release, each year, the bondage of self, which was more than just sin. I found myself moved by the idea of the ancient ritual, akin to snakes' molting: shedding the self in order to grow.

Seb drew on his Singha, gazing beyond the pond into the darkness. Soraya, too, seemed magnetized by it, that void. Then she turned, eyes wide, as if possessed, to say that *Loi Krathong* was her favorite night of the year.

—You get to start everything again, all new, she said.

There was uncomfortable silence. She grew still, staring blankly at the dark. Our earlier conversation returned to me, things she'd said simply, without irony. Her sadness seemed more than her own. Maybe it was mythic sadness. She wore it beautifully. It was in her face, lit by the candles she'd placed along the deck. It was patterned into the colored scarves she draped around her shoulders. Usually, I saw only her passion and energy, but tonight, with her gaze lost in the darkness of the plantation, she was sadness. I didn't see it. I *felt* it as my own.

At the far end of the deck, the administrator lit a cigar.

We watched the moon come into view. Distended, drunk with light, it pulled at the frail strands of our conversation.

18

I SCAN ELLA'S PAGES, SOFT, WORN. There's something of her body in them: oil from her fingers, cells of her skin. From the binding's crease I take a strand of her hair. My first thought is to tell Siobhán. But a relic might upset her. I hold the hair up to the autumn light, rusted as Paris stretches in its bed of shadows. The strand is amber-colored, gold. I pluck a hair from my head to compare. Hers is coarse, mine finer, warm, darker. I tuck them together between the pages.

The self is the past is desire, Ella wrote. *Rituals are real.* She seems to believe that things will be different as soon as her *kra-thong* sails into the river. The world will flow through her, and she'll be open to it, finally free. Her *Loi Krathong* entry is eight pages in copious blue ink. It begins with what looks like an epigraph: *Death is linked with love because death, like love, symbolizes our fear of letting go of ourselves as well as our desire to let go of ourselves.*

In other entries Ella mentions a book called *A Buddhist History of the West,* by David Loi [*sic*]. I found the book by David Loy, a scholar of Buddhism and psychoanalysis living in Japan. The line is from page seventy-four. I order this book and two more on Buddhist philosophy, then look again at the entry. The prose is drunk, strange: . . . *rivers flow east over land like a page.*

River cut earth skin. Not-self is the world. River mouth, dark hollow, asks without uttering a sound. Words, faint fictions by which experience, long dead, guides us with afterimages . . .

19

ACROSS THE STREET AT ANTHONY'S, torches flared and Chinese lanterns danced color to the dusk. *Loi Krathong* falls on the full-moon night of the twelfth lunar month. Lunar months, unlike solar months, drift through the seasons, more fluid. What better way to divest oneself of the dying year, Anthony reasoned, than by honoring Dionysus? He was throwing a party.

Béa's house, across from Anthony's, has the only working oven in the village, so we did the cooking for the party there. As we chopped vegetables and roasted chickens, Béa told me about a brilliant local artist who, out of the blue, won the Bangkok Prize for photography. He couldn't afford materials, and he taught photo classes at the Alliance française just to have a camera. Béa was arranging an exhibition of his work in Chiang Rai.

—Everything ready? Anthony asked, emerging from the shadows of the road. Koi and I will carry over the ice for the bar, WON'T WE, KOI? We've had a row. He's bought fish. I said there would be plenty of food. Thai people won't eat *falang* food, he says. So now we have three large fish—we're keeping them warm over the burners. He says it doesn't matter if they're cold, but what is worse than a cold fish? And now, because of this, he's petulant and—

Koi appeared in the halo of the porch light. Dodging the hand reaching for his waist, he slung two bags of ice over his shoulders and strutted back across the road toward Anthony's.

—He's in a mood, Anthony said, speaking fluidly, distractedly. We've been to the flower market today. There's a lovely flower market in Chiang Rai. Have you been? ISN'T IT LOVELY, KOI, THE FLOWER MARKET? They had roses for one hundred baht—one hundred baht for a dozen roses! I bought three dozen!

We heard the surge and sputter of a motorcycle. Anthony hurried off, worried a guest had come early.

In Béa's kitchen, a candle swelled and crackled, dripping wax into an herb pot. Countertops were piled high. I peeled lychees for an experimental pie, and Béa rolled dough with a wine bottle. We were laughing over something when we noticed Soraya, oddly still, framed like an icon in the doorway.

—*Sawatdee ka*, she said in a hollow voice.

She moved through all parts of the space, unsure where to pause, pulling her red scarves around her shoulders. When she finished her circle, she stood in the center, fixing me with her green eyes. Her bottom lip quivered, her skin taut. Her face fell into her hands. Her shoulders shook.

Béa asked what was wrong, but Soraya couldn't answer. Her chest only heaved.

I listened to the sharp inhales of her sobs, not knowing what to do. Béa, more humane, hugged Soraya and smoothed her hair.

When Soraya looked up, her eyes met mine. I felt guilty, not saying anything. She passed a hand across her cheeks and chin to brush away the tears.

—Anthony said you would be here, she said.

I nodded. I wanted to be as warm as Béa, but drama made me anxious and skeptical, as if the display of emotions made them less real.

Béa took Soraya's arm and led her around the kitchen, showing her the tray of toasting peanuts and Kaffir lime leaves, roasting chickens, bubbling greens. Soraya grew calm.

—We need someone to do the cranberries, Béa said.

She'd asked for a dish connected to where I was from, so I'd gone to the Western grocer in town and bought imported cranberries for sauce. It was the best I could do.

—Okay, Soraya said, like a child who wishes to be obedient.

—All you do is wash them, add sugar and water. Pick out any rotten ones.

Soraya sat listlessly at the table, trying to read the package instructions. Tears returned.

—I could smell it, she said bitterly—smell sex when he came home. He's away again now.

I looked at the floor. I'd hated the administrator when I met him, aloof and uninterested. Joining her at the table, I held Soraya's hand.

—The worst part? she whispered. This has happened before. The first time, my husband, it was almost the same! I *knew*. But I couldn't believe . . .

Some days earlier, Anthony had salaciously revealed the full story of Soraya's escape from Bangkok. The daughters, daddy's girls, hadn't questioned their father's story about Soraya's running off with the administrator. The true tale was that Soraya had caught her husband entangled with a younger cousin of hers in the most compromising *positions*. Anthony had touched his teeth to his lip with relish at this part. When I pressed him for his source, he said he'd gone to the driving range with the vice president and the other administrators. *It was all they could speak about. Men are such gossips!*

Béa handed Soraya a tissue.

—Thank you, she said, wiping her face. I'm fine. It comes and goes. Some days I mind less. I do my work . . .

She sniffled.

—But my daughters . . .

Soraya's face fell into the cup of her hands.

—I don't care about him—*either* of them—but my daughters . . . They think I left *them*. They are still so angry at me. They don't know why . . .

Soraya's body shook.

—They try to cut me out, to pretend I'm not their mother. To forget me! Where do they think they come from? From *her*? Who is nearly their age?

Soraya ripped open the bag of cranberries with her fingernail, spilling them onto the table. She laughed, throaty and shrill.

—They believe the lies. Like dogs. They're not mine. I don't want them.

Her expression hardened. She began sorting the berries. As her pain transformed to focus, I saw that this anger, betrayal, and humiliation—an old refrain—drove her many smiles.

Béa put sugar and water in a pot. Soraya added the cranberries. We waited for it to boil, for their skins to break.

—I see their seeds, Soraya called, looking over the pot.

She'd brought pineapples for the party. Slicing them, she told us about the two kinds: *Sapparot* Chiang Rai and *Sapparot* Phuket.

—It's the soil that determines the taste of the fruit. The soil in Chiang Rai is mountain soil. Phuket is by the sea. You taste the sea in a Phuket pineapple. There are different seeds, but it's the soil that matters, she smiled sadly. The soil is the mother.

Seb came to help carry food to Anthony's. We used dishrags as potholders. Flashlight beams lit our shoes, patches of earth, and the foil coverings, from which steam was escaping.

—A veritable caravan! Anthony called from his veranda. How magical!

His house had filled with people. A young man, tall and delicate, like a feather, stood apart from the group, watching us as we walked up the drive.

—Lek, Béa called to him, we were just talking about you!

—Talking about me?

His voice cracked boyishly.

Lek bowed as we approached, his long hair falling across his face. He removed his glasses to wipe the lenses. His eyes were large and bright, taking everything in, so much that I felt exposed.

Later, when the meal had finished and the dancing had begun, Soraya took me aside to show me the *krathong* she'd made.

—I cut a banana leaf from a tree and decor*ated,* she said, putting emphasis on the last two syllables, prettily. I thought you would like it. We must release it in the river.

I was thrilled. Soraya knew how much I wanted to do the real ritual, to release a *krathong* in the Mae Kok. Béa offered to drive us to town, and Lek and Seb, whom we found smoking in the driveway as we walked to the car, came, too.

The drive was short. We parked by fairgrounds next to the river. Women on parade floats with sequined dresses and glittering eyes waved abstractly, blinded by floodlights. Soraya said it was the Nopomas Queen contest, to honor the most beautiful woman in Chiang Rai. As we walked, the lights faded and the horizon became a joint between two mirror planes, points of flame reflected in the blackness of the sky and river, a planetarium of sharply magnified stars. The Mae Kok, turbid by day, flowed fast, energized, its surface lit by a crowd of jewels. I linked arms with Soraya, pointing to flying lanterns in the sky. I asked if they were also *krathongs*.

—*Khom loi*, Lek said, stopping at a cart to buy one from a vendor.

He showed us how to light it, and it whizzed into the night, lighting our faces as it flew.

Soraya drew her scarves around her shoulders. Her eyes were moist.

The air was cooler by the water. People gathered in the dimness, families with picnics and half-clad children making forays into the water. People were putting coins in their *krathongs*.

—Offerings, Soraya said when I asked. It can be money or something from your body, like hair or clippings from a fingernail. You release a part of yourself to remember that you are greater. You will survive your body.

Seb snorted. I knew what he was thinking: Body *is* soul, and nothing survives its death.

Soraya handed me the *krathong* she had made. I plucked a hair from my head, intertwined it with the petals of the marigold. Soraya lit the candle. There was a whiff of fire and jasmine.

—Sebastian, go with Ella, she said. Release it together from the sandbar.

Removing my sandals, I followed Seb to the water's edge,

my toes sinking in the mud. The reflection of the full moon trembled. *Krathongs* floated by. Their incense tempered a dried squid smell from the snack stands Then there were the odors from the river, silt and sand, plant and animal.

The Mae Kok was wide and shallow. I waded in, feet sticking in the silt, skirt hitched to my thighs. There were shouts and children splashing. Cold pockets of mist collected in spaces unlit by the *krathongs*. Seb was in front of me. The waterline cupped the globes of his calves. Around him, moonlight made sharp sparks of the ripples. An extinguished *krathong* tangled itself at my ankles, causing me to jump. The candle in my *krathong* blew out.

Soraya hurried toward me with a lighter. Her face glowed.

With one hand protecting the new flame, I walked into the river. Only when I reached the sandbar did I notice Seb had turned back and was rejoining the others on the bank. No matter. I stepped onto the sandbar, wind on wet legs. A child next to me said something in Thai. Wild dark eyes and tangled hair. She ran away. I held my *krathong* over the water. Candlelight scattered my reflection: hair, nails, sins, coins, flowers. I gripped my *krathong* as the current rushed under it. Others floated by, tiny funeral pyres. Soraya's voice in the dark: *Life is beautiful even if it is also sad.* Muddy fingers relaxed, and the *krathong* danced swiftly downriver. My body began to tremble, maybe from the cold.

20

ERRATIC SUNLIGHT SPLITS THE GRAY, lighting flower boxes and outdoor tables beneath the café awning. Inside, tourists point to croissants in golden rows. I take a mouthful of coffee, lukewarm. The blue journal ends with *Loi Krathong*. The yellow journal beckons like a new country, alluring and still strange, but I can't concentrate on it. I'm drawn to the longest of Ella's entries, fifty pages composed after her return from I don't know where, after ten missing days in July. It's at the end of the black journal. What happened during those missing days? Why doesn't she say where she was, Ella, who divulges everything in the journals?

I pay for my coffee and walk back to the flat, so absorbed that I'm slow to notice the man standing with his suitcase on the place Marcel-Aymé, a clean-cut man in his early thirties. My heart stops.

Z smiles at me sheepishly, pleased at the success of his surprise.

We stare at each other. His being here feels good but alien, as if he has come from a world I'm beginning to lose. How dare he show up, uninvited, returning me to myself, undoing my slow absorption into Ella's life. For months, Z has been asking to visit. I kept forgetting to answer. It wasn't that I didn't want him here, just that this task demands a necessary suspension of my own life. And there is a different existence emerging here. Life does that—it can't *but* emerge, much as I've tried to stop it for the sake of finding

Ella. Rhythms developed, then rhythms added to rhythms. Exhibitions changed at the Ormeau, and this time I went to the opening, the vernissage. I talked more with Zoë, bright-colored nails, pink lipstick, the force behind *Nulle part ailleurs.*

Z and I rent a car and drive to the countryside. When we reach the Loire, we hike. Winter woods, naked trees. Z's cheeks are pink in the cold. I ask if he is tired, jet-lagged. He says he isn't. Familiar feel of his gloved hand. He says that Paris seems to agree with me. He asks when I'm coming home.

Instead of answering, I begin to tell him about the monstrous fifty-page entry, made in one sitting (the same "mood" in her pen strokes) during the monsoons. No mention in so many pages of where she had been the last ten days.

—You'll crack the case and come home, Z says, linking my reply to his question.

He says it lightly, a joke. He goes on:

—I wasn't sure you'd be glad to see me. I almost didn't come . . . but it's better to know.

—Know what? I say, feeling sharper.

—Are you happy to see me?

—Of course.

—Then why didn't you answer about visiting? It's been four fucking months, Elena.

Z is blurry, like a stranger. Part of me knows that four months are significant, our longest separation. Another part isn't sure what interest this adult, smartly dressed man holds for me.

—This project is demanding, I say. I just want to focus on it entirely, at least for this year.

—*This* right now is distraction? Z says.

—In the best way, I say, feeling trapped.

Z looks at me suspiciously. He asks if I can picture the extra room in his apartment, the one with the window onto the courtyard. It could be my study. He asks me to think about it.

We walk on, leaves crunching under us.

—Are you sure you're not becoming *too* involved? Z asks. What about *your* work?

—You mean the dissertation . . . I say, trailing off, proud of myself for remembering, for being able to have this reasonable conversation with him, as myself, as Elena.

It feels tedious to explain to him that I can't go back before finding Ella. I know that she has more to give me, some secret to being alive.

—And what about us? Z asks.

I want to be grateful to him for having come so far. The ticket, purchased at the last minute, was probably expensive. I know he came to save our relationship. But my mind is stuck on that gap in July.

On our last night in the countryside, full moon over an unfamiliar landscape, Z breathes beside me in the dark. Awakened by a sense of terror, I go to turn over, stop. Something is wrong. Like her, I don't want to know. Like her, I am full of dread. The bed is sticky, wet. The smell is too much, a smell of the body, nauseating and intimate. I turn, warmishness spilling. . . . No physical pain. Just shock. Another wave. Thighs sticky. Top sheet blackening in the moonlight. I try to push myself to a sitting position. Afraid of what's flowing out of me. I try to stand. Legs not my own. They don't support my weight.

—Elena? Z's eyes are black in the shadows. What's wrong?

I show him my hands. I gesture to the blood soaking through the bed.

—What's wrong? he repeats.

—The blood. It's—

—Where? Z sits up, alarmed, runs his hands over the mess, pulls back the sheets. Where?

I shake my head to show that it is everywhere.

Suddenly wide-awake, he takes my shoulders and pulls my face close to his. His eyes are very wide, serious.

—Look at me, he says.

He shakes me.

—There's no blood. Do you see? Elena? No blood. Do you see?

Sensation of falling—a body falling somewhere, not my own.

In the morning, there is sunlight in the room. I look for traces of the mess and can find none. We have breakfast on the winter porch and drive back to Paris.

III

Aurelia: The Hot Season

21

THE NEW SEASON BEGAN IN FLUSHES of colorlessness. The Mae Kok turned a thicker brown, the electric greens of the rice fields dulled, and the deep purple hills gave way to lackluster clays, earth tones for the roving eye. In the last days of the cool season, a band of white appeared on the horizon, a tide readying itself to rise. It choked the blue with a sickly gauze, a translucent pane against the sun.

My skin and mood informed me of these changes, irritability with the temperature's rise, sensitivity in the linings of my lungs. I felt dry like the landscape, and brittle.

—The hot season is nearly here, Muay observed one morning as we stared across a windless sky. This is what it will feel like. They will burn the trash.

—The trash?

—On the side of the superhighway, they make piles. You cough. They think they are getting rid of it, but it stays in the air. Until the monsoons come. Every year it gets worse. Many teachers—especially foreigners—they go somewhere else.

—Because of the summer holiday? I asked, distracted and obtuse.

—Because of bad air, Muay said harshly.

The hot season brought change—a housemate and a new

house away from Muay and the university's serene sterility. I was desperate to move to Ban Du, more a part of the country, more alive.

Seb lived there.

I met Aurelia on the first days of the hot season, and she became its emblem—as much a part of it as the heavy air and parched earth. She came cracking with need.

The day was hot, white and windless. Classes had been canceled due to an international conference devoted to fostering educational and economic friendship among the countries of the Greater Mekong Subregion. My students, in white and black, transformed into caterers, airport taxi drivers, and tour guides for delegates from Cambodia, Laos, Myanmar, Vietnam, and Yunnan, China. It was a day of compulsory plenaries in the administration building on top of the hill. I hated sycophantic diplomacy. My face grew tired from smiling. After an hour, I slipped out of the auditorium—overly air-conditioned—and crossed the foyer to a deck overlooking the hills. The dry heat coaxed down my goose bumps as I stood blinking, restless, in bright sun.

At the far end of the deck, a figure was pacing, hardly visible in the sun glare. She was a Westerner, and she was smoking, exhaling white clouds into the whiteness. Something about her movements, a casualness, told me she lived here—she wasn't a tourist, nor had she flown in for the conference. She paced with purpose across the deck, intent upon her solitude.

I retreated to the coolness of the vestibule, taking refuge in the restroom.

As I was washing my hands in front of the mirror, a stall door opened, and a blond figure appeared, bending over the sink, studying her lips. Our eyes met in the mirror; brown eyes reflected back as if they were mine. I turned to dry my hands, breaking our stare.

As we walked out of the bathroom, she lit a cigarette, crossed her arms, and looked at me like a shy animal.

—Aurelia, she said, extending her hand. I'm not Spanish. Most people think I'm Spanish. Because of the name? She shrugged her thin shoulders. I'm not.

She had slight creases around her eyes, evidence of a life spent in the sun. But she was slight and dressed like the students in a white blouse and black skirt. It was impossible to guess her age. I asked her what she did.

—Oh, teach some. Like everyone here.

She brushed a wisp of hair from her face. She had a flippant, raspy way of speaking.

—I also work for the government? she said, inflecting her voice as if it were a question. The U.S. government? she added, blowing out smoke.

The Thais who knew us only in passing would often confuse Aurelia and me. The woman selling *som tam* at Ban Du Market rarely failed to make me believe I'd been there hours earlier.

—Ah, you! Hungry again?

—No, that wasn't me, I would say, doubting myself.

—Yes, you. *Som tam* extra spicy. So many chilies for *falang*! *Ped mak maak!*

She would laugh, crushing chilies with her pestle. Aurelia liked her food so spicy, it must have burned her insides—it made her feel full, she said, after eating only a little. This alone made it urgent that I distinguish myself.

—No. That was Aurelia. *Chan bpen* Ella. Different person.

The vice president, who, having studied in Frankfurt, knew German, and, for obscure reasons, a bit of Italian, would ask me, Where's your *doppo-gang*?

It turned out that Aurelia and I had grown up in neighboring towns. We'd shopped at the same chain stores and had similar ways of saying things. She told me she'd been contracted by the government to write a report on the hill tribes. She'd been here a few months but didn't know many people. Her job required her to attend this conference, but it bored her. Also, she was looking for a house in Ban Du Village. *Love affair gone wrong,* she said flippantly.

After three days of knowing each other, Aurelia and I decided to live together in Ban Du, in a house with a wall of glass. It had a veranda and a gravel yard. Mango and papaya trees grew along the gate that separated our property from a dirt track that bordered the rice fields.

—I'm so happy for you! When can I see your new home? Soraya had been effusive.

Muay had been nonplussed, unable to understand why I would give up my suite at the university. Béa, who I thought would be delighted to have me as a neighbor, demurred:

—You've only just met this woman, she said. Are you sure you want to live with her?

I told Béa I was good at reading people. The truth was, I found Aurelia familiar.

In the house by the rice fields, Aurelia became my mirror. On hot-season evenings, I'd watch her pace our veranda, sucking at cans of sugar-free Pepsi Max with the intensity of a person starved. Or else, having chewed a pack of gum, she would spit out fist-size lumps and stick them back to the packaging.

She clung to cigarettes with nervous fingers, shuddering with each inhale, as if she wanted to be filled in a way nothing could. She was insatiable, she told me once, which was why she had to be so careful.

I'd watch her through the glass wall, her thin body seeming unconnected to the mass of cigarette butts and crushed cans growing on the ledge beside her.

Aurelia didn't like the feeling, in general, of being seen. She'd whittled down her flesh, canceling hunger by means of discipline. If discipline faltered, if the body gave a sign, the craving was silenced with Pepsi Max. It wasn't that she didn't feel hunger; she felt it all the time. But if she gave in to it—even once—she'd never be free. After confessing this, she disappeared and returned with a silver pack of peanuts in her outstretched hands.

—They're for you.

—Really?

—I bought them for you. At the store? The one down the road?

I found myself accepting the logic of her world, a logic of desire denied.

—A snack after work. Happy hour, *ha-ah!*

This utterance of hers, *ha-ah,* doesn't lend itself to writing: a laugh cut in two by a glottal stop and the vowel repeated to affirm the agreement it sought to secure, as if really asking were unbearable.

I tried to close her hands around the peanuts, but she thrust them at me fearfully. Points of her shoulder blades emerged like rock ledges under her loose tank top.

Aurelia's violent vulnerability riveted me day after day. I'd watch her—animal, volatile, at war with herself—legs against the balustrade, regulating, sensitive and proud, closing around her the narrow corridor of her cage.

On the other side of our wall of glass, I saw her, so different from myself—from who I thought I was—but it took a moment to be sure the image was not my own reflected back at me. Something about Aurelia frightened me. At her core was something feral, volatile. It was in me, too, this thing—maybe in all of us. But I'd been taught to bury it deep beneath the skin. Aurelia didn't seem to understand this. She had everything inside out.

22

THE GERANIUMS IN SIOBHÁN'S FLOWERPOTS will not survive the winter. Petals cling to spidery limbs in the cold. Siobhán has made tea, as usual, but there is something haphazard, less controlled about her. A few tea leaves are stuck to the side of the pot. I wipe them away with my napkin.

We never mentioned Siobhán's sudden departure from the restaurant. After her return from Basel, we simply resumed our meetings. Professional. Less personal.

—They've issued Ella's death certificate, Siobhán says.

A shudder passes through me. We knew it would happen. Still, a part of me hoped to find her in time.

—Have they listed a cause? I ask, to remind Siobhán she still needs me.

—Dead in absentia, she says quietly. As you know. It's usual after seven years . . .

She trails off. She has forgotten to bring out cups. I go to the kitchen.

—Thank you, Siobhán says as I begin to pour. You must tell me what happened to Ida.

The tea spills. Siobhán, sighing, takes the scarf from her shoulders to absorb the liquid.

I look at her, shocked.

—You think I'm luring you down some path that isn't good for you, she says, dabbing.

—It was irrational, I say, ashamed at myself for having suspected her. I'm sorry.

—Finish your story, please. What happened to Ida?

I tell her about my mother's institutionalization. I can picture both times, crisp and clear. Siobhán absorbs this, asking:

—You think you're genetically . . . predisposed?

Shaking my head, I tell her about the months after my mother's death. It's these months that terrify me most of all. That I could be alive without living—without memory.

—So you think the journals are dangerous for you, she says.

—No, it—I had just finished reading them. I just . . . wondered if you knew that my mother had struggled in similar ways.

—Oh, Siobhán says.

She is quiet so long, my mind begins to wander. Aurelia, bleach blond, barely visible, squinting in the sun glare.

—I didn't know that she was institutionalized, Siobhán says. Aidan and I were discussing this . . . her whimsical side. Even when I knew her, she was imaginative and could go too far. She could have trouble deciding what was real. Oh Elena, this has gotten too complicated, hasn't it?

—It's the point, I say, suddenly wanting at all costs to finish the project, to find the instant when Ella's sanity starts to fray, its etiology, somewhere in the pages.

—I am sure there is something in the journals, Siobhán says, shaking her head. But the idea is not to put you in danger—

—I'm not in *danger,* I say quickly. The death certificate will be revoked when she is found. It would be terrible to stop now. We can't give up. I'm close to knowing.

Siobhán sighs and goes to the kitchen. She returns with dish towels and a sponge.

—Maybe she *can't* be found, she says.

23

KOI FOUND THE HOUSE—just hours after I'd told Anthony I was looking for a place in the village to share with a foreigner. He'd heard that the cousin of the mother of the woman who ran the comic-book store across from Ban Du Market was looking for foreigners to rent her house.

—Foreigners keep things tidier, Anthony said, and pay more.

He winked at us in the rearview mirror. He'd offered to drive Aurelia and me to visit the house. From the passenger seat of the truck, Koi sighed.

We wandered inside while the owner of the house stood in the yard, throwing grains to the roosters. She would smile as they scuttled in the gravel and dust. She drew circles in the gravel with a stick. She spoke no English, but with Koi as intermediary, it was agreed that Aurelia and I would move in with our things in three days. On the drive back, Koi explained:

—She lives with her sisters now. She doesn't have much money. She lost her husband.

He reminded us to have the house blessed as soon as possible.

Koi had refused to go inside, waiting on the veranda, ignoring Anthony's insistence that any bad luck accrued would be retroactively wiped clean once the blessing took place.

Cursed or not, the house absorbed Aurelia and me and our few possessions, wrapping us in its ambient calm. What did the architect know? Or was it an accident of angles that the rooms glowed colors on bright days, as if a prism were breaking and scattering light into every corner?

We swerved, passing a motorcycle on the narrow road. Aurelia slid into me. As I reached for a handle to steady myself, I noticed a pattern of white dots painted on the truck's interior.

Anthony was testing a shortcut from Ban Du to my place at the university. He was lost.

—Turn around. Go back, Koi told him.

—Koi, quiet! Don't be impatient!

Gentlemanly once more, Anthony picked up the strand of our conversation.

—How are they going to arrange a blessing, Koi? They don't know any monks.

—I'll arrange it, Koi said, his breath quickening.

—He's spooked because a man died there, Anthony said. The husband of the nice owner we just met *succumbed,* shall we say, in the back bedroom. Did you not see the Buddhas?

To overlook them would have been impossible. The back bedroom held dozens of fat, smiling Buddhas in different sizes, robes and rolls of skin lacquered in colors, folds of clay kiln-fired to look like flesh. Unlike Thai Buddhas—eyes closed or at half-mast, thin fingers extended in reverent *mudras*—these Buddhas looked like fat cabaret dancers, their beady eyes full of mirth. Their purpose was to cheer the dying man in his final weeks and ease the transmigration of his soul to a better body—man once more, but wealthier, or *diva.*

—Laughing Buddhas are Chinese, Koi said when I asked. The owner's family is from China.

Aurelia, who turned out to be nine years my elder, though she could pass for twenty, took the master bedroom. This meant that the back bedroom, with the laughing Buddhas, would be mine. Full of trepidation, I carried the gaudy god bodies to the storage room. Superstition urged me to replace them with a Buddha head in the Thai style, more to my taste. I bargained for it at the weekend market. *Chin like a mango stone*, the craftsman said, running his fingers along its wood. *Skin so smooth that dust cannot stick.* It was a Sukhothai Buddha with a sharp nose and a pointed crown that looked like the stinger of a scorpion. I felt peaceful whenever I looked at it. The laughing Buddhas made me seasick. Life was too strong and sweet as it was, and what use did I have for an ironist's wit, cut on the sharp edges of despair?

In the rearview mirror, Anthony's lips were moving, mocking Koi for propitiating the ghost of the man who'd died in the house. Koi's eyes flashed with anger.

—*No!* The house has to be blessed anyway. It's usual. Just like your car, eh?

Koi motioned to the painted white dots on the ceiling of the truck.

—Oh, *you're* right. Koi, you always know best, Anthony said, patting Koi's knee. Talk about propitiation! My little *god.*

—You treat him like he's a child, Aurelia burst out.

—On the contrary, Anthony said cuttingly, I treat him like the *diva* that he is.

A howl, raw and ragged, escaped Koi's lips:

—*Chaa bpa na sa thaan!*

He repeated the sounds, again and again, compulsively, as if their syllables might neutralize what terrified him.

—What *is* it? Anthony asked, slowing the truck.

Desperate, Koi gestured to a hut ten paces from the road, from which clouds of smoke were rising in controlled bursts. A vague sweetness reached us through the open windows of the truck.

—Keep going, go, go! Koi gasped.

Aurelia looked terrified, and I began to feel afraid, too. Koi kept gesturing to the hut and saying over and over the Thai words with a strangled voice. Whiteness was beginning to envelop the car. Koi rocked violently, from side to side, his body shaking the seat in front of Aurelia.

—What *is* it? Anthony said, refusing to drive forward until he'd understood.

—*Chaa bpa na sa thaan. Chaa bpa na sa thaan!*

—English, Koi!

—Smoke from dead bodies, Koi said, pointing to the hut.

—But Koi, how could they *possibly*—

Anthony paused a moment, then his hand fumbled over the gears, and we shot forward.

—*Crematorium*, Koi, is the English word. It's where they burn the bodies of the dead.

Anthony's didacticism calmed us. But crematoriums were supposed to be hygienic places, where care was taken to keep the dead out of the air, out of the lungs of the living. I gulped in clean air along the long, familiar road. Aurelia had a small scar on her forearm, and her nails dug absently into the skin around its edges.

24

O N THOSE FIRST MORNINGS IN OUR NEW HOUSE, I'd set off from Ban Du by motorbike—Aurelia had one and convinced me by example to get one, too. I'd arrive at the university with legs caked in dust from the pyres of trash burning on the shoulders of the superhighway. I'd brush it from my skirt as I crossed the parking lot, my mouth full of ash. The hot season became the taste of the air and the newly brown hills, earth stretched fine and tense like skin over their slopes, each day more cracked and wrinkled.

I bought water from the convenience store. The bottle perspired on the lectern. A second hand spasmed across a clock face. Students greeted one another, talked. The clock stared with its bald iris. I judged how far the hands had to travel before I'd meet Seb in the parking lot and we'd ride together to Béa's for dinner. Three hours. Interminable.

Last week's lesson was about Faulkner's melancholia, possibilities dead forever and corpses clung to for years in attic rooms. This week was Hemingway, a tale suffused with the unsaid.

A student read:

—The hills across the valley of the . . . el-bow were long and white.

—Ebro.

She looked up.

—Ebro. It's a place—a river in Spain.

—In Spain, she repeated.

Her eyes grew large, and she turned back to the page.

—*On this side there was no shade and no trees and the station was between two lines of rails in the sun.*

I picked up reading where she left off, exaggerating my cadence so the students would internalize my rhythm. I saw the flies and the bar. I could smell the beer in their glasses. I asked about the American and the girl.

—Are they lovers?

—They have nothing to say to each other, a student replied. They are boring.

—They are *bored.* Is that what you mean?

The girl-woman in the story seemed to lean against the back wall under the clock, upset, unsatisfied, twirling the straw in her drink. *That's all we do, isn't it—look at things and try new drinks?* The girl had Aurelia's face and my voice.

The minute hand jerked forward. The room was very hot. I wanted to sit down, but there were too many eyes on me. I asked:

—What is a white elephant? Let's think about the title.

—It is the dream of the mother, a student said. The mother of the Buddha dreamed a white elephant and the Buddha was born. When she was pregnant.

—*And?* I asked, trying not to show surprise.

—It is a gift you do not want, another student said. It's probably what Hemingway meant.

Fatigue hit. My limbs went limp, as if they belonged to a puppet whose strings had snapped. The clock face, glaring in the heat, pulled me upright.

—I feel fine, I read aloud. Does she mean it? Is she okay?

—It's irony. She's not fine, a student said.

Anthony, who had taught in Thailand for many years, passed on what I discovered to be a myth: that Thai students were incapable of divining sarcasm in literature or in life. *Americans are deficient in this, as well,* he added—it was during a lunchtime conversation—then said, *Oh, come now, Ella, don't look crushed.*

—Then why does she *say* she's fine?

Others joined in: *She wants to make her boyfriend happy. She doesn't want him to worry.*

—She wants the world to think she wants for nothing. Perhaps it's expected of her.

Silence settled as the class turned to look at the student who had spoken. He said little in class but turned in papers in flawless English. He was tan and slight, with a mole above his lip.

—Yes, I said. But the reason isn't explicit. Hemingway forces us to speculate.

I wrote the word on the whiteboard, watched it scrutinized and copied into notebooks. *Speculate, speculum, speculate* turned over on my tongue till it lost its taste. It was very hot. I loosened my collar. I could talk about Hemingway's life, influences, style. I asked instead:

—What is the operation?

A student drawing in her notebook sighed. There was a sheen of sweat on her face.

—It's an abortion, said the quiet one.

The other students looked confused. He said the word in Thai. *Ohhh.*

We read on. I asked questions. Why does the couple drink so much?

—Alcoholics. Jig is a party girl!

Laughter. The bead curtain and the railway tracks replaced the classroom and the courtyard outside the window. Later with Seb, on our motorbikes, I saw the hills around Chiang Rai, rough and cracked like the skins of pachyderms.

On Béa's patio, we sipped pastis from tall glasses and watched the sun redden along the village road. Aurelia had declined my invitation. *They're* your *friends,* she'd said. I told her it was ridiculous to think that way. *My choice.* She shrugged. *Anthony is immoral.* She brushed me away with the wisps of her cigarette smoke.

—I hate the taste of licorice, I told Seb.

—Then why are you drinking it? Have a beer.

We were alone. Béa was inside on the phone, Anthony and Koi running late. We sat so close, I could feel the heat from his body layering the heat of the evening. He finished his pastis and moved off, opening a Singha, which I thought he might hand me. He took a drink instead.

—It's something different, I said. That's all we do—look at things and try new drinks.

Seb rolled his eyes.

I looked at the reddening sky, rotated the glass in my hands. I felt bored, tired.

—There's an Indian legend, I began. It says white elephants bring rain.

Seb never asked why I was thinking certain things.

—Today, I went on, trying to interest him, my students told me that the mother of the Buddha dreamed of a white elephant before the Buddha was born. So, white elephants are sacred.

—*Sacred,* Seb snorted. They would say that.

I said nothing, which was the only condition on which he would say more.

—White elephants are a fucking liability! Believe me, no girl wants a god in the belly. And then there's the historical side— white elephants have probably paralyzed kingdoms. They aren't workable because they're "sacred," but they *eat* as much as working elephants, so they're expensive. Sacredness is bullshit.

Seb's tirade was weird and excessive. We were all irritable. It was because of the heat.

He finished his beer, wiping his mouth.

—You don't believe in symbolic meaning? Meaning that you don't see at first but comes later, that you have to wait for?

—If it ends up having meaning, it's because you've *given* it meaning. Jesus, things've always got to *mean* something with you. Just let it be.

—I don't know, I said, pretending not to care about the derision in Seb's tone or the way his body turned away from me. Sometimes you invest without knowing the outcome.

Seb lapsed back into his customary silence, staring at the patio, concrete covered by woven mats. Words hung between us . . . like what? Like the wings of dead butterflies. Seb opened a second beer. I felt my own boredom and frustration added to his. The evening was too hot.

Time staggered. There was too much of it suddenly. Not knowing how to care for it, I listened for the geckos, wanting to be rid of this not knowing what to do with time. Béa would come out soon. Anthony and Koi would arrive. We would get noodles from the market.

25

ON THE DAY OF THE BLESSING CEREMONY, we woke to a blue sky out of season. After weeks of chalk haze, the light, reenergized, sparked across the living room as we waited for the monk.

Muay brought rambutan from the market. Anthony arrived short of breath, explaining that Koi was buying supplies. *Supplies?* I asked him. *Incense, voodoo dolls,* he said. He settled on the couch next to Seb, who was playing with his phone. Soraya seemed haggard, hair loose around her face, a sheen in her eyes as if she had been crying. After *wai*'ing to everyone, she pulled me aside and said she had good news: A monastery near Chiang Mai accepted foreigners on retreat. (She pronounced this word beautifully, accenting the second syllable.) She had a contact and could reserve me a spot if I liked during the hot-season vacation. I looked over at Seb. We'd made vague, drunken plans to travel together. I told Soraya I'd think about it.

Glancing through the glass wall, we saw Koi, making a show of having hurried, filling a plastic orange bucket with incense and flowers. Aurelia joined him on the veranda. She lit a cigarette. When she came back in, she was full of energy.

—Coffee? Who would like coffee? The monk? He'll want coffee? He's probably tired.

She disappeared into the kitchen. I wished she would sit down. Seb ate a rambutan. We couldn't settle into waiting. Anthony kept checking his watch.

Muay, having overheard my conversation with Soraya, whispered:

—Those retreats! You sleep on boards. The food is terrible, and there are insects, big spiders. Don't do it. If you want to learn Buddhism, I will give you a book.

Finally, after what seemed like a long time, Seb gestured to the road. A figure in earth-colored robes was making his way slowly behind the mango and papaya trees that lined the road. The monk was carrying what looked like a broom, its straw fanning out from a long handle.

Koi went out to greet him, making a low *wai*. I felt a shiver of excitement, a hope that the ceremony would free me of rage, perversity, dreams of Seb. . . . Aurelia and I would be free of the white obsession driving us—both of us—if it was coming from the house. My critical faculties retired themselves. It felt better to believe.

Sweat beaded on the monk's bald head, and he wiped it away with a handkerchief. His eyes were black pools set into a face the color and texture of walnut shells. Declining Aurelia's offer of coffee, though he did look exhausted, he set his cushion by the eastern wall of the living room and began chanting in a language I'd never heard before.

Koi set before him offerings, flowers and incense, which the monk worked into his ceremony. With slitted eyes, I stole glances at Seb, whose eyelids twitched as if he were dreaming. He had new stubble on his chin. It suited him.

The monk beckoned, and Aurelia and I inched forward on

our knees, bowing. Water particles hit our backs and arms as the monk scattered blessings with the straw of his broom-fan.

Then the seconds charging forward seemed to stop. The throaty chanting of the monk, tired and too human, created composites of pasts and futures, communicating in a secret language of association. *All* time, Buddhists say, is wrapped in the present moment. We are the ages we have been and will be. In Aurelia's body, I could see the seed of her future: her hair darkening before going gray, her eyes growing wise, and wrinkles creasing her skin like an ancient map. Then the monk's chants began to mix with vibrations from another set of lips—Seb's as he would sing the refrain of a Thai pop song that played at the club. Seb's tune, his little phrase, would project onto memory what the fog of whiskey had erased—time revived by his ironic humming of the pop tune: *Dum dee dum dee dum, dum dee dum dee dum, dum dee dum dee da dum.*

Later that night, we went dancing. Even Aurelia came. The walls in the club were dark, with infinite edges, and Seb and I stood as usual at a table in the fishbowl of its center, strobe-lit, staring at each other over whiskey and sodas, not dancing, almost afraid of each other, of something growing between us. Singers on stage lip-synched syllables over the beat that gathered itself and leaped forward: *Dum dee dum dee dum, dum dee dum dee dum, dum dee dum dee da dum.*

We declared an after-party in our living room. A traveler we'd met at the club came with us—a man from New Jersey, a town Aurelia knew. But as soon as we got to the house, energy waned. Aurelia disappeared, first to the kitchen, then to her bedroom. Seb fell asleep on the couch. The traveler and I shared whiskey and went on talking, Seb snoring softly at intervals.

—He laughs in his sleep, the traveler said. It's cute. And weird.

The traveler wanted to know if I knew people with whom he'd gone to university, and vice versa. We traded superficialities like worn coins, comforting because they came from a world I thought I was losing. He was the kind of North American male Seb wasn't: earnest, sure of himself, brusque, with a burly confidence that occluded whatever lay beyond the sphere of his light. In Seb there was a softness, a desire to get a little lost in what was not himself. He shared my wish to be a little destroyed by life. I knew he hated this part of himself, the part that drew me to him, and was always seeking to root it out.

The sky was lightening outside the living room's wall of glass. The traveler lay back, his eyes lightly closed, his hand on his stomach. There was no question of his driving back to his guesthouse. He was drunk, and it was almost dawn. I saw the open door to my room, then Seb, still asleep, breathing evenly on the couch. He looked innocent, like a small boy, hands folded under his cheek like a prayer. Feeling the traveler's eyes on me, I looked up. We sat, gazes locked together in the dark room as the sky brightened over the fields. Dark lashes around the traveler's eyes. Then the electricity went out of the moment. I got up, light-headed, and set blankets and towels on the other couch. Blankets were useless in the heat.

I heard the traveler sigh as I fell onto my bed, sweating.

When I woke, it was to the sound of Aurelia's voice, answered by a male voice, groggier.

—She made us *breakfast,* the traveler was saying, stupefied, when I emerged.

—I always want eggs after a night of drinking. Mmm . . . the greasier the better . . . *ha-ah!*

Seb shook his head as if shaking off a spray of water. He went into the bathroom.

Aurelia never cooked. She didn't keep food in the house. She'd thrown away my cereal once, afraid she'd eat the whole box. I followed Aurelia to the kitchen.

—I made eggs and a papaya smoothie. You should sprinkle the smoothie with instant coffee? Gives it *kick.* I do it.

Her eyes didn't meet mine.

—*Eggs?* You went to the market?

—I couldn't sleep. I never sleep. I'm worried—it's okay, but I'm starting to worry about things. It's okay; it's just worry.

Loose chords of anxiety in Aurelia's voice made me uneasy. You can catch anxiety like an illness. A pan on the stove gleamed with oil and bits of egg. She stared at the floor.

—Hard partying, drinkin' dancin', you need breakfast. Also, I had to get out of the house. Smelled like . . . I don't know, with them sleeping in the living room?

There were five cans of Pepsi Max next to the stovetop, empty.

—I was crazy once, Aurelia said. I'm getting old! Old woman! Take out the coffee?

She thrust a thermos into my hands.

—You're not eating? I asked her.

She dodged my gaze. Her hands moved nervously over the countertop.

—I wanted to cook, you know? That was the pleasure. Making it. For you.

I felt nauseous and embarrassed by Aurelia's behavior. It

revealed something too intimate. Taking in the coffee, I sat beside Seb on the couch where he'd slept.

—She brought us chilies? the traveler asked.

—For the eggs. Aurelia likes spice, I said, feeling suddenly defensive concerning her.

—She's not eating?

The traveler eyed the food suspiciously.

—Welcome to the madhouse, Seb said cheerfully, pouring himself coffee.

The traveler forked the eggs, looked at them, and frowned.

—I mean, it's supernice of her, supernice, he said, shaking his head.

Something about Aurelia's gesture made me terribly sad. We drank the coffee. Watery.

In the weeks and months to come, Seb would seek out the traveler, befriending him. His delicate manner would harden, give way to something cruel, almost sadistic. It wasn't the traveler's fault or intention, just his effect. And maybe it was Seb's real face revealing itself, his sensitive solicitude a mask he donned, with effort, for my benefit.

When they left, I threw away the eggs and went out to the veranda, where I could watch the rice fields glowing green, absorbing the clean, uncomplicated energy of the midday sun.

26

PURE NERVES, NO SKIN, oddness of channeling the hot season in the dead of winter. Her world springs to life: *Scenes* crack the cold with their meanings, charging the grayness. How boring it must have been when I had only one body. Now I'm Ella most of each day. Checking the address in my phone, I step into the cold, feeling the oddness of my own skin again in the winter air.

Buildings on the narrow street hunch forward slightly, as if to listen. Cold chalks the concrete. Flurries hang in the frigid air. Time is out of sorts in the journals. It's worst in the black and green books, but what I missed on my initial read are these first cracks. The yellow and red books contain the etiology of what comes after. It starts, perhaps, with Ella's conviction that all time is contained in the present moment. Buddhist commentaries I found call this "presentism." (If time is present before it's lived, are Buddhists fatalists? Commentaries say no.) But if Ella were testing this simultaneity of time in her writing, it's possible that her first disturbances are deliberate. What is *sense* but agreed-upon order, a separating of then and now?

The Japanese tea shop where Zoë works is in a part of the city near the Louvre, on a tiny street webbing out from the rue Sainte-Anne. The idea to consult her came from a conversation we had about *Nulle part ailleurs*. She told me she wished she had titled it in

189

English: *Nowhere Else.* She liked that the coordinate of presence—now/here—contained its opposite. We remember and imagine all the time, she said, but these pasts and futures don't exist except in the present from which we access them. Her way of collapsing photographed and painted space in her artwork was inspired by a book she'd read about religious philosophies of time. It discussed presentism as elaborated in the most arcane of the *tripitakas*, the *Abhidhamma.* Zoë said she retained only what interested her and was far from expert, but she agreed to talk with me further.

The tea shop is airy and bright, and the shelves of the tasting room are lined with ceramic bowls, teapots, yuzu vinegars, sake, and tea canisters. An English-speaking couple watches Zoë mix matcha with a wooden whisk, her polished nails matching the bright pink of her lips. The couple detects herbaceous notes in the tea. Zoë tells them they have sensitive palates and should return for a sake tasting.

—Herbaceous, she says when the couple leaves.

We laugh, and she makes us a pot of sencha.

—At first, I thought Siobhán hired you to work in the gallery. She needs help desperately and won't accept it from anyone but Aidan when he's here. You're not doing that, are you?

I frown. Zoë never asked what I was doing, so I assumed Siobhán had told her. And Siobhán had never asked for discretion. I didn't have the sense our work was secret.

—I'm not a gallerist, I say. Siobhán hired me to find her daughter.

Zoë puts down the teapot in alarm.

—Siobhán has a *daughter?*

The words tumble out: Given up for adoption. Siobhán never

knew her. Adult child. Twenty-three. Disappeared. Siobhán haunted by it ever since.

Zoë listens. She says the story makes sense. It explains why Siobhán is so hard to know.

—What are you, she asks, a *detective*?

Shaking my head, I tell her about the journals and the book Siobhán has commissioned.

—Ah, the press! Zoë says, then grows solemn. It means the girl is dead.

—The goal is to find her alive, I say, surprised at the sharpness of my voice. If I rewrite the journals, then I get inside her head a little, figure out where she went.

Siobhán's arguments take shape on my lips, believable. It's flattering and intimidating to think the press may be for me—for my work. But Zoë looks puzzled, so I get to the point, describing Ella's interest in Buddhism.

—So either she's performing this "presentism," running events together in her entries, or something is starting to go wrong with her mind, I say.

I've been staring past Zoë as I talk, conjuring the journal world from remembered script. When I find her face again, it has a faraway look.

—There's beauty in *looking* for someone, she says. You're a writer?

—Not really. Siobhán knew my mother.

Stalled out by the strangeness of Zoë's question, my mother's illness, and my old vow not to become an artist of any kind, I take out the journals and flip to a passage in the yellow book I want to show Zoë. She runs a finger along the fraying spine of the red book and says it's delicate. She doesn't insist, nor does she

mention it again, but it unsettles me to think that she believes
Ella is dead. Maybe it was just something to say, a passing idea.
She doesn't really think so. The entry is in red ink, parts washed
out by water stains,

Jan. 22

> *Too hot to do anything but lie here. Seb. Strong sensa-*
> *tion, all body. What pulls me to him, this man sealed in*
> *indifference? Dreamed we were camping by a lake. Too*
> *much rain. I was screaming. He couldn't hear. Black*
> *pen gone. Time begins to scatter. Now, now, now. Hap-*
> *pens now, now, now while I'm missing it. Aurelia, des-*
> *perate to wake the stillborn within her, murders it with*
> *Pepsi Max. Animal, solitary* [illegible]. *Flood when it*
> *breaks. Instinct. Rub out the face that is eager to please.*
> [illegible] *pulse on skin, electricity quickening at life's*
> *edges, evidence of its inner source.*

—Oh, god, Zoë says. Why do you think it has to do with
Buddhism?

Embarrassed, I point to the bit about time scattering and the
now, now, now. When I was alone, Ella's words made sense. Now,
I can't find the collision of times I identified before. We look at a
few other entries, this time in the red book. As we study them, trying to decide what is when, Ella's words dry out, lose their shine,
like the rubbery bodies of jellyfish dead on the sand.

—What's clear, Zoë says finally, is her sense that spirituality
can be a cure for obsession. It's really common. You see it also with
addiction. It's how I started. It saved my life.

The owner of the tea shop calls, and Zoë disappears. When she returns, I see she has to tend to other things. As I gather my coat, she invites me to a concert she's going to with a painter friend, giving me the place and time before I can refuse.

On my way back to the flat, halfway up the rue des Martyrs, jasmine plants press against a florist's window. I go in and buy one. At first there is only the cold in my nostrils, then the faint, cloying odor of the pearls. I carry the plant like a child up the hill to the flat, wanting to know what it was to be decked in one of Soraya's jasmine necklaces, to smell it on the breeze at night. *Did* Ella go mad, or did she just know something most of us don't? At the writing table, I separate things I've done today as Ella and as Elena. The last sun rays make narrow shards on the floor, grow thinner, then close into shadow.

27

EVERY TUESDAY EVENING during the hot season, I would find Béa amid the stalls of Ban Du Market, and we would pick out snacks to take to our Thai lesson. One Tuesday, well into the season, when the heat was fiercest, I arrived at the market desperate for anything to distract me from Seb—fantasies like firecrackers, fevers, he'd appear behind windows, desks, and doors. The heat-mirage Sebs had multiplied because for weeks the real Seb had been distant. The arrival of the traveler had brought out a hardness in him that wasn't there when it was just the two of us. Seb was polite—I had nothing to reproach him for—but he'd stopped *confiding* in me. Our old intimacy was dying. If we could be alone together, I was sure it would return. But the traveler was always there. With no job—was he living on savings? a trust fund?—he'd moved from his guest-house downtown, taking a patio apartment near Ban Du Market. He planned to stay awhile. So my fantasies had become richer than life and were getting harder to control: Seb's face, his voice, his smell at the ends of all my nerves, flushing my skin. In my office, in class, I couldn't think of anything else. It was in this agitated state that I arrived at the market, longing for little rituals, language games.

Our teacher, Ploy, had strong preferences and loved pork with sticky rice.

Channeling Ploy—the way her mouth would swell with the taste of Thai words—I asked for two bags of *khaow niaaow* and two of *mu ping*.

—*Falang pood Thai gaaeng maak!* The wrinkles on the seller's face lifted into a smile.

She charged the usual but gave me four bags of sticky rice with the pork. I thanked her.

Ploy lived close to the market in a house that opened almost onto the superhighway. Cars, trucks, and motorbikes passed at great speed, making lines of light in the dusk. We rang the bell. Ploy called to us to come in. We pushed, but the door didn't move. It was an absurdly large door, painted metal, out of proportion to the house. It took the full weight of Béa's body and mine to open it. Once ajar, it gained momentum, swung on its own, and we tumbled into the house.

Inside, a dark eye, amused, peeked out from behind the kitchen wall. We slid off our shoes. As Ploy crossed the room, her wide-necked shirt slipped from her shoulders. She pushed it up casually. Her walk was slow, both flirtatious and making fun of flirtation. Admiring this, I'd become a student of her style as well as her language, thinking her charm could be mine if only I got the cadence right.

Ploy laughed when she saw how much rice I was carrying. Her laugh was a dam bursting, surging between words and syllables. Béa laughed with her. Thai came easily to Béa, who could endure moments of nonunderstanding as if there were nothing other than laughter to be learned. Béa didn't sanctify language, but I wanted it perfect, like a god.

—You have brought us a feast! Ploy said, gesturing to the rice in my arms.

Ploy's English was meticulous, errorless. Maybe she considered it part of her job to demonstrate that *attention* as well as submission was necessary to mastering a foreign tongue. All sound play, all glossolalic poetry (usual byproducts of forays into linguistic unknowns) got referred, in Ploy's case, to her Thai. She reduced words to phonic textures, twisting meanings into spasms of sound. Ploy instructed us mostly in English, so we had to intuit the eccentricity of her Thai from the way she spoke on her cell phone and her frequent admonitions: Do as I *teach* you. Never speak like I speak. Then the laughter would come, spreading from her body into Béa's and mine. We never knew if Ploy had a curriculum, but her laughter told us if our tone, pronunciation, or grammar was awry. Her laugh wasn't derisive—just pleasure at hearing Thai phonemes oriented on axes that weren't their own.

Taking the bags of rice from my arms, Ploy led us to the kitchen.

—Too much *khaaow*. How do you say *cow*, I mean the meat?

—*Néua,* we replied, familiar with the game.

—*Néua,* Ploy said, correcting. High tone, *néua!* Beef.

I handed her the pork.

—How do you say pork?

—*Moo,* Béa replied from deep in her throat, like a cow.

—*Moo-what-tone?* Ploy chanted in unvarying pitch to test our memories.

The sound was out of my mouth before I could cycle through the five diacritics.

—Rising! *Chaaaiii!* Ploy said to me. Right.

Smiling, she disappeared into the darkening garden, letting in a warm breeze and the smell of the superhighway. She came back with bunches of bird's-eye chilies, red and green.

—We will cook something to go with so much rice! *Som tam, tam eng. Malagaw,* she said, taking shredded green papaya from the refrigerator. What do you make with this?

—*Som tam,* I said, my lips vibrating *m*'s like the skins of hand drums.

—*Chaaaiii! Tam eng?* Oh! *Tam eng* is to make yourself. Homemade.

—*Som tam, tam eng,* I said.

—It's just like language, the food you eat. In Thailand, it's the way people are together. How spicy? she asked, her black eyes teasing as she tossed chilies into the mortar.

We sat on the floor mats in the living room, scooping up sticky rice, pork, and papaya salad. Béa lit a cigarette as the meal drew to a close. Words were streaming in my mind. I felt them in my sinus passages, their nasal sounds: *khao niaow, moo ping, som tam, tam eng.* Ploy was saying sentences, leaning toward us, sweating. She put sticky rice and *som tam* on her plate.

—*Tam eng. Arroy, na?* I said.

—Yeah, *right?*

Ploy's reply struck me. Familiar. Unable to place it, I felt unsettled.

—*Ahaan maak, gern bpai,* Béa said precociously.

Ploy explained:

—She says there is too much food. It is true, but don't worry! My friends will come later. They eat a lot. Boys.

She laughed.

It must have been the chilies from the *som tam*. I must have let the seeds linger too long on my tongue, because a slow burn began in my mouth. My skin grew hot. Ploy fed me a spoonful of palm sugar to dull the pain, and when that didn't work, she mixed a cordial of honey, lime, and ice. I took gulps from the glass, greedily pressing its coolness to my burning lips. All the moisture left my mouth. I picked out ice cubes with the crook of my finger and rolled them on my tongue. Ploy couldn't help herself. She found my intolerance to spice hysterical.

I got up, trying to regain my sense of comfort, my whole body burning. In Ploy's bathroom, there was only a thin grating over the window, and sounds outside were overly clear: trucks and cars on the superhighway. I sat and tried to breathe evenly. Tears came to my eyes from the spice. Then, in the semidarkness, came the sound of voices, familiar, and footsteps on the drive.

—It's weird, dude. You see it, right? It's, like, pretty fucking there. Full on—

The traveler's voice and heavy step, crunching gravel. Then Seb's soft laugh, click of a helmet clipping onto a frame. Voices amplified between tile walls. I didn't dare turn on a light.

—The whole fuckin' village gets it. They're like, dude, that *falang*'s in *heat*.

—Yeah, *right?*

That phrase, said like that, inflected, is Seb's signature. It means he gets you, he agrees. I needed more context, but already I wanted to throw a sharp object at the traveler.

—So you *do* notice? the traveler asked.

—We're good friends, Seb said evenly.

—You fucked her?

I climbed up on the toilet seat to try to see them through the grate. It was impossible. Strobe patterns from the super-highway flashed in the space.

Seb said something muffled, to which the traveler gave a full-throated laugh.

—Don't repeat that, Seb said. It'd be, y'know, *messy.*

—I wish you *would*—

—Why? Seb said, snorting. Worried *someone*'ll have to?

—Yeah *right?* the traveler said, Seb's imitated phrase fitting him poorly.

Shame and anger added to the burn in my mouth. As crude as Seb's reaction had been, I forgave it. It was the traveler's presumption that enraged me. How could he think I'd want *him?* Burly, crude, yet what he said hurt because it held some truth—tightness in my throat, shortness of breath when Seb was near, it wasn't clean or pure. Deep down I knew it had no necessary tie to Seb. Still, I clung to him with a bodily obstinacy that was the enemy of good sense.

The traveler laughed nervously.

—I don't know—if it's a *falang* dude she wants, since you're settled and all.

—I'm not *settled*, Seb said. This isn't . . . *lasting.*

—Why not? Ploy's supercute. She's funny as hell, too.

—Yeah, *right?* But she's—they're all *clingy.*

I flushed the toilet and went back to the living room, my mouth in pain, eyes watering. I tried to gather my thoughts, but they foundered, waiflike. The traveler's words stung: *Falang in heat.* Seb's: *messy.* Seb with Ploy? Ploy gave us our assignments for next week.

—*Falang suay,* she said to me with a wink.

I stared at her, confused. I'd thought *suay* meant "beautiful."

—Next time we will add fewer chilies, she said kindly. You are too delicate, sensitive.

My head still throbbing, I picked out my sandals from the pile of shoes by the door. I was bent over, fastening the strap, when the doorbell rang. There was Ploy's melodious "*Come in*," a strip of green evening light, then space collapsed into a black-red nugget. Crack of metal against a hard object. My hands reached out, grabbing at nothing. In the door frame was Seb, warm cedar of his smell, breeze behind him carrying scents of the summer night and the rushing highway traffic. Thud of a body falling, terrible taste in my mouth.

—Dude, is she *out*? Did you knock her *out*?

Voices, sharp intakes of breath, feet coming from the kitchen, pain at skull base, moving like a wave to the fingertips. Familiar gray eyes checking over my body, long in meeting mine.

—Shit. I'm sorry, Seb said.

Pain came in beats with my pulse. Seb's warm hand. Hungrily, my fingers laced with his.

—Can you get up? he asked. Are you okay? Open your mouth.

Something spilled from my mouth as I lifted my head. Ploy's eyes bulged. She left and returned with a damp towel. The sight of my blood snapped me to awareness. I turned my head to the floor. More liquid escaped. Ploy tucked the towel beneath my jaw. Afraid, I squeezed Seb's hand.

—She might have to go to the hospital, Seb said, freeing his hand from my grip.

—There is a lot of blood, Ploy agreed.

—She should sit up, Béa said. If she stays like that, she's going to swallow it.

They lifted me, supporting my head. I moved my tongue over all of my teeth, relieved to find them in place.

—It looks like it's her tongue that's bleeding, Béa said, inspecting me. I'll call the hospital.

I tried to protest, but no sound came. My head ballooned with pain, but the thought of a hospital made everything worse. Béa was calling. There was no answer. Seb looked miserable.

—You know the sound of the metal door? Ploy asked, trying to make things light. The sound is *khlaaaang,* she said, drawing out the long *aaa,* Do you know what *khlaang* means?

I shook my head, breaking a clot. Blood on the towel made me gag. I wanted to go home.

—It means "love." Not love between two people, but the love of a crazy person. *Klang-klai!*

Ploy's laughter rang out, innocent. Seb gave her hip a little shove.

—I want to go home, I said, surprised at the sound of my voice.

Ploy took two Singhas from a small refrigerator and held a cold bottle to my cheek before handing one to Seb and the other to the traveler. Béa said she'd call a taxi. I said I would drive.

—You're not drinking? I heard the traveler ask Ploy.

—It will give me a belly like you! Ploy said, poking him.

—Are you sure? Béa asked me, raising her voice over their laughter.

I got to my feet, pain firing from every nerve. Ploy found my remaining shoe and bent down to fasten it for me.

Outside, patches of unblackened sky hung over the super-highway like sores. We walked to the market, where we'd left our motorbikes. My head felt large, oversensitive. Béa's lighter exploded in the darkness; our steps in the gravel were avalanches of sound. Passing cars ricocheted in my nervous system like electric shocks. My mouth was gummy and dry, the rest of me swollen from embarrassment. Headlights on the drive home seemed unremitting.

February 22

With every word swallowed, you inherit a history. Seb's words in Ploy's mouth. Horrible night. Head splitting. From a body cut open, no soul escapes, only passions, appetites. Now, in my room, protected, alone, I am this sequence of thoughts like vapors in candlelight. Here I let in only so much, just enough to metabolize. Myself is what I know of it. Desire acts without the will, breeding itself like a virus into systems of signification. Desire is the ass of language. We clothe it with words and it bulges beneath them. Unfastened from its object, loose in the world, it will eat us alive. Aurelia is home. In the kitchen. She has knocked over a pan and is foraging. Crackle of food packaging. I'll hear her later, repentant, doing sit-ups on the chaise cushions. Aurelia doesn't age. Obsession protects her from time. She keeps white nights so that her days never end. Her body sheds no blood. Her periods don't come. Ha-ah? She cannot sleep. Don't have cigarettes before bed, Seb told her. No, they don't affect me. Aurelia, afraid of being seen, is disappearing like a photograph on a tin roof in sunlight. Nothing ever passes, enters, or leaves her body, which is always circling so as not to change. Maybe she has long understood what I'm coming to learn: unbearable weakness of a body in want. Desire is humiliation. Whittle yourself down and there's less you, less want. Roosters picking in the yard. A breeze, quickening, smacks the window against the side of the house.

28

SWEET COLD LIGHT OF A FEBRUARY MORNING in a bed under skylights dirty enough to hide the sky. It's a paradox that everything I do to know her hooks me into this life, different from the life I lived with Z. After the concert, after drinks, Zoë trailed us, her face half-hidden behind the corner of a building, one brown eye visible, laughing like a spy, making sure that this is what I wanted. Yes. Now the painter is rinsing a small coffeepot, turning it in his long fingers on the other side of the studio as winter light from the skylights slips into the room.

Tout dans le même endroit, he explained last night. His canvases, paints, and kitchen are in the same large room as his bed, where I am wrapped in blankets, my clothes over a stack of easels. I wanted to be painted so I'd *feel* like Ella, my body becoming not words, but something fixed, other.

The painter speaks very fast and says he is sorry, but my French is slow, so I just smile when he asks, *Tu veux un café? Des oranges? Je te peins encore ce matin dans cette belle lumière, si ça te va?* I grasp at the threads of his phrases, unable to compose a response in time. How does it happen, this coming of a voice? Will immersion, will submission cast us up to the surface one day, and all at once?

Our breakfast is efficient and mute. The painter has a habit of smiling with one side of his mouth, as if overwhelmed. At first,

I thought his offer to paint me was a pretext, but it seemed to engage him more than the sex, not in a perverse way. Now his glance flicks to his easel, and he indicates the ratty divan. The floor is gray rubber with energetic stains of dry paint.

—*Tu n'as pas froid?* he asks me.

I shake my head, less nervous now. His painting is abstract and solid, telluric even, terra-cotta and turquoise layered to give the work hints of a third dimension. Like sculpture. I'm no judge of talent, but what he showed me of his work was calming, sensual: self-portraits, jugs, bathtubs, his father's face, disordered and somehow compelling. When he paints me, I don't have to talk or plan out what to say in French. I can think. I like the look of his face, absorbed, so different from most faces. I find an odd pleasure—a sense of justice—letting myself be translated like this, from flesh to acrylic and pigment, back to earth.

From my supine position, I think of Ella filling herself with words, submitting herself to Thai, repeating the sounds to discover how *else* one might live. I am witness to her picaresque pickings among ways of being. She's apprenticing herself to the world, and I to her, despite her youth, because of her guilelessness. I know she is taking on words so that one day she'll decide, as if by magic, to make them her own. She isn't usual. Most often we live in foreign words until we die.

In the journals, Ella asks. *Is the old concept "self" anything other than a mosaic of other's words?* I am becoming her words, as much as I fix her in mine. We're connected now, and I've only to close my eyes to find myself far away from this white city where it has again begun to snow. It's getting harder to tell which of us is creating the other.

29

A FEW DAYS BEFORE THE HOT-SEASON VACATION, a familiar figure appeared on our veranda with an oversize backpack and two camera bags around his neck. His shirt was dark with sweat, and he wiped his face with a bandanna as we spoke. I recognized him from the costume party my first month here, when every encounter, because of its newness, had uncanny staying power.

—Weren't you moving to Mongolia? I asked, hesitating to hug him because of the sweat.

Aurelia slipped away, saying he must want a glass of cold water. The native photographer removed his backpack. I helped him with one of his camera bags, lifting it above his head.

—Thanks, he said, wiping his forehead.

He explained that he'd gotten a job subbing photo classes at the Alliance française, since the regular teacher was preparing his own exhibition. I smiled. I knew the regular teacher, Lek— Béa's friend, the soft-spoken man with a gaze so intent that it made me feel exposed.

—Mongolia is still definitely next, the native photographer was saying. Béatrice gave me your address. I told her I knew an

American girl who works at the university. She said it had to be you. Can I crash a few nights while I look for a place?

Aurelia came back from the kitchen with chilled water and a lemon slice. The native photographer emptied the glass in one gulp and shuddered from the shock of the cold.

She lit a cigarette and studied him. We were part of a travelers' culture where everyone seemed to know everyone, at least by degrees, and it wasn't unusual to colonize others' couches. We talked it over and decided the native photographer should stay through the hot-season vacation. It would be nice to have someone to look after the house. The native photographer, happy with this arrangement, promised to plant a garden while we were away.

—A rock garden, he added, looking at the gravel of the yard.

The next days were full of departure preparations. Soraya had reserved a place for me at the monastery—initially for ten days, since she didn't like the idea of me gone a long time. I asked her to extend it, not liking to do things halfway.

—Okay, my Western daughter, she said, a whole long month. Then you will be in Chiang Mai for Songkran. Songkran? Oh, it's the Thai New Year. Chiang Mai is the best place to celebrate. Everyone goes out in the street and throws water.

I knew this, but I let her tell me anyway. Soraya had reconciled with the administrator, who was sending her to a spa in Japan over the hot-season vacation. I asked if he would join her.

—For the last part, she said, unfolding and refolding more neatly a shirt I'd laid out on the bed. He has work responsibilities, she added, her eyes lowered, very urgent ones.

Aurelia and I caught the same bus to Chiang Mai, where I had dinner plans with Seb (who was on his way to a beach town with the traveler), and Aurelia, I suspected, had a tryst. She'd been coy when I asked about her plans, saying something about a villa and asking to meet up after my retreat, since we'd both be in Chiang Mai. After the retreat, and after Songkran, Seb and I had plans to backpack through Vietnam. With perverse melancholy, I feared something would happen to prevent the trip, which I looked forward to with unhealthy fervor.

In Chiang Mai, later, at Seb's favorite of the riverside restaurants, I watched lantern light flicker across his cheeks and forehead.

—No one but you ever *suffers*, he said, arcing his body toward me across the table.

His eyes narrowed, challenging, prodding me out of myself. He was mocking me, but the word sounded strange in his mouth, as if he'd been given a swab of cotton to chew. I swilled Singha. It was warm and flat. Heat of these nights made the mind soft with longing.

—You take yourself so *seriously*, he continued, raising an eyebrow.

Colored lanterns quivered on their suspension wire, reflections flickering in the river.

Signaling with his hand, Seb ordered another round. He crossed and uncrossed his legs. The beer girls probably thought us coupled and bored, empty of stories to tell each other.

—Fine, I said. Tell me how *you* suffer. *Un*seriously.

—Darling, I never do.

Emptying his glass, he leaned in again, resting his chin on his palm. He made me think of those Greek statues that change their demeanor with your angle of view.

—Everything's clear when I'm alone, he said. Most of the time, I find people boring.

A beer girl approached. She plucked ice cubes from a bucket with silver tongs and dropped them in our glasses. She opened a large Singha and poured.

—You're here *why*, then? I asked sharply, though his tone had been soft.

—Me? I'm here to watch the beer girls, he said, sardonic again. A better question is why are *you*?

He fished his ice cube out of his glass and threw it in the river. Heat gathered beneath the skin of my face. Then Seb leaned in again, serious.

—You're different. You feel real to me. Other people, it's like they forget what life is. . . .

—And what is it? I asked. Or am I supposed to remind you?

With no notice, his eyes were full of intensity.

—To me, you're interesting, he said softly.

For a moment I thought he would lean even closer, kiss me. But he broke my gaze and looked down, fingers moving over the keypad of his phone. On a small stage, a singer-guitarist duo began a cover of Norah Jones. I asked Seb who besides the traveler was going with him to Pattaya. I wanted to know if Ploy would be there.

—Few guys, Seb shrugged, tapping his foot to the music.

—Are you coming back after, for Songkran?

Our flight to Hanoi was from Bangkok, but I wanted Seb to be there when I got out of the monastery. I wanted to spend the Thai New Year together. I wanted the bus ride to Bangkok, Seb restless, pressed against me in the small seats.

—Oh. Right. We'll see, he said, leaning back in his chair.

—You have a thing, I asked, a thing with Ploy?

He nodded, not meeting my gaze. He said it was nice but not that serious, and he seemed about to say something else, when a new message lit up his phone. I saw it was from the traveler.

—Up for a club? he smiled at me. What time do you have to be at your *convent?*

—It's a monastery. Eleven. Not too early. Not four A.M. Every day is four A.M. Wake-up.

I was sounding like Aurelia, my thoughts disjointed.

—Monks, Seb said, shaking his head. Just after I arrived for the first time in Thailand, I was out on Khaosan Road, right, in Bangkok. It must have been five in the morning, and in front of us was this giant flock of monks, a *gaggle,* like birds, or like *creatures.* We waited until they passed us—we couldn't move, stupid with awe. They had these begging bowls, already full, and orange robes glowing against this pale green light. I think I saw God, you know. . . .

He laughed, but the vision animated his body, energized his hands and eyes.

—To the detox of your spirit, he said, raising a glass.

The tempo of the music quickened.

The club was hot. I don't remember its name or anything about it other than patches of arms, legs, and stomachs as mirror balls scattered light over Thai women and Western men. It was smaller than our club in Chiang Rai and smelled of sweat and cologne.

The traveler was there with friends, all men. He ordered whiskeys, and we stood in a circle as the lights spun around us. They were talking about the hill tribes. I don't know why. To make conversation, I told them about volunteer work I'd done with Muay and Aurelia. I described Thai Women of Tomorrow, TWOT for short, an organization to protect village girls against the sex trade. Something about the club made me say this. There was awful silence.

—Can't stop a force of nature, one of the men said finally.

The others laughed. Tension rose, but I kept talking, my body flushed with indignation.

—You are fourteen years old, I said to the man who had spoken. You are no longer legally required to go to school. A man comes to the village. He tells you and some of your friends that you can work in the city for a year—just one year—and come home with money for your family. Your family needs that money—

—*Baht* for *twat!* another man said, interrupting me.

He had a round, doughy face and small beady eyes. I looked to Seb, who was covering his face, trying to hide that he was laughing. Still, my rage was only for the dough-faced man.

I left them, shaking with anger, and began to pace the area around the dance floor, faster and faster, until I crashed into a man moving slowly in the opposite direction. His sour smell reached me before I saw his greasy hair, a grin floating on spit-coated lips, hot glare of yellow eyes. In a humid, cramped room, my heart beat in my ears and my vision blurred as I heard the clink of his belt buckle and felt the sour damp of his pubic hair, his sticky white saliva, the terrible taste of him. I stood as if caught in the man's stare, until a girl in blue platform heels swept by on a breeze sweet with perfume, linked her arm in mine, and led me to the dance floor. We danced to Thai pop. Despite it all, ashamed, I was energized by the thought that Seb might be watching.

At the end of the night, last chords sputtered in the speakers and the lights came up, revealing a sad, bleak room full of sweaty people. Around me, hands smoothed skirts and hair. The dancing girl disappeared. I found Seb leaning against a wall, his arm around another girl.

—You're still *here*, he slurred, seeing me.

—We figured you bailed, the traveler said, emerging from a cluster of foreigners.

—We're going for *pad thai*, Seb said: *Luna* knows a place. . . .

The girl laughed, slipping a finger between the buttons of Seb's shirt. He batted her hand away, then reached his hand under her blouse, clipping her nipple. She sucked in breath.

—I don't think *Loona*'s your name, he said, his face in her neck. The problem with Thai names is they're too long. You can't use them.

A middle-aged *falang* nodded to Seb.

—No more than fifteen hundred baht. They'll talk you up. Don't go for it.

My cheeks began to burn. I glanced at the traveler.

—Not my thing, he said, shrugging. But if it were, I'd double-bag it.

A laugh sputtered at his lips and died.

Outside, I pushed through throngs of Thai women with money belts. Seb's image stayed with me in the streets amid the burned-garlic odors of noodle stands. I hailed a *tuk tuk* and gave the name of my guesthouse. Bends crashed me against the sides. Heat closed in as the engine vibrated. Fumes of petrol made the streetlamps, palms, and city walls seem large and close.

I wanted to believe that Seb *wouldn't,* that it was the traveler's influence. But the traveler, seeing me make this calculation, had headed it off.

The self is a crack in a glass globe. Seb again in the guesthouse lobby, on the stairs, in my room, where a ceiling fan churned slowly through the stale heat. I opened the window and looked out. In a lit room across the courtyard a man on a bed was masturbating. I watched until the body jerked in orgasm, then drew my curtain and fell asleep.

In the morning, the sun on the black curtains unlocked the smells of everyone who'd used the room. My sinuses were blocked. I folded my clothes into my backpack and walked outside. White sunlight. Guesthouses mirrored each other on the threadlike streets of the old city. It was a desert of lit concrete. Cafés for backpackers advertised on laminated menus: *Flesh fruit smoothly, banana ban cake.* Choosing one, I sat down with my things and ordered an egg, *sunny-sigh up.* Newspapers on the table: *Terror ravages. Madrid. Europe's worst attack since '88.* Snot dripped onto the copy of the *Bangkok Post.* A morgue had been set up in an exhibition hall. Relatives had to identify remains. *The government blames the Basque separatist group ETA for the bombings, which come three days ahead of Spain's general election.* For the first time in a long time, I began to cry. I didn't know anyone in Madrid, had never even been there. But I put my face on the table and sobbed. The server set a box of tissues beside me with a glass of water. Maybe he thought I was Spanish. Maybe he thought I was crying about the papers. Maybe I was.

The crying stopped as abruptly as it started. I was left with a hollow feeling, the feeling of having seen the other side of the world's Janus face. I wanted to hold my breath for as long as those families had to search the rubble for their brothers and children and husbands and wives. I needed to start moving. It was late, and I still had to buy temple offerings before my arrival at the monastery: *eleven lotus blossoms, eleven orange candles, eleven incense sticks.* I dried my face, puffy and swollen in the mirror of the cafe, and hailed a *tuk tuk.* Traffic was stalled all the way to Payong Market. The heat of the day was already suffocating. The stoplight turned green, hardly visible against the bleached sky. Inching toward the market, I read the retreat handbook. *Rules: 1. After midday, no solid food. 2. No reading of newspapers or other material. 3. No writing. 4. Speech is not allowed. 5. White clothing will be distributed upon arrival and must be worn at all times.*

30

—It wasn't ETA, Siobhán says flatly, waving my pages in the air. It was a local cell with ties to al-Qaeda.

From her white couch, I watch the winter sky, gray and unchanging. Siobhán is driving at something I don't yet see. To me, it's clear that Ella dwells on the attacks because they feed her wider sense of catastrophe. What more?

—The conservative government in Spain was voted out of office for blaming the separatists, Siobhán says. The public felt manipulated. Then al-Qaeda claimed the attacks, called it Operation Death Trains.

She lights a cigarette and walks to the window. I have the unnerving sense that she is acting out something, or that she has said this before. Why tell me about the bombings? I didn't ask. Ella's distress over them is symptomatic of her sense of a world violence. Micro, macro, it was all mixed up for her.

—Ella didn't know that, I say. So why does it matter?

—She found out later.

Siobhán looks away. The contents of the journals now are more familiar to me than parts of my own life, and there is no mention of al-Qaeda.

—How do you know?

She opens the window to smoke. Cold air rushes in.

—She told me.

Siobhán turns, tapping her cigarette on the ashtray, her face pale.

—Over the phone, she says. She called from the monastery. The news upset her.

Her words pin me like a specimen to the couch.

—You *spoke* to her? I ask, shocked.

—I thought it was important that you base your work on her journals, nothing more. But, yes, we spoke, and now it's relevant that you know about our conversations.

—How often? I ask, hating that she can divulge crucial information on a whim. It feels like a betrayal.

Siobhán regards me, displeased.

—It started in November, exactly a month after her birthday. She called four more times, monthly, on the twenty-third. The twenty-third was the day she was born. There was no way to call *her*. She used a calling card. All that came up was a string of zeros. I could have gone through her mother, but . . .

Siobhán's affect is so unusual that it takes me a moment to realize what she's doing—*justifying* herself—and to *me*, as if I had the authority to declare her innocent.

—In March, she called sooner. On the fifteenth.

She shakes her head. Her skin looks ashen, but her eyes are alive, full of light and pain.

—She was upset, Siobhán says. She wanted to talk about how the terrorists blew themselves up when they were found, not weighing their chances to survive. I didn't know what to think. It was the last time she called.

Siobhán lights another cigarette. Her hands are shaking.

—She *confused* everything, she says, her voice trailing off.

I churn through remembered script, looking for some reference I might have missed to their conversations. Nothing. Ella felt she was expanding into what was around her. *I don't know where I end,* she wrote. *I am too much.*

—What else did you talk about? Was she angry? Did she ask things like *why* you gave her up? I ask, thinking it would be like Ella to get straight to the point.

Siobhán closes the window.

—She asked about my family origins, Irish, Scottish, that kind of thing. She wanted to know why I lived in France. I also told her about the London years, about the strength of my friendship with her adoptive mother—with your mother, too.

—Did she ask about her father?

Siobhán looks at me, as if to say she understands my game and will play along.

—Yes, she says. After all, she has a right to know. He was a philosophy student. From Germany. He doesn't know about her.

—What color is his hair?

—Very light. Long when I knew him.

—Were you in love?

—No.

—Why didn't you tell him?

—I was very young. I wasn't sure what I would do, but I wanted it to be my choice.

Siobhán moves away from the window, breaking whatever spell we'd fallen into.

—Ella and I spoke five times. Now you know. Her last call was from the monastery. She said she was breaking a vow of silence to do it. She said she found the meditation difficult.

Siobhán seems at peace, but I'm agitated, shaken, having taken a role that isn't mine.

31

I'S HARD TO REMEMBER THE MONASTERY. The month is splashes of color and angles of light. My journals are my memory, and I didn't write much. A few words every few days. I had to play by the rules if the experience was going to work. If it was going to change me.

> *The* bikkhuni *says not to cry for lost worlds. They are not real. Only presence is real.*
> *Flesh has worn off the world and I'm wandering among its old bones, listening for lonely whistles of the void.*
> *No sick, no intestines, no stomach, no anus, no vomit, no dizziness, no suffering, no heat, no thirst, no clamminess, no consciousness, no muscles, no bone.*
> *Tomatoes. Life seduces. Strange fruit.*
> *The Man from Augsburg says I'm a scorpion.*
> *Gone so wrong in this selfless place of stone and bone and no difference, only whiteness.*
> *Punished by floods and the tiny dead for company, weak mind that was mine flayed by the moon.*

Each day there was reporting with the head monk, Pra Ajarn. It was the only time speech was allowed—a time to pose questions, confess doubts, and discuss our practice, its difficulties or ecstasies. At my first reporting, Pra Ajarn—ancient body, baby-smooth face—sat under a photograph of his teacher. Rings of incense dissolved above us as I bowed, holding my palms at my chest, thumbs pressing hard against my sternum.

—*Ella,* Pra Ajarn said, glancing at a notepad for my name, How is your practice?

That I didn't get it was obvious from the way I moved: from one courtyard to the next, to the library, to the *bikkhuni* huts, to my room, unable to find stillness, peace. That morning, I'd endured the gongs at four thirty and at seven, falling asleep again until the white sun began to sear me alive on my wooden-board bed.

—Walking meditation is easier for me than sitting meditation, I said, saving face.

Pra Ajarn's eyes closed for a moment. He adjusted his earth-colored robes. I stared at the weave of the mat, any desire I had to be precocious made ridiculous by how little I understood.

—*Samsara* is joy, too, he said finally. It is strong. Most English speakers say it is suffering. It is not *only* suffering. *Samsara* is everything attracting us to life.

Even—especially—when I thought I'd made progress, grasped some facet of the Way, reporting would undo the new certainty. So, when frustration boiled over in the heat of the afternoons, I would often seek out the young monk, Pra New, who had led orientation, chipper, chatty, different from Pra Ajarn.

—Use this, here, he would tell me, pressing his stomach. Do you know about *vicara*? It is practice, steady pressure, like the ringing of a bell. It is what you learn *only* by practice. It is the only way to take away your doubt.

—But how do I know if I'm doing it *right*? I asked. What if I practice *wrong*?

—From here, Pra New said, pressing my gut, then shooing me out of his welcome office.

IT WAS AGAINST THE RULES TO CONSUME solid food after midday, but each night at dusk, a woman came to the temple gates with vats of steaming soya milk, which she ladled into plastic bags, plugged with a straw and tied off with a tiny rubber band. It was customary to drink the milk at a cluster of picnic tables with plastic tablecloths, under a tent where fluorescent light strips attracted insects of all kinds. Sitting at the tables, I noticed, each night, one of the other meditation students doing a vigorous walking meditation in the main courtyard. He had white shoulder-length hair. His walk was razor-sharp, fast, and riveted to some goal. He fascinated me because he moved without doubt. Perhaps he had found a way, through practice, to banish it. It became my habit to watch his meditation every evening, when incense snaked from the feet of the sleeping Buddhas and lanterns flung their brassy light against the stupas in the courtyards.

One evening, I arrived at the picnic tables and found the main courtyard empty and the man seated in my usual seat, three bulbous bags of soya milk in front of him. I sat across from him (we weren't allowed to speak). His body was thin and hard, old enough to be my father's. He consumed his first bag of soya milk, its shape collapsing under the pressure of his mouth.

—Breast milk, he muttered, as if to me.

I chewed my straw, then sucked through the slit I'd made. He consumed the second bag.

—Always hungry here, he said. They want you to forget your body. It's impossible.

I said nothing, thinking of how we'd been advised to eat lightly to avoid desire. Sensual appetites cannot be quenched and will just grow if you give them fuel.

A sucking sound, and he was gone. In his place were three crushed bags with milk traces.

THE PRESENT, HOT, MAKES THE JOINTS of the world disengage. Salt tears in the library. Can see no humanity past my own. Mind, blown open, turns, returns. Fingernails on the buttons of Seb's shirt. Meditate on rotting flesh to combat lust. Intestines voided themselves regularly, my body a hollow tube: secreting. Mind bound to sickly flesh, bobbing, rocking on uncomfortable seas. Skin chalk white as the sky.

The *bikkhuni* brought me tomatoes, saying I needed color in my cheeks. I refused, wanting the full experience. She sat before me, patient, a tomato in each upturned palm. Finally, I took one and sucked at the skin indifferently. With the burst of seeds and juice there was sensing, taste! Lethargy broke. Pure exuberance for the rest of the day.

ONE DAY I ASKED PRA NEW ABOUT the other meditation students.

—The man who walks more quickly than the others?

—Yes, yes. He signs the ledger as the Man from Augsburg. He doesn't give his name.

—Why? Is he really from Augsburg?

Pra New shrugged. He didn't know.

—Every year, he comes on the same day and stays three months. His practice is not typical. He does no sitting meditation and walks too fast. We have to warn the novices not to imitate him. They always try. He builds to twenty hours of meditation per day. In his last week, he stays in his room and sees no one. We bring him food, but he won't eat.

—And no one knows his *story?*

—Look at how he walks, Pra New said, exasperated. It's there, his story. You want more than that? You are nosy. Worse than *I* am! He laughed. Now go, meditate!

GONGS ANNOUNCED THE MORNING MEAL: mouthfuls of Pali prayer, laminated transliterations of Thai and English on the tables. Word designs like serpents would slip into the tympanum through the cavities of the eyes. Breakfast was rice in a watery stew of what may have been vegetables. I left with my usual hunger, which felt like nausea. There would be another meal at noon, then no solid food. Some afternoons there would be ice cream, which is only artificially solid. Like all things.

Words scooped of meaning collected against me like cicada shells. Whey of words. Sibilance just sensation when its semantic privilege peels away.

Language carries dis-ease in the form of desire.

When the noon gongs sounded, I lined up at the refectory, thinking only of tomatoes: skin, color, taste on my tongue. Feeling a hand on my tunic, I turned, wanting to fall against this body, anybody, so as not to have to stand. White hair shone in the sun. He beckoned. Hesitation was brief, ineffectual in the face of my curiosity. We crossed the temple grounds and slipped between the bars of the north gate. His presence focused my thoughts.

His smell was patchouli wood. Outside the monastery, a sidewalk curved through conifers and palms.

—You won't survive like that, he said, walking ahead of me. Rules are important, but you must break them to oblige the intuition. Otherwise, you lose it.

—Isn't that the point? I asked, struggling to keep pace with him.

—To lose your intuition? He turned to look back at me. No.

—But fasting lessens sense desire. It's a way toward freedom.

—Discipline and moderation regulate sense desire, not murdering one's natural instincts. Do you listen to everything one tells you?

I said nothing, concentrating on the path.

—Proper care of the body *and* its desires is necessary to a full life. Asceticism on retreat is maddening. Turns out pliant fools, he said, turning to look me up and down, or messes.

The walk was invigorating once I learned to lengthen my stride to keep pace with him. We crossed the street, veering away from the monastery. The street was deserted.

—Where are we going? I asked.

—Oh, *now* you're curious! I was starting to worry about you.

A *tuk tuk* careered around the bend and accelerated past us.

We came to a clearing by the road where there was a bamboo thatch hut and plastic tables on packed dirt. A plump woman was frying noodles in a large wok. I felt relief. A restaurant.

—*Sawatdee ka*, she called.

Aromas woke the senses: herbs frying, the snap of shrimp as they sweated and turned pink. We sat at one of the tables. My hunger was a hollowness that was almost painful. The Man from Augsburg was speaking. Words echoed. The world looked large, like a fishbowl.

—Ignore the body, he was saying. How without nutrients? We have a proverb. The Thais would agree, but it's German: *Der Mensch ist, was er isst.* You can't forget your body, because what is living, other than desiring, dying, eating, fucking?

My body cringed at the blow of each of his consonants. Black dots danced before my eyes

—Beautiful stuff, he said, leaning in.

—They say you fast in your last days here, I said.

—I fast to feed my hunger. Like trimming the wick of a flame.

The woman brought us steaming plates of *som tam*, *pad thai* with succulent shrimp, and *pad krapow gai*. It was simple food, but the colors and smells sent me into raptures: tomatoes in the *som tam*, greens of limes and basil. Hunger burned through my body. My hands felt clammy despite the heat.

—I don't have money, I said, looking dazedly at the Man from Augsburg.

He threw his head back, laughed, then fixed me with his pale eyes, as if I were some interesting, suffering specimen. He curled his golden hair behind his ears.

—We'll put it on my tab, he said, gesturing to the food without dropping his gaze: Please.

My body won out. I tried to be delicate, but the tastes were consuming: crispness of young papaya, sweet-sour tamarind, textures of *pad krapow*, everything intense, herbed, spiced.

When I looked up, the Man from Augsburg was staring at me. He plucked a shrimp from the plate and chewed it thoughtfully. Sweet mango arrived in a glaze of warm coconut milk.

—It is the most sensuous of fruits, he said, taking the slippery flesh in his mouth.

Guilty as I was at having transgressed the rules of right alimentation, at having answered the needs of the body and taken pleasure in it, I felt a chemical restoration occurring. I was energized, uninhibited. Exuberance flowed into my limbs and animated my face and hands. Language became coherent again, leading somewhere, ripe with possibility. I was chatty— and wanted to know the story of the Man from Augsburg. I posed bold, naïve questions, which seemed to amuse him: *Do you believe in goodness? Do you believe in home?*

—In the last seven years, he said, I've lived in fifteen countries. Not counting the navy. To me, moving is like sleeping with women of all different ages and cultures. You are different in each place, with each body. Then there is the chance to distill whatever survives the changes.

He sounded eccentric, yes, but who could blame us for speaking of essences when all we did every day was sit or walk alone with our breath? I thought of my journals, record of my plural selves. I imagined finding in them an overlap, a verbal Venn diagram of my essence.

—Except in my case—he began to laugh—there's nothing. In my quest to find a core, I disappeared. Most invigorating thing I've lived. You lose personhood; then it's raw possibility. . . .

He was still laughing, withholding the story I wanted but telling me something all the same, in control of his words. Still, I was frustrated, unable to know him ordinarily.

—Your questions, *Ella*, he said, sensing this. You want to find a *man* in front of you. Oh-*ho*, there isn't one, *Ella*.

Each time he said my name, he seemed to gather some ritual control over my reaction.

—Why the monastery? I asked, needing to say something. What are you trying to find?

—Or lose? I'm peeling away *occasional* selves—he smiled ironically—layers of masks. I'll be honest with you, because you're darling and earnest. I don't believe in karma as a model for responsibility, but I love expiation. It's an old addiction, from my childhood. It . . . *feels* good.

A FEW DAYS LATER, I OPENED MY EYES from a sitting meditation to find the Man from Augsburg sitting cross-legged in front of me, staring, his pale eyes as blank as the sky.

—What is your astrology sign? he asked with utmost seriousness.

When I answered, he said:

—A scorpion. Of course! With you it's clear. You desire, you repel. You're doing it now. I can feel you, afraid.

—I'm afraid of *you*? I asked, indignant.

—No, he said. Of your desire.

DECAPITATION OF THE *I* YIELDS THE IRRATIONAL *i* like the square root of negative one: imaginary.

THE *BIKKHUNI* CUT MY HAIR IN THE STREAM. It washed away, and we watched bougainvillea blossoms falling into the brook and water sliding over the smaller stones. Body so light as to be elsewhere. Here everyone is alone, the *bikkhuni* told me. Lay-people come to the gates with orchids, lotus buds, gifts for the temple: forms fading among fading forms, arising and passing away. The monastery is a simulacrum more real than living, magnified, so the feeling is more.

TO KEEP MY HEAD IN THE MONASTERY, I began attaching great impor-tance to small things. In the heat of the afternoons, when medi-tation was hardest, the promise of a shower kept me sane: rush of cool water, sloughing off debris of dead days. I plunged on, walking, sitting, teeth clenching at image obsessions after which I trailed, wanting word labels to fix to their calamities.

When the timer sounded, giddy with anticipation, I undressed in my room, shivering in the heat, and stood under the shower-head. With the flow of water, the moment would open. I'd climb inside. Stay. Present. I turned the knob.

Nothing. I jerked harder. I turned the knob back to its start-ing position, counted to three, twisted again. Hard. A single drop, brown and putrid, fell to my cheek. Shaking, with chills in the heat, I stretched myself across the floor tiles, pressing my skin to their cool surface.

It was still too hot. I dragged myself up. Still no water. I went to ask Pra New about it. But he was busy, speaking to new arriv-als, retelling the story of his name.

—Past is *past!* he said, flicking his wrist. So we start again. So I'm New.

I walked on. By the time evening fell, I was calm, meditat-ing in the library. Fans blew breezes across the space. Marble tiles were cool. Monks murmured chants from dark corners.

Lamps were lit as the night advanced. I left with the last of the monks, down the stairs flanked by *naga* statues, glass mosaic bodies glittering in the moonlight. I carried my sandals, wanting to feel the roughness of the pebbled walk on my feet.

As I approached the row of bungalows, I saw that the inside of one was silver, reflecting the brightness of the full moon. It was mine. It looked like magic. When I opened the door, water rushed around my toes. After turning off the shower in the bathroom, I stood very still, guilty. Then I began a walking meditation, sloshing through the shallow water. Hundreds of ants had been killed in the flood, their corpses in the water like specks of dirt. Then, later, I dragged my backpack to a shaft of light in the middle of the room, lay in the water with my head on the pack and laughed, looking at the moon.

WHEN MY RETREAT WAS OVER, there were details again, things to arrange. I apologized to Pra New for flooding my room. I would miss him.

My street clothes sagged, loose sandpaper against my skin. My hair was short.

Pra New found me a ride on the back of a monk's motorcycle to Tapei Gate, where I was having dinner with Aurelia. Mobile phone turned on again after so long.

Aurelia's hands shook as she picked at her food. She talked in bursts. She asked about the monastery. But her questions came too quickly and didn't correspond to what I was saying. When I asked how and with whom she'd spent her time, she looked intently at her spicy vegetables, as if sight alone were the right way of ingesting them. It seemed cruel to press her.

—You don't want to flow time, she said. You want to—not stop it, but slow it, so you live more, better? Flow is what *they* want us to think. It's a stupid trap!

—They? I asked, worried by her rapid, disjointed way of talking.

—You know, everybody—everybody who wants to hurt us? Aurelia said.

I noticed, maybe for the first time, how frail she was, her chest bones sticking out under her necklace of beaten gold. Emotionally, too, I felt her craving a vague thing she had to keep herself from having. Although I hadn't touched anyone in a month, some instinct guided me around the table to the wooden bench where Aurelia, quivering, forked the vegetables she couldn't eat. When I hugged her, I felt the sharp ridges of her shoulders, the frailty of her bones. She pulled back. Awkward, I hugged harder. She began a quiet sob into my stiff clothes. I held her until she stopped shaking and excused herself to go to the restroom. She said it was nothing.

—It's just life, you know? *Ha-ah!* Just life. No, nothing happened. Just life.

The Man from Augsburg had given me his address and instructions to ask the building concierge for keys to his highrise apartment. I hadn't planned to go. My plan was to check into a guesthouse and wait for Seb, who had texted to say he would come to Chiang Mai after all, for Songkran. But the monastery's fragile serenity was slipping, replaced by a sad, worried separateness. I wanted to feel close to someone, if only by being in his space. Aurelia's fear and desire always reminded me uncomfortably of my own.

Inside the apartment, everything was urbane, clean. There

was a balcony with nice views, musk-smelling soap in the shower, patchouli cologne in the bathroom. There were soft sheets but no personal details: no pictures, letters, not even bills. He must keep other apartments in other cities, I realized. There were Buddha heads in the living room, sleek candles, a large TV and stereo, meditation books in German, and tapestries in black and red. Wished for something more human. Nothing in the refrigerator. I lit the candles.

Sometime in the evening, my mobile phone buzzed. There was a creaking in the hallway. Blood rushed to my face. I grabbed the phone. Would he say *I am outside, open the door?* Would he come in with his smell, patchouli like the cologne in the bathroom? Want what? Eighteenth floor. No escape. *Fear,* yes, only *fear* of his presence, body taut, intentioned—magnetizing all space.

His message demanded a response: *What are you trying to tell me?*

I looked at the clock, as if this information would help me. It was late. *What?* I messaged back, inelegant, clumsy—when I could've said, *I'm in your room in the dark, thinking you'll enter, impossibly, that I'll learn who you are and be afraid. . . .*

But his first message turned out to be a sort of summons; he wanted me in front of my phone, looking at his words as they appeared.

You visited me tonight during meditation. You were asking me something in a language you made up that only you could understand. When I got back to my room, for the first time in the seven years I've been coming here, I saw . . . Can you guess?

His reply was quick:

Scorpion on the wall. Just above my bed.

The phone flashed again, insistently.

So what are you trying to tell me?

Had I sent the scorpion? What did he want me to say? Things felt animated, live symbols connecting us. I looked at the phone.

What did you do with it? I texted.

It took him a long time to respond, enough so that I worried. I was right to.

Smashed it. Stained the wall with its guts. Still twitching. Shouldn't have been in my space, the nasty thing.

In his bed all night, I dreamed of flooding, water cascading into spaces it shouldn't go. The next day I took my things, blocked his number on my phone, and checked into a guesthouse. I never saw or heard from the Man from Augsburg again.

32

CROSS IF POSITIVE. LINE IF NEGATIVE. The worst is waiting, plastic stick on the back of the toilet while the timer ticks down. I think how stupid I've been. Guilt over Z. When I went home with the painter, I wasn't myself. Now the idea of something growing inside me—unknown—terrifies me.

There is an image that will not fade: a long sand beach under hot sun. Horizons mingled, blues. A strip of sand into water. It is very real, more like a memory than a scene from the journals. My memories have a gray aura, a cast of reality, like a tarnish. Hers are brighter. Which is this? It might be my missing year.

The stick is a mess of blurred lines. I can hear my heartbeat in the empty flat. There is a second stick in the pack. I try to pee in a straighter line. While waiting for the second reading, I try to put my panic in order, map if/then scenarios, but I think of her instead. Who would she tell? Muay? Goody-two-shoes. Aurelia? Unstable. Béa? Yes, ordinarily, but too busy with Lek's photo exhibition, which would travel next to Chiang Mai. Only Soraya would understand.

Pink line, sharp and clear. I throw myself onto my bed with relief.

Z is at work, but he picks up. He whispers for me to hold on and takes the call outside. I have the impulse to hang up, no explanation. It has been a month since we've talked.

—Are you okay? Z asks in full voice. How is Paris?

I hear wind behind him. Maybe there's sun in Boston. I feel terrible and have nothing to say. I ask about work and he tells me. I ask when he'll quit and become a philosopher. He laughs. Our conversation is strained, too polite. He asks about the project. He doesn't ask when I'm coming home.

—I think I'm starting to see things from the months I don't remember.

I hear him draw in breath, annoyed by the sudden intensity. But he was with me during that time, almost every day. I have to ask:

—Was there a body of water, a sea, an ocean, or even a very large lake, where there may have been waves? Was there a beach we went to? Someplace we visited?

—No, he says. Why?

—I saw a beach—

I stop short, confused. *Is* it mine, this vision? The journals create memories, but usually I know they're hers. This one is at the edge—I don't know where it comes from.

Z sighs. He's working. He has to go.

—Do you think you can just . . . maybe concentrate on moving forward?

—Of course, I say, wanting to seem in control, the sort of person who is aware of her excesses and recovers quickly. Maybe . . . we can talk more often?

—I'm here, he says.

When he ends the call, I feel an unbearable sadness—discomfort, too, at the image that hides its source: a beach, low waves. Dusk is falling. Raw breeze through the windows. It will rain again tonight.

33

THE MONASTERY HADN'T FREED ME from earthly attachment, still less from desire. When Seb appeared, hunched under his worn backpack, gray eyes scanning the stalls of the weekend market, the force of his familiarity was too much. I ran through the crowded aisles, falling into his surprised hug. He was glad to see me, too, and he sized me up with careful eyes.

—The monks starved you, he said.

I laughed. It was true. My clothes were loose, baggy since I'd left the monastery.

Seb bought us mango and sticky rice, which we sat on the curb and shared, and it was like old times, conversation bubbling between us. Those few days in Chiang Mai were halcyon. We played like children, celebrating Songkran with water guns and buckets, and happiness hit with all its force—too bright, too joyous, too unlasting.

In Hanoi, we spent most of our time apart. Seb reasoned that you encounter a city more deeply in solitude. Under a leaden sky, I watched tai chi in parks, drank Vietnamese coffee in lakefront bars, and smiled at children who asked for money, buying them baguettes from an ancient woman wheeling a bread cart. In quiet spaces, I listened for the flow of fountains and the slender strokes of bells. Some things Seb and

I did together, like squatting in line to see the corpse of Ho Chi Minh and eating *bo bun* on stools so low, our knees were higher than our bowls.

There were nights on a wooden sailboat in the Gulf of Tonkin, then Haiphong, Hội An, Hué, Da Nang, Ninh Hòa, Nha Trang, Ho Chi Minh City. From each place name hung a smell, like the street of spices in Hanoi, where banyan trees plunged their wooden arms into the earth.

The gray sky dissolved as we made our way south. In Hội An, a textile town and old trading port, Seb grew annoyed at the tourists and felt the urge for solitude. He hired a motor-bike for the day and drove into the hills to look at Champa ruins. Respecting this, or at least accepting it—creature of harmony that I was postmonastery—I set out walking, past the Chinese shophouses and temples, the Japanese Covered Bridge, the French colonial buildings and narrow Vietnamese houses, past the tailor shops, once, twice, along sand beaches and wharves, covering the city with my steps. In one of the tailor shops, a woman was drawing. I stopped and asked if she would make me a dress.

She took my measurements, and we picked out a Vietnamese silk that was pleasantly coarse, a shimmery peach color. She asked how I wanted the dress, sketching options to give me inspiration. It would be strapless, tucked at the waist, and fall below the knee. I had nowhere to wear such a dress. I asked if I could watch her make it.

—It will take time, she said. There are other orders I need to finish before yours.

I didn't mind. She cut the fabric to my dimensions, pinning it to a mannequin. She worked with quiet concentration,

methodically. Her name was Minh. Her presence stilled, a little, the turbulence I felt around Seb. I asked if she'd been born
in Hội An.

She nodded and asked how old I was. We were both
twenty-two. I was two months older, though she seemed the
more adult, running a shop. She said it belonged to her family.
I asked if she liked her work.

—I want to study in Da Nang, she said, but it's difficult.

—Is it expensive? I asked.

—My father died, she said, but people think he took the
wrong side in the American war, so there is a black mark, and
my brothers and I cannot study.

—He helped the Americans, I said.

She asked if I was hungry and brought us two bowls of *cao
lâu,* herbs, noodles, pork, and broth. She said her aunt made
it—at a restaurant in the alley behind us. We ate and talked.
She told me she was engaged to a man from Da Nang.

—New city, new ideas. New name. She smiled.

—New name—does that mean you can study?

—It depends. I have to work hard here, so if it does work,
I can pay for it.

After lunch, Minh finished the dress. I took a picture of
us together. I never do things like that. She took one, too.
When I met Seb back at the guesthouse, he said the dress was
gorgeous.

We journeyed on, farther south, skirting salt fields and rice
paddies. We stopped to swim and to pick mangoes by the
beach, and we slept in a bungalow by the South China Sea. We
stayed too long in the seaside paradise we'd found, so there
was no time for the Mekong Delta. Ho Chi Minh City would

be the end of our trip. We were growing tired of each other and tired of traveling.

We arrived in the city at midday and napped through the heat of the afternoon, in a blue guesthouse room with a cherrywood floor. The whirring ceiling fan disguised the traffic noise and gave us some relief, for we'd grown unused to cities, to wearing shoes, to the structure of a day (voyage out, then home).

Wandering the streets that afternoon, we were like two boats unhitched from a mooring but still tied together. We banged against each other in our indecision. We studied the peeling paint on building façades as if it were something of beauty. We spoke of going to a museum.

We found crossing the flow of traffic, never easy in Vietnam, impossible after our time at the coast. We didn't have the energy to calculate our course against the cars, bicycles, and motorbikes—what Seb called the "erratic tide of the human." I hated him, desired him, changing course all the time. Bit by bit, without meaning to, we inched our way into a network of side streets, where a lone motorcycle kicked up dust in its wake, where there was almost quiet.

—Beer? Seb asked.

It was something to do.

Two more bends in the narrow road led us to a café with no sign. From a corner table near a cracked window, we ordered *bia hội* and set up a game of checkers. We slid the plastic coins across the board and slipped into the rhythm of our game.

The man behind the bar was tall and gaunt, drying glasses with a dishrag and replacing them on shelves. He had the look of waiting for someone he knew would never arrive. When he brought us rounds, he looked at Seb's shoulder, as if he might rest a hand there, then went away.

For hours we sat, squaring off against each other. Seb resisted my moves, and I felt oddly satisfied by the slow accumulation of my chips on his side of the board. I was losing, but our glasses were full and the sky outside was inking blues. The bartender brought us two glasses of plum wine.

—On the house, he said.

We nodded our thanks, our bodies already tired, dried from the sun, the heat, and the beer. The plum wine was sweet and bitter. It tasted of fermentation.

In the hours we'd been in the bar, only a few other customers had passed through: solitary men who came, drank something, and then disappeared up a wooden flight of stairs. I wondered vaguely what could be up there, but my mind didn't feel like puzzles.

Lights came on when it got dark. We would search out dinner in this part of the city before retreating to our guesthouse. The floor spun as I stood.

As Seb moved to put away the game, the bartender approached with the pitcher of plum wine. He asked if we liked it. Sitting at a table by the bar was a man with a fleshy face and a woman creased by wrinkles, her frail body swallowed in a large black dress. The bartender filled everyone's glasses. We toasted.

The woman seemed older than the men and carried herself with a poise that made it seem as though she were looking down at us, though she came to the height of our shoulders.

—Your mother? Seb asked the bartender.

He laughed, clinking glasses with the fleshy man. The woman was impassive.

—You think I am a young man, the bartender said. Cheers to that! She's my sister, he said, then put a finger to Seb's chest, asking:

—American?

—No, Seb said, clearing his throat.

He hated being mistaken for an American.

—My brother, her husband, is dead. You look like him. All of us think so.

The woman didn't smile. The bartender patted Seb on the back and went behind the bar.

—Papa in the war? the fleshy man asked Seb, motioning for us to join him at a table.

—Her husband was American, he reminded us, gesturing to the woman now disappearing up the stairs.

The bartender joined us at the table with a jug of amber liquor. Seb's smile seemed to say, *Let the games begin.* We drank more. The liquor was strong. I got used to it.

After a time, the bartender put his thin arm around Seb and pointed at me.

—Your wife, he said.

—No.

—Aha, girlfriend! You have a wife at home, in Canada?

—Maybe *you* have a wife in Canada, Seb said, grazing the man's shirt with his index finger.

Fresh laughter erupted from all sides.

—Your sister? the fleshy man asked, flicking his eyes from Seb to me, appraising. She can work here? he said, rubbing his thumb across his fingers. The money is good. For you, too.

He laughed.

My face felt hot as I waited—enraged by my passivity—for Seb's response.

—Light-haired girl, the man said, very popular.

Seb's hand flew to his face. He was laughing.

—Come upstairs, the bartender said to Seb, as if he'd been thinking of something else.

Seb stopped laughing long enough to ask the fleshy man:

—How much? He motioned to me. More or less than Vietnamese?

In the roar of laughter that followed, the room ballooned with sound and contracted, swallowing Seb and his guide up the narrow stairs. Heat rocketed to my face. I stayed rooted to the chair, my back very straight, hand spreads across the table. The fleshy man rubbed his eyes, tearing from laughter. I wanted to follow Seb up the stairs and grab him so that he'd have to face me. I wanted to strip out the streak of cruelty that *wasn't* him.

The expression of the fleshy man was biting into me like an unpleasant odor. I pushed back my chair. The floor spun. Fleshy fingers clamped my thigh as I tried to stand. I was pinned. Rocking the chair back, I fell to the floor, freeing myself. As I scrambled up, the room spun again, more violently. I made for the door. *Think,* I urged myself. Seb was wearing the satchel with all of our things—phone, wallet—all that I hadn't wanted to carry in the heat. I'd run until I found a busy street, then—I remembered the blue room but not the *name* of the guest-house! We had been there only hours.

—Don't do that, the fleshy man said, sounding sober and authoritative.

—Why? I asked, pausing in the doorway.

—It is not safe for you, he said calmly.

He stooped to pick up my overturned chair. I gripped the door frame, prickling with terror but not wanting to make a scene. Were these threats? If I ran up the stairs, it was possible that I wouldn't find Seb, that I would get lost in corridors that flowed through the whole city.

The screen door banged as I ran into the alley. The night was humid, hot, and wet. It must have rained while we were inside. Other alleys branched from where I stood. I feared they would dead-end. In the empty street, I paused, unsure which direction to take. Then, finding a crevice between two buildings, large enough for a person, I slipped in and tried to silence my breath.

Stung by Seb's complicity, not knowing what he was doing, I thought how stupid I was to have depended on him. I would have to wait until he came out, then follow him back to the guesthouse.

The door of the bar swung open, then slammed. Sharp sounds in Vietnamese. Bartender's voice. Labored breathing of the fleshy man. Sweep of a flashlight beam. I considered running. But if I chose the wrong alley . . . I listened to the lights and sounds fade in the opposite direction.

—Ella!

Seb must have come out of a different door. I emerged from my hiding place.

—Ella, what are you *doing*?

He rushed toward me. His shoulders collapsed in relief as he recognized me. He gripped my elbow, and a swell of tears conveyed my fear, my disgust.

—C'mon, he said, stop it.

I couldn't stop the tears but tried to smother them away with my arm.

—Shhh, Seb said, and pressed me to him.

I let the side of my cheek rest against his chest. Then he took my hand and we crossed the alley, going back the way we'd come that afternoon. Streetlamps lit our way. The terror I'd felt moments ago had gone. Gathering strength, I pushed him hard with the palm of my hand.

—What *is* it? he asked, startled. What's *wrong* with you?

—You left me *alone* with them! I whispered, anger making it hard to speak.

We walked through patterns of shadow, Seb's face visible only in little squares.

—I'm sorry? he offered.

—What did you do?

—Hmm?

—Upstairs. When you went upstairs.

—I used the toilet.

—You're lying—

Tears threatened again. My breath came in gulps.

—You're crazy. It was a few minutes. When I came down, no one knew where you'd gone. They said you took off running. What the hell?

—You came out another door.

—Yeah, there's another door. I checked the house to see if you'd disappeared that way. No one had any idea where you were—

—You were . . . My voice faltered.

—What?

—It was a brothel, I finally managed to say. The upstairs, and you were . . .

Seb's body collapsed in laughter. He put a hand on my shoulder.

—Ah, how could I possibly— He laughed again. I was gone less than five minutes. Is that really what you thought? He was showing me a picture of my *American* father. Remember? They thought I looked like some brother or husband or something?

I studied Seb's face in the darkness. His sigh made me feel ridiculous.

—It's a family. What did you think—that they wanted me to deflower their daughter?

—I thought you were with a prostitute, I said quietly.

—Jesus, he said. It happened *once*. Get the fuck over it. I let them show me the photograph and I used their toilet.

Seb's tone was stern and logical and fed color to the sick world that had enclosed me moments ago. Things around us began to seem more normal.

—Did he look like you? I asked.

—Hard to tell in the photo. He was next to a plane, in a military uniform.

—It was a family?

—Of course.

—It wasn't a brothel?

—What do I know? Seb shrugged. Upstairs it looked like a family home.

—It was a family, I repeated numbly.

—If it makes you feel any better, I thought that, too, at first. Seb laughed a little. They were worried about you—

—They wanted to sell me as a prostitute! I said, but it seemed funnier now.

—It was a joke! Kind of flattering, he said, teasing me.

I started to smile but remembered how afraid I'd been. My anger returned.

—How long did you leave me there?

—Five minutes, if even. You're upset, okay, but there was *really* nothing to worry about.

He patted my back as we walked.

—It's funny, he said. The man they kept saying was my double looked *nothing* like me.

—You said you couldn't see his face.

—Yeah, but even so, you know . . .

I nodded, and the events at the bar seemed very far away, almost unreal as we snaked our way through the tiny streets. We found a brightly lit snack shop and stopped for rice bowls with flavorful sauces. The food and the light made the events recede even further, and Seb and I did what we should have done earlier: retold each other stories from the trip. We delivered our tales with new animation and energy. The veterans at the bar became another episode, my brush with prostitution a diverting detail. The *Belle du Jour* of Saigon.

After leaving the restaurant, we descended back into the streets, walking on, both drunk, not minding the stench of the night—a smell like rotting meat, garbage overflowing bins. The pavement seemed to steam before us, humid. Part of the alleyway was decorated with mosaic and mirrors. It made me think of mazes. We were looking for another drink, though it must have been late. I was on the point of asking Seb if he knew where we were going, but part of me liked being led through the tangle of dark streets with no sign of a major road.

I reached for his shoulder, ahead of me, his skin warm under his T-shirt. He turned and in a single gesture twisted my arm against my back, pinning me, his mouth hot against mine. There was the warmth of him, excitement, and the pain shattering through my arm, all together. A scream came on its own. Then his hand was across my mouth, smelling of the spices at dinner. His body pressed into mine, flattening us against the wall of the alley. Mosaic pieces pricked my back. My arm was still pinned, but no longer hurt. Seb found with his free hand the place on my neck where my breath would stop if his fingers pressed even a little bit harder. Consciousness flickered, and fear shot through me. Before I could say anything, his fingers relaxed, as if he knew my limit. But he was looking behind him, his collarbone level with my lips. I gulped in air, dizzy. There was confusion and only his smell in the dark before I followed his gaze, lifting my chin over his shoulder. There seemed to be figures in the shadows, a cry, shrill, quickly muffled. Four men, maybe more. One girl, struggling, between overturned bins.

Fear surged back with near-shattering force. How many minutes passed? I shut my eyes but couldn't keep out the sounds, amplified by the narrow walls of the alleyway: half-stifled cries, words among the men, grunts, slaps of skin on skin, banging of bins. Seb's eyes glittered in the dark. Then there were no more cries. Only a raw smell of semen and rotting garbage, Seb's heart beating fast against my chest.

A car passed on a nearby street, and its beam of headlights flashed across us. Everything was as if underwater. Would they leave her like that, between the bins, her legs bent under her? I could smell her horror, her shame—smell it on my body as if it were mine. Seb guided my elbow, urging us to move. I resisted. What if she was hurt badly? How could we help her? Then I heard the footsteps of the men returning. One hoisted her over his shoulder. I strained to see her face, or any sign of life. In the shadows, only her long dark hair fell across the back of the man who carried her.

We returned to the guesthouse in slow motion, my mind lingering far behind my body. I felt walled in by glass, thick shards. Mix of shock and the strange liquor. Seb's slow step and hunched shoulders. Our large key turned in the lock.

We had booked one room to save money. We would share the large king-size bed, like brother and sister. The bed was flanked on one side by a low bureau, on the other by a chest of drawers, on which someone had set a glass vase of white orchids. Seb put his wallet and passport on the bureau. The sheets were wrinkled from our siesta. A book with its spine broken lay open on the bed. I felt calm, lucid even, in the dim light.

—We should talk about this, I said reasonably.

—You okay, yeah? Seb said kindly, pulling my ponytail.

I flung away his hand and crossed the room. We glared at each other across the huge bed.

—You *asked* me to, he said, defensive.

—To what?

I was worried about the girl, wondering if and how we might contact the police. Before I could say anything, Seb shoved the bureau with the back of his hand. It rocked against the wall.

—We don't *have* to talk about it, he said. Do you want to or not?

—Yes.

—So talk. I'm listening. But I'm tired, so—

—Maybe we should—

—I *told you*, he said, cutting me off, not listening. I said it wasn't a good idea. You said, *Really good ideas never seem like it at the time.*

Seb tried to speak with his hands, then looked around, as if for a way to escape.

—Are you pretending not to remember, is that it? he asked me.

—No, I remember. Of course I remember.

—Okay, he said, relieved.

—How could I not? It was horrible.

—For fuck's sake!

His hands searched for something to tear apart. He grew anxious. I missed his calm but was pleased to have caused agitation. I was so used to crashing against his indifference.

He took a long breath. His voice became rational again.

—*You* said to do it. *You* said to get it over with—so it wouldn't be between us. You said you didn't want anything more. You *said*—

He went into the bathroom. I heard the tap run. He came back with a paper cup of water. He drank it in one gulp, shook his head, as if he could make me disappear. He spoke slowly, enunciating each word:

—You promised it wouldn't be a big deal.

He looked at me meaningfully, as if to implant a memory of things I didn't think I'd said.

—In the street, I said slowly, words from my lips like insects.

—Yes, he said. I thought we would see. And that it would stay here. In Vietnam.

As the air left his body, I thought I saw something in his face like desire. I thought he might hug me. Then the tenderness, desire, whatever it was, fled.

—On the street, he said, defensive again. Like you wanted, like you begged—

—Begged? I frowned.

—You said *please:* you begged.

The word grated against me. *Begged.*

—I didn't—

—Fuck it, Ella. What is wrong with you? I knew I shouldn't've—fuck.

His eyes narrowed. From opposite sides of the bed, we stared. Then Seb looked down.

—Look, we had a lot to drink.

—That has nothing to do with it! I hissed.

—At some point you decided the bar was a brothel, he continued in the same tone, not angry, but incriminating. You thought the men were after you. You freaked out and ran.

I sighed. He was narrating things, as if I'd been too drunk to know what was going on.

—*You* left first, I said. *You* left me alone in the bar with those men while you went to go fuck someone. Don't make me feel like I'm crazy.

My skin was burning.

—You're perverse, he said. It happened *once,* in Chiang Mai. Doesn't mean it happens all the time.

—And at the beach, Pattaya? I asked, mocking. Never there?

—Fuck you, Ella. For Christ's sake, I never should have—

—What? You never should have what?

—What?

—What were you going to say?

—I don't know.

—You're making this up. You're sick.

—No! His voice rose sharply. *You're* sick. God, I *knew* better—

—You're making me believe things. You held me against a wall because—

—Because you begged me to—

—Stop saying that!

My voice had gone shrill. It echoed between the bare walls and floor. I saw Seb start to shush me and then think better of it. I felt the tension in his body on the other side of the room. The water in the orchid vase trembled, then silence.

—Look, he said, so earnestly that I trusted him again, I'd never take advantage of you.

Then, before I could answer, something flashed across his eyes. He muttered:

—If I didn't care, I would've done it a long time ago. Not like I didn't have the chance.

The air left my lungs. The room felt suffocating.

—Turn on the fan, I said.

He ignored me.

—I thought it would help you. I thought we could leave it here.

—*Help* me?

—You *wanted*—

I'd lost the thread, remembered only vaguely about the

woman in the alley. Why weren't we speaking of her? And Seb was adopting some strange idiolect, full of euphemism.

—There was the woman, I reminded him.

—What woman?

I thought back to the alley, the mosaic, the humidity, the amplified sound of men's shoes.

—The woman at the bar? The *proprietress*, he added, trying to make a joke of it.

—The young one, I said, frustrated that he wouldn't talk about it.

—I know that's what you think I was doing upstairs. It's your dirty imagination.

—No, I said evenly. The girl in the street—in the alley. She was hurt.

A smile appeared and disappeared from his lips in the same instant.

—What are you talking about?

—You saw it first. You covered my mouth.

—You're being crazy. Let's talk in the morning. You'll be calmer. You'll remember.

—I remember fine. *You're* the one who won't talk about it.

—We *are* talking! When *all* I want to do is sleep! Let's give it up for tonight. You're not acting right.

He squinted at me, as if a better view might help him make sense of me. I sensed his anger and something stronger, like disgust—at himself or at me, I wasn't sure. I thought again of the girl.

—It was horrible, I said listlessly.

—For God's sake, I regret it, too, okay?

—Four men, maybe more. It was so dark, hard to count.

—*What?* What are you talking about?

Seb's eyes grew large. He began to back away slowly from his edge of the bed.

—You remember. It was horrible to watch, to hear. They took turns. They spit—

I tried to cover my face with the crook of my elbow. My nose was stuffed up.

—Jesus, Ella. What do you want from me?

—I want to know *why* you—

—You want to know why? *Why?* I felt *sorry* for you. I was drunk. *That's* why.

Then Seb's indignation evaporated, and a taunting smile took its place on his lips.

—You want to play it this way—you're kinkier than I thought. He laughed. But let's give up for tonight, yeah?

My head was pounding. Seconds passed before I could choke out the necessary words.

—A girl, I said. We saw her. You were making sure I didn't scream. . . .

I couldn't get the rest out, not from tears but from something else, something volatile in me. I saw the fleshy face of the man at the bar leaning over me as I lay among the overturned bins. He lifted me over his shoulder. My head hanging, I saw the world upside down. I stared at the bed, wanting the visions to stop. My body felt strange.

—What if it—what if it *was me?* I whispered, vague horror obscuring the room.

Seb cracked a strange smile.

—What if it was you? he taunted me, an edge to his voice. Part of you wants it. I feel it in you, he whispered.

Some force was goading him on, some ancient hurt. I froze in the sticky heat of the night, searched his face for any sign of the old kindness. Light sparked off the vase. Adrenaline coursed through me. It was a mistake to look up again. When I did, I saw only parts of a person: gray eyes in shadow, arms crossed complacently, as if none of this mattered. Then images of the girl, legs folded beneath her. I remember only a tightness before, in my right arm, and a trembling after, shuddering with the shock of sudden effort. Blood racing the surface. Skin very hot. No memory of contact, just water moving down the wall with terrible slowness, and Seb's face ashen, devoid of smugness. He stood very still, staring at the mark on the wall. But for a few inches, he might have been killed. Neither of us moved. We watched each other with gaping mouths.

In the morning, Seb was gone, glass shards glittering hard on the cherrywood floor.

34

SIOBHÁN IS LATE FOR THE FIRST TIME since I've known her. When she arrives, she is restless, not knowing where to put her hands. She doesn't feel like coffee, so we walk along the river, though the sky is threatening rain.

My suspicion is that Siobhán has known all along where Ella went at the end of July. I want to know why she didn't tell me everything at the start, why she chose to undermine our search. But now, with her discomfort so obvious, my nerve dissolves. There's only the instinct to shield her, to reassure her that her daughter hadn't lost hold of *all* that is beautiful and real.

—Let me read you something, I say, showing her to a bench. Ella is safe here, delighted by everything.

I sit beside Siobhán and take the black journal from my bag. To comfort her, or myself, or to protect Ella the only way I can, I flip pages, taking her back in time up the coast of the South China Sea. I read to Siobhán from the book to comfort her, like a mother to a child.

> —*May 11. North of Ninh Hoa there is an outpost for travelers, palm-thatched huts on the beach. Once upon a time, the owner, from Dalmatia, built himself a wooden sailboat and sailed until he stopped and*

*lived. Seb and I played "beached" in blue dusk. We
swam out, pretended we were dead, and let the waves
wash our bodies to shore. Whoever is beached first wins.
You're on your honor. No swimming. No breaking out
of jellyfish pose—Seb calls it the "dead whale position."
Tides turn you, just your body, wave-tossed. My body
wouldn't stick to shore. Tumble-dried in the shallows
and scrambled in sand. I looked over at Seb, still bobbing. I stood and declared myself the victor. We changed
for dinner and gathered on the terrace, talking with
travelers from Italy, Switzerland, Ireland, Denmark.
Then we moved off to a terrace closer to the sea. He's at
a table with a lantern. I'm in a chaise longue, borrow-
ing his light. We're writing to capture these days. Days
that will soon become others. Leather binding on his
book is worn. The moon is full, marbled. It leaves pale
streaks on the water. Waves are crashing, softly now.*

Siobhán tries, like me, to be objective, but we're in love with
Ella—Ella who exploded into living, without knowing where she
ended and where the world began. Siobhán is smiling, so I go on
to describe how Ella loved one of Lek's photographs, the one that
won the Bangkok Prize. I'm saying how elated Ella was when Béa
surprised her, buying her a print, when Siobhán stops abruptly and
clasps my hand. She drags me up the rue du Vieille Temple, weaving among tourists in raincoats. My first thought is that she has
forgotten something: to lock the house, to shut off a gas burner.
We walk too hurriedly to speak. Fat drops fall, spattering the sidewalk and the street, but we're safe inside the Ormeau's back room

by the time the sky opens. Rain flies against the pane of the high skylight.

From a large drawer, Siobhán takes a frame wrapped in newspaper. The black-and-white newsprint is of a long-tail piercing a river silvered by sunlight, the back of a rower straining at the oars. I remember her writing: *Rower's brimmed hat is a silver moon in sunlight. Oar spinning eddies. River ripples like muscle. River rower. Perfect.* Siobhán and I agree that the photo is deft, classical. Most exciting, though, is the chance to see what Ella saw, to compare her descriptions against a sort of real. Our worlds are so separate—materially—except for the journals.

Siobhán explains how the print traveled from Chiang Rai with the other journals. Ella's adoptive mother, finding it melancholy, asked that it be sent to Siobhán.

Taking advantage of Siobhán's stable mood, I ask directly if Ella visited her the summer before she disappeared.

—Why would you think that? Siobhán spins to face me, genuinely surprised.

I remind her of the break in the journals at the end of July.

—Ten days. Ella leaves and goes I don't know where. She needed help. . . .

—You thought she came *to me?* Siobhán says. Because I didn't tell you about the calls, you think I could—that I could have met her and not told you?

I nod.

—I wouldn't hide that from you, she says evenly. As for Ella, *home* was the mother who raised her. It's as it should be. Besides, she wouldn't have come to me in her situation.

Siobhán is testing me. She wants to know if I know. My dream from the Loire shudders back to me. Even then I knew. But how?

The journals never say. Ella's words swerve around an empty center, the secret that sets the code. Now that I know, it is obvious: *I came back empty, scraped clean of futures.* It's not a metaphor.

—Her decision was going to be different from yours, I say.

Siobhán refuses to look at me, but from her lack of surprise it's clear she knows.

—Why didn't you tell me? Why keep secrets if I'm doing this for *you*?

As I speak, I'm torn between fury at Siobhán—thinking her deranged for asking me to find a missing person while withholding crucial information—and anticipation of her response: everything I learn I should glean from the journals. The idea is to live in them to discover what happened. Siobhán, following her own thought, says with sudden feeling:

—She *could* have come to me! I would have helped her if she'd asked me.

—She went to the United States, I say, still seeking confirmation.

Siobhán nods, annoyed, perhaps, to have to disclose any information at all.

—Same-day ticket, almost ten thousand dollars on her credit card. Her adoptive father told me.

Ella gives no record of this. Ten days of turbulence. Nothing. In the green journal, far into Ella's delusions, there is mention of a child figure I'd read as fantasy, a metaphor for something, the source of which I couldn't fathom. I ask Siobhán:

—Did she go through with it? There was no child?

—As far as anyone knows, Siobhán says.

—You're not sure? I ask, mistrust rising. Do you know or not? Aren't there records?

—Probably, yes. Only her adoptive mother was with her. Her adoptive father was out of town. They were, I think, separating. I don't know. As you're aware, we don't speak anymore, Siobhán says, her cadence suggesting closure. I thought *you* might illuminate the situation.

I look at the skylight, rain still shaking down from the sky. It feels as if the city and world are flooded.

—How can I find her if I don't have all the information? I ask.

—It's better that you learn from Ella than from anyone else, Siobhán says. And you did.

When the rain stops, Siobhán offers to walk me part of the way home. As we're leaving the park in front of the Ormeau, air heavy from the storm, I let myself imagine that Ella *had* come to Paris, and that she is *here,* holding the park's gate open for Siobhán instead of me.

35

The house was full when I returned from Vietnam. Aurelia had been back awhile, and the native photographer was staying in my room. He moved his things to the spare room when I came back but was so spooked by the laughing Buddhas that he slept on the living room couch, which he assured us was insanely comfortable. Having him there was like having a radio on for background noise. He'd go on about something, and Aurelia and I would exchange glances, smiles behind our eyes. The rock garden he promised never materialized, but he made us coffee in the mornings, and the three of us fell into a comfortable routine.

I knew that sooner or later I would have to see Seb. In the weeks since our return, we had managed not to encounter each other outside of work. At the start-of-semester faculty meeting, he'd smiled stiffly across the room, a stranger in a blue shirt and tie. There was a tender fear of running into the real Seb, white T-shirt and dusty sandals, but Anthony, who would have insisted on a group dinner, wasn't back yet. I didn't go out much. It was a time of tiredness. I told Aurelia about it. Freakish fatigue, she said. She had it all the time. Lek had told her that certain people can feel the monsoons coming. They grow tired in every limb, preparing for the season in which one turns inward, retreating from the outer world. The monsoons are for meditation, contemplation, gestation, our bodies following the rhythm of the rice crop, seedlings germinating under the flooded fields.

On the day of Lek's photography exhibition, I was sick to my stomach all morning at the thought of seeing Seb. I craved reconciliation, but it was impossible. I was nervous, confused, couldn't trust myself. After work, I crawled into bed, but the native photographer dragged me out again, wanting my opinion on his latest photo series. The pattern of his Hawaiian shirt gave me such bad vertigo that I leaned on him until I reached the couch.

—You're not sick? he asked me.

—Aurelia says it's anticipatory monsoon fatigue.

He frowned, then went about setting up the display on his laptop. His photo series was of rice planting, for which he'd spent long days knee-deep in rice paddies with the farmers.

—Shouldn't we go to town? Aurelia said, coming into the living room.

—Art opening not opera. Come look. It'll be quick.

He was excited, proud. Images filled the screen: rice seedlings in blurred bundles, a woman with longing eyes in red rubber boots, a metal bucket she must have been swinging, a farmer's hands, gesturing, fuzzed in whitish haze. The native photographer cursed under his breath. He clicked faster, searching for an exception, one clear image, without the blurring.

—Could be the gear, he said, looking at the digital camera attached to his laptop.

—Technology's just a tool, Aurelia said, opening a can of

Pepsi Max. People feel what you see. It doesn't matter what you use.

Aurelia's wisdom always caught me by surprise.

The native photographer was saying that if the blurs had been more visible in the digital camera display, he could have corrected for them. I thought of his archive in the United States, his parents indexing image files, following his instructions. He hated that things could be lost. I sympathized with the desire to capture *everything,* to fit what's fleeting into frames of view. But I also loved that the farmers, the seedlings, and the fields had flooded his aperture in rebellion, insisting on their right to be lost, unfixed. Since my return, the world seemed unstable, colors richer, smells stronger, everything watery and out of focus. Overcome by frustration, the native photographer slammed his fist on the coffee table, rattling our wall of glass.

LEK'S PHOTOGRAPHY EXHIBITION WAS HELD in an old warehouse by the river, which Béa had converted. She'd set up plywood partitions from which the prints could hang. This had the effect of making the exhibition resemble a sort of labyrinth; viewers would enter the plywood enclosures to see the photographs. She hoped it would work.

By the time we arrived, the makeshift gallery was crowded. I found it exhausting to greet everybody. Soraya was circulating with a microphone, trailed by two cameramen. Lek seemed very nervous. He was shy, he'd said once, and considered it bad luck to be the center of attention. He made a stiff *wai* and signaled to Aurelia with a pack of rolling tobacco.

They reappeared outside, through the windowpanes, pacing together against the electric blue sky.

Muay caught my arm, breathless. On my first day back at the university, she'd come to see me. *You've gotten ugly,* she said, laughing brightly. I understood it was my tan—an old joke between us—but I began to tremble. *Oh, you think it's lovely,* Muay went on, not noticing. *You look like a farmer. Open it!* She'd gotten me Walpola Sri Rahula's introduction to the Pali *suttas.* I smelled the pages near the binding, the way I did with all new books, even the journals, thanked her for the gift, and then began to cry. Her face took on a look of concern and worry as she comforted me. I tried to reassure her that I was just very tired.

Now, she nodded toward Soraya, laughing and whispering:

—I'm going before *she* traps me to do an interview! We're having dinner in town. Will you join us?

I was telling her I'd only just arrived, when all people and sound crushed out in a silent vacuum. Seb was standing at the far end of the room. He looked well. Still tan. He'd shaved the beard he'd let grow in Vietnam.

—See you soon, then! Muay patted my arm and left with a few Thai teachers.

I watched Seb, who hadn't seen me, guide Ploy to the entrance of the plywood structure where the photos hung. They disappeared inside.

Béa greeted me with kisses, eager to walk me through the exhibit. I stalled, soothed by her high energy, half taking in the black-and-white photographs of fishermen netting catfish, of fish eyes staring up from sun-spattered hulls. In the next chamber, two prints showed the back of a man on a motorcycle.

He was leaning into a turn, hair whipped to one side, sweat patterning his T-shirt.

—It's Lek's brother who died, Béa said softly. Motorcycle accident two years ago.

Ploy's laughter rang out from another of the partitioned spaces. Dread in every limb.

The exhibit was building to *Loose Boat,* the photograph that won the Bangkok Prize. It hung by itself at the center of the plywood labyrinth. Standing before it, I watched a thin long-tail cut across the river, dimpling eddies in its wake. The rower's back was tense, muscles taut. The stillness of the image made me feel the boat move, gliding upriver with each thrust of the oar.

I asked Lek later if the title was ironic. The image was so focused, anything *but* loose.

—No, he replied. Only with tight focus can you capture something loose.

Now, coming out of the plywood labyrinth, I saw the native photographer looking at a photograph of fishing nets that flew through the air in sharp lines. He cocked his head, as if searching for the secret of motion unblurred. I thought of *Loose Boat,* how the river could flow because its ripples were still.

THE IMAGE OF THE LONG-TAIL DISSOLVING in sunlight stayed with me at Cat Bar, where we ended the night. The owners, Lek's friends, a Franco-Japanese couple who also made pottery, brought out whiskey and soda and joined us on the cushions. Toasts in Lek's honor continued into the night, while he rolled cigarettes with too much care, keeping his head down.

—Poor Lek, Béa said to me. He's miserable. He hates attention.

Where was the joke? The quip? I was craving satire in my too-tired mood.

—When does Anthony get back? I asked. I heard he's still on vacation.

Béa looked at me strangely.

—No one told you? That's just the story Seb told the university so they'd hold his job.

I frowned.

—Koi went missing.

Béa's words slid against me, indigestible. She told me how Anthony had awakened one morning and Koi wasn't there. He waited for him for two days, not leaving the house, until finally, terrified Koi was dead, he called the police. They told him to look through Koi's things. Sure enough, many of his clothes were gone, and a few little valuables, too, from the house.

I wanted to protest that they loved each other, even as Koi's expressions of restlessness came back to me, the way he'd bristle sometimes under Anthony's touch. I was very tired.

—Did Anthony—was he okay? I asked.

—He left so suddenly. I didn't have the chance to talk with him really.

—He went after Koi? I asked, imagining Anthony in one of his impeccably ironed work shirts, running through spiderlike streets in Bangkok, calling Koi's name. Will he come back?

Béa shook her head. She didn't know. I felt devastated by the news of Koi's betrayal, sad for Anthony. Our little band was beginning to unravel. I felt unbearably tired.

One of the owners of the bar began mixing cocktails. Ploy

looked on like an interested scientist. Seb was scowling at the
native photographer, whom he hated for being loud and American. Seeing his gaze lift to Ploy, I tried to see her as he did:
long brown legs, lips drawn to tease him. It must be this that
Seb liked: someone to make light of him, to mock him.

Béa went to turn up the music. She knocked a few balls into
pockets on the pool table.

All evening, Aurelia had been speaking earnestly to the
female owner of the bar. She took a break to smoke. I noticed
Lek's gaze, like mine, riveted to her restless pacing. I motioned
for her to sit down next to me.

—What? she asked.

—What were you talking about? I gestured to the bar
owner.

—You know, she said. Men.

—What about them?

—I'm calling a cab, she said.

—You mean a *tuktuk*? You're *calling* it?

—Hailing it? Whatever.

She waved her hand, then said suddenly, as if picking up a
conversation we'd just left off:

—He said he was retired, but he could have been lying.
Sometimes they lie? He retired young and wanted to live
somewhere beautiful for the rest of his life.

—Who?

—The man in Chiang Mai? With the villa? she replied, as if
asking. Once they're old news, I can talk about them. *Ha-ah!*
Chiang Mai man is old news. He was French, like her guy? she
motioned to the bar owner. So I was warning her. She should
leave him.

The bar owner was smiling at something her lover had said. I looked back at Aurelia.

—*Tuk tuk,* she said. Share?

I shook my head. Despite my fatigue, my limbs drained of energy, I wanted to linger at Cat Bar, among friends, in the last stretch of an era I feared—because of Anthony, because of Seb, because of many things—was ending.

—Wait, I called after her.

She turned, surprised.

—Will you stay?

—Here? she asked, looking around the bar.

—No, I continued, embarrassed. In Chiang Rai, you know, for a while?

I wanted Aurelia to stay, Seb to stay, Anthony and Koi to return. The native photographer planned to move on in a few days, and I wanted him to stay, too. I had a terrible sense that everything was slipping away and wanted to hold it all near me like a scared child.

Aurelia paused in the doorway.

—You look tired, she said, sizing me up.

I nodded.

—Maybe you should date, she said. I have a date, *ha-ah*! In Bangkok.

She came toward me then, and said in a low whisper:

—I know what it's like. You can't let this beat you. Find your strength.

Her gaze met mine squarely. I tried to look puzzled. She motioned to Seb.

—Forget him. He's immoral. You're too good for him.

She held my gaze a moment, then turned abruptly and disappeared.

When I gathered the courage to look at Seb, I found him staring, gray eyes expressionless. He looked down as soon as our eyes met. My heart began to pound in my ears.

The air was thick in the bar. Stars in my vision when I got up from the cushions. Looking for the bathroom, I walked with exaggerated care, focusing a spot in front of me so I wouldn't fall. It was odd to feel this dizzy, this tired. Did everyone know? Seb wasn't the type to tell, but perhaps it was obvious from the way I looked at him. Were they sorry for me? I didn't care. All people, even those I loved, could only slow my way to becoming like trees, like rivers, like earth. The toilet was a hole in the floor, sucking in the whole room, walls bending and shrinking into it. Vision swirled. Colors bitter, overripe. Musty, cloying. Floor floated to meet me until I threw up.

Feeling better, fresher, I splashed my face with water, rinsed my mouth, and walked back into the bar. It must've been the whiskey, too much food or not enough.

I must have been in there longer than I'd thought. The number of people in the bar had dwindled. Seb and Ploy were nowhere to be seen.

IV

Monsoons

36

the last day of July

Drops drumming. Hungry. Bruised sky. Rain on the tin roof like a sonata of the dead. Now and forever. Smell of rains. Humidity attaches to things, gets inside. Gecko on the wall. Candlelight shadow. Here in the house by the rice fields and elsewhere in another time, rain . . .

Rain on the place Marcel-Aymé pelts the statue of the man in the wall: his protruding head, his hands, his knee. It slides across windowpanes into lines that signify nothing and point nowhere but hold the light like vials of mercury. Distance punctured by the rhythm of the rain, here as it was there, now as it was then. Delight in coincidence.

. . . The house was empty when I returned. Glass doors locked. Aurelia gone. I'm lying on her bed, in her room. Couldn't face my own. Sleeping for days. Lit incense to keep away mosquitoes, candles to ease the dark. Pages damp, soft to pen touch. The monsoon is our fault. We made it rain. In April, it was so hot. We threw water on the cracked earth, like a ritual. Months later, heat broke, rains came. Now the house by the rice

fields crumbles like a ruin in the flood. It will burst at
its stone and wood seams, fold into the earth, dissolve
under skins of moss. . . .

The heat has broken, but last night Paris seethed in it still. My computer heaved like a tired child. Fingers tapped out the sound of the rain that wouldn't come. Windows open on the city like mouths gaping, wanting something without edges or ends, restless. I wrote:

Flew around the earth in not enough time, far from gravity. No memory of the first flight. No memory of stopping in Singapore or arriving in Newark. But I can still see the face of the woman at the airline counter, professional and blank when she charged my credit card. No questions. No baggage. Return in ten days.

Now the dark and damp conduct smells easily: wet flowers, jasmine, incense, melting beeswax. It's the same orange candle you light in temples for the dead, Muay told me once, horrified to see it in my room. At the time I was so light, I laughed.

When it was time to go—Mom wanted me to stay—I felt the shudder that comes over you when you know you're seeing a place for the last time.

The Paris heat wave lasted five days, the radio urging checks on *les personnes âgées* so they wouldn't die in their apartments. I took cold shower after cold shower. Heat made it impossible to think. The only time it was cool enough to work was at night. I would work until late. Last night I fell asleep in my clothes, still hoping for the storms forecast on the radio. The first drops came down as I was falling asleep. I thought I was dreaming as Ella, but the parquet was wet when I woke in the night, undressed, closed the windows, and prepared for bed. Now, morning, the heat has fully broken; summer rain streaks the windows, closed for the first time in days. Breathing the rain, even in the closed room, I reread what I wrote last night (it was very hot), and go on:

No sooner did I shut the glass door and lay down on Aurelia's bed than the rains began again. In waking dreams, the house crumbled. My bed sailed out of the ruins, bumping against the remains of our tin and tile roof, washing out into the flooded yard by the banana and mango trees. A wave sent the bed-boat out the gates and into the rice fields, where, squinting through sheets of rain, I saw the house in the gray light that slid in silver needles from monsoon clouds.

Monks say the season isn't one in which to travel; footsteps puncture the earth, damage seedlings. There is violence to the monsoons. Edges dissolve. Foreground becomes background. The monsoons are a time for rest, contemplation, meditation, and study. Three months of rain.

A long time ago, shortly after we'd met, Seb explained the monsoon by saying it keeps people close to their lovers. Some storms are over quickly, but others go on for days. *What about you?* I'd asked. I'd just arrived and wanted to learn as much as I could about him and about the country. (They seemed, in the early days, oddly connected.) *We didn't leave the bed,* he said, grinning. *Day after day it rained.* It made me think of him now, with Ploy.

There are respites, I learned, when the black and battered sky is shot with sunlight, which glistens on the wet leaves of palms and makes mirrors of the puddles. The air is clean, washed, and the colors of the landscape brighter, as if the color settings on a camera had been adjusted.

As I slept, the rains spilled down the roof, making waterfalls of windows. Release like a loss finally grieved—that's how I heard them in my sleep, full of despair, saving nothing, sparing nothing. All out. The sky wrung out. No one knew how far I'd gone, so there was no one to tell I'd returned. To Béa and Muay and whoever else cared, I was with Soraya in Bangkok. Seb proctored the exam for my class, and then the students left to spend their midterm break in cities. Soraya arranged it, hugging me. But in Bangkok I couldn't: the cold in the clinic and the foreign tongue spoken whenever anyone wasn't speaking to me.

From the feel of the house, Aurelia has been gone a long time.

On the night of her return from the United States, Ella wrote for hours, fifty pages in the same mood and hand. Odd smell to this journal, faded black cover, infused in the monsoon. Last night, we were writing together; we were listening to the start and stop of the rains. It's the longest entry in the journals, dated "the last day of July" and full of memories: Songkran, the Thai New Year, which took place three months earlier, in April, then the terrible morning in Saigon at the end of May. I sense clearly now what happened in Vietnam—what happened physically, concretely, between bodies. It comes together, narratively. But Ella is falling apart. She remembers in the present tense, as if it were all still happening there in the dark. It makes me worry, imagination drawing her back with too much force, blending fact, memory, and figment.

In the beginning, I had only to take her words and shape

them. Now, I invent and cut away. I'm stepping on her, crowding her, sealing over what's raw and real and true. We're in combat. There is my narrative—ordering days and months—and her journals—radically particular: *the smell of wet wood in the city with two names.* My narrative has yet to yield a reason for her disappearance. Vietnam seems crucial, but the journals are far from clear. *Not much pain from the night before,* she writes, *body an echo chamber for sensations, especially smells.*

The secret of her disappearance is very close to the surface in this long entry with its three scenes: the monsoons, Songkran, Saigon. What is the connector? A line from Ella's journal returns as if in answer: *Story of Seb.* The *story* of Seb, as if by writing and writing she could tame what happened.

But does memory change, chameleonlike, with its setting in words? It would explain why my father will not speak of the past. He's modifying it to protect the future. We fear, by secret accord, that talk of my mother's illness will trigger in me the same affliction. If we are quiet, *it* will stay quiet. My mother's sort of trouble can develop and worsen at any time; she was thirty-four the first time she was taken away. Similarly, we don't mention the time when I reach in memory and find only blankness. Z's strategy is different. Z speaks often of my missing months, implanting in me *his* memories, hoping I'll annex them as my own. It doesn't work. Stories foisted on me from a time I don't remember feel like alien skin.

By the end of the summer, things had become grim in Ban Du. Soraya was gone, having joined an order of *bikkhuni* in Bangkok. She left a voice message on Ella's phone, which Ella received on her return from the States. The message wished her beauty and peace in this life, the next, and all the others. Ella copied the voice mail into her journal. A few days later, she learned from Béa where Aurelia was: in a hospital in Bangkok. She'd been in a motorcycle accident; the man she was with had been killed. Lek took the first bus to Bangkok and did not leave her side. There was still no word from Anthony, who had left months ago in search of Koi. Ella's problems might have shrunk in comparison. Instead, they mushroomed. The world became strange and sinister.

I get up from the writing table and open the windows. The sky exhales into the room. It's hard to imagine that a year has passed since that first meeting with Siobhán, a year of a life that has grown comfortable. I wake each morning with a task. I defer Z. There is a clear purpose, something specific to wonder about. What will happen when the project is over? Or will I extend the story for the pleasure of weaving, warding off what I don't want to face: my missing memory, the great hole in life into which everything loved can be lost?

37

October 4

> *Space grown sick. House by the rice fields unliv-
> able. Monsoons have ended. Pomelos and mandarins
> in the markets again, and green papaya. The mangoes
> have gone. Mangoes are a summer fruit. Grown too
> ripe and have rotted. The sky is the azure of the day
> I first arrived. Now toeing a line. Right side of okay,
> but one false step could ruin it all. I smelled something
> today in the spare bedroom, where all the laughing
> Buddhas are. It reminded me of the Thailand that
> greeted me a year ago: smell of rough magic.*

The sun was overhead when I came upon the sign, which
is what I'd been looking for. Mist from the morning hadn't
entirely evaporated, so the path to the pavilion was green,
live and fresh. Doubt struck as I walked among the birds-of-
paradise and wet leaves of palms; *I am wrong to leave.* But Ban
Du felt like a wasteland. Everyone gone: Koi, Anthony, Aurelia,
Soraya—I should've gone with her, become a nun. The house
by the rice fields, haunted and lonely since Aurelia's accident,
had been permanently blackened by the days of rain after my
return, when I didn't leave the bed, horrified by my body,

wanting out of my skin. If I hadn't been so afraid of everything, I'd have gone with Béa to see Aurelia. She took the bus with Lek, who resumed classes once Aurelia was through the worst but still went to Bangkok as often as he could. On his most recent return, he announced that Aurelia was walking again. He was so glad.

Muay helped me pack up my office at the university. She promised to keep my postcard decorations and lesson plans, photocopies and whiteboard markers, for when I came back. She was angry with the university. I didn't care.

The last two evenings, I'd gathered courage and looked for Seb at his house. He wasn't there. Since we barely spoke anymore, I had to learn from Béa where he was.

—You shouldn't follow him, she'd said. He's with Ploy. You'll only hurt yourself.

Béa was always too careful. Besides, she didn't know. No one knew.

So I took the motorbike up the winding dirt paths into the hills. The colors were brilliant, the sky an impossible blue. At turnoffs to waterfalls, the air grew cool. Bamboo groves turned to deciduous forests and back again. Boars trotted off the road as I approached. I got off and walked the motorcycle when the road got too steep to ride. Finally, I reached the wooden sign with gold letters: NAAM JAI SAI. WATER OF THE CLEAR HEART.

Many months ago, when Seb and I were exploring the region's waterfalls, we'd stumbled upon the place by accident. I was new at driving the motorbike, and Seb was getting tired of having to stop so much. We thought at first that it was the entrance to a hill tribe village, but then we sensed the

Her Here 277

stillness and rare quiet of the place. We walked down a lane of birds-of-paradise to a Lanna pavilion. Breezes blew through the space. We could see all the way to Myanmar.

We met the owners of the resort—a young Thai couple who took an immediate liking to Seb because he spoke both French and Thai. The couple had worked for a year in Bordeaux before deciding to give up their jobs and use what they'd saved to build a paradise. After a year of searching, they found this site in the hills of Doi Mae Salong. It was low season, and they offered to give us a tour.

All of the villas had been built with the region's finest teakwood. The architects and builders had designed the space in harmony with the landscape, in Lanna style. One of the villas opened onto a deck with an infinity pool: bright blue of water and tile against the valley below. I could have stared at it forever, but the couple invited us for jasmine tea and lavender cookies. I was Seb's sister. We never bothered to correct them.

Now, I reached the resort's pavilion, its view causing my breath to catch in my throat: tea plantations, orange orchards, pineapple fields, and villages tucked into hills creviced by waterfalls. Still, I spent my days in the valleys, not at these heights.

The female innkeeper kissed me on both cheeks.

—Sebastian's sister, she said, smiling with warmth that made tears gather, hot and hidden, behind my eyes. Yes, yes, he is here.

She offered to accompany me to the villa, but I said I could go alone. I needed to compose myself. She drew her hands to her chest. I *wai*'ed in return.

I drew in breath on the walk, juniper, jasmine, and teakwood on the breeze. I knew Seb wouldn't be alone. I'd come with a sense of urgency, but would I know, once he and I were face-to-face, how to ask him for a word? I was braver in mind than in body. Still, I knew that if I didn't tell him, something inside me would always gape. The path narrowed as I approached the villa.

A Lanna house has no borders. Walls are doors, open to breezes blown across rice fields, orange orchards, and tea plantations. Teakwood gave the room its odor, rich and sharp. A breeze touched my face and arms. Seb was packing, suitcase on the bed. His back was turned, and his white shirt stood out against polished wood walls. Behind him, through wall-size doors, hills stretched into Myanmar.

Silently, I floated into the room, closer to Seb, who was folding a shirt. With the odor of him—familiar—my heart squeezed. My throat grew tight. All of Vietnam came rushing back. Where was Ploy? Had Béa been wrong? Had Seb come not with Ploy but by himself—to be away from things, to think? Hope swelled in my chest.

There was the humidity of his body, carried to me by the breeze.

—I thought Ploy would be here, I said, inches from his back. Even to my own ears, my voice sounded raw, accusatory.

Seb flinched so hard, he almost hit me as he wheeled around, his eyes the gray of polished marble.

—Jesus, Ella. How did you get here?

—I had to speak with you, I said.

—*Now?* he asked, performing incredulity, to shame me.

—I didn't know when you were getting back.

—I'd have been in Ban Du in an hour, he said.

—I didn't know that. Béa told me you took a trip with Ploy.

I tried to stay calm, but my voice was accusing again. He sighed.

—The idea was to have a mini break before the semester began. The owners—

—They gave you a discount?

—Of course. He smiled boyishly—a flash of the old Seb— then grew serious. Ploy is overworked. She has all these new students with the start of term, and now she is leading tourism visits to the tea plantations, the botanical gardens—

—Where is she? I asked, cutting him off, looking around.

—She had a lesson at noon. I stayed on a bit. I'm going now, he added.

It was time to say what I had come to say. But just then there came a sudden, delicious sense of peace. I could barely remember what I had to tell Seb or why it had seemed important.

—It's good to be up here, I said, up in the hills. I should've come more often.

Silence ballooned between us.

—I went to the States, I began, then looked at Seb as if this alone were enough to make him understand, without speech, without words that would make it more real than it had to be.

Seb placed a last shirt in his suitcase and looked around the room.

—Your book, I said, pointing to the deck by the infinity pool.

I watched him enter the panorama of the landscape, then followed. The deck edged dizzyingly over the valley.

—Sublime here, I said, wanting banalities, phatic niceties to steady myself.

He reached for his book, keeping my position in sight, nervous. His movements were stiff. The old comfort was irrecoverable.

—I came to say I'm *sorry,* I said helplessly.

It was not at all why I had come, but Seb came toward me, an opening. It was time to tell him.

—What are you reading? I asked, changing the subject.

—*The Magic Mountain.* Hard to get into—look, this couldn't have waited until I was back?

—I'm leaving Chiang Rai.

I studied his face for surprise but could find none. Only his eyes seemed to darken.

—Tomorrow, I added. For good.

—Ah, he replied, still without astonishment. They asked you not to teach.

I nodded, studying the edge of the pool.

—It'll be okay, he said. Maybe they'll ask you back next term, after you've rested some? Muay told me. It's not fair of them, is it?

—I'm going to the south, I said, to the Andaman Sea, to "take time for myself."

I tried to laugh, but the laugh came out bitter.

—I came to say good-bye and to tell you—

Seb held up his hand as if to shield himself, the way he'd shielded himself from the vase.

—You were upset, he said gently. A lot happened. I know you didn't mean . . .

His eyes were clear. I forced myself to look at him until I

felt I would crack. Then he put a hand between my shoulder blades, holding me upright. I looked over the hills, wishing I could jump and fly over them, be a fleck of dust in the light, dancing down into the valleys. I'd driven two hours, hauling the motorbike up steep inclines, to tell him. I'd vowed to tell him, to say it even if it had to be in front of Ploy. But now the chance was here, and the words wouldn't come.

—Ella? Are you okay? I felt him shaking me. *Are you okay?*

I said vague things about Bangkok, the States, and looked at him meaningfully, hoping he would guess. Wasn't it obvious? My voice came in shudders, breath too fast.

Seb frowned, puzzled and a bit afraid.

—I should go, he said. We'll ride down together, yeah?

I thought of how to say it on the way down, though every jolt of the hillside made it feel as if an organ would spill out through some hidden opening. The doctors had advised me not to return to Asia. They said I should stay at home in case of complications. Mom insisted that my obligations to the university didn't matter, that my health was more important, that they would find someone to take over my class. We'd find a way to get my things. She said all this, and yet I felt it would be certain madness if I stayed: no job, no sense of identity outside her care. So I flew eighteen hours over desert and ocean and slept for a week in the house by the rice fields, telling no one. Soraya was the only one who knew, and she was gone.

When we reached the superhighway, Seb leaned toward me, his eyes naked, full of feeling, and kissed me on the cheek.

—Take care of yourself, he said, cupping my shoulder in his palm.

I nodded, and he sped away.

October 5

Dusk descending over waters multilayered in blues. Sands are marble-colored, sticky in the mist. The Andaman is smooth, drifting to sleep under my gaze. I'll cross it tomorrow, on my way to where the sea gypsies live. These skies and sands are too vivid to exist in life. They must be images. I've stepped inside a photograph or between the frames of a film, crawled into a space that is neither life nor art, but the zone created when they reflect each other infinitely, like facing mirrors. This is more real than regular reality. Can feel the earth, magnetic, under my body. People born in the year of the rooster (I heard this) must scratch the earth to feel secure. Feet dug like claws in the sticky sand. The moments keep moving, yes.

October 7

Whose fault? Fault lines. Anything nuclear, fissures in family. No borders or bounds; any breast can nourish anyone's child. Fault in the idea that home exists. Utopia buried in rubble. Here: salt, sea, nomads. Two miles from the bungalows, Angus says, are the chao leh, *also called the gypsies of the sea. Unwritten letters to my birth mother on my walks: I'll be cured, salted, like a sea cucumber, strung up in the sun. Sapped of humors by the magic of the sky and sea.*

Grade upon grade of blue, then the white gold of sand. Bungalows stretched two hundred meters along the coast of the island, near the place where I washed up in my hired long-tail, hoping for deserted shores. The driver tossed my pack from the boat and came aground with me. I scratched the sand with my toes, rooting myself in the cool beneath the sun crust of surface.

I wished the driver would go. But he secured the boat, and we walked a hundred meters along the shore to a bungalow set back from the coast, the space around it crowded with clay statuettes, hammocks, dartboards, and sculptures made of wood and beer cans. A man with smooth skin, no shirt, dark dreadlocks, and silver rings on his large hands paid the driver what I thought was a commission. Later, Angus told me it was for marijuana from the mainland.

The driver stuffed the money in a pocket.

—*Kap khun krap,* Angus said, and, turning to me, priced the bungalow in British English. He had a gentle way of speaking. His face was broad, with high cheekbones and a flat nose. He looked half Asian. (I learned later he was half German, half Malay.) I paid a month up front. I wanted to be relieved of the money I'd brought, to carry less. Angus offered me cold beer. We drank it in his bungalow before he showed me to my own.

I watched the old words float to the surface of my thoughts and spill away into the space around us. Your accent—have you lived in England? How many people live on this island? What is its circumference? Will you be here always? Or will others come to replace you? How do you live your days? Where have you come from? Why did you leave? Giving voice to even one of these questions would have meant slipping back into the old ways. Here, I would not need others. They distract from looking within. The questions died away unasked. Finally, I was elsewhere—far enough that *here* wouldn't find me. The island

teemed with unmarked paths, raw possibilities. It was a place
to live forever.

Hours ago, I'd left Krabi, the mainland shore, where monkeys placed their tiny hands in mine and laughed and screeched,
for this island I didn't know existed until I arrived. I lay on the
threshold of my new bungalow, heels inside and hair spreading into the sand: relief of displacement. Could I do it forever,
dump my excess of self into larger and larger containers, until
the pressure of enclosure would become negative and the
skin of my body would burst? I would empty out at last into
the world. Chiang Rai was too full of me. Familiar places only
chanted back regrets. I needed unscratched sand with nothing
of my impression. I wrote:

iiiiiiiiiiiiiiiiiiiiiiiiiiiiiiiiiii

ooooooooooooooooooo

to sound the void. I liked the o shape best and made more.

The nuts and dried fruit I'd brought from Krabi were not
enough. I was hungry all the time. In my mind's image of the
island, I could pick papayas from trees and net fish in the sea.
Instead, a gnawing in my stomach brought me to Angus's bungalow. Unsurprised, he led me down a small concrete road to
a town that further jarred with my vision of the island. We
bought what we needed and returned to his bungalow. He
made Malaysian curries. His father was from Malaysia, which
surprised me. I'd assumed it was the other way around. Maybe
it was. It didn't matter. He offered me beer again, and the first
sips eased a dull emptiness of hunger that was beginning to
feel like pain.

Angus was saying something about the low season, the restaurant in the town being closed. His voice was reedy and

rough, like wind through a pipe. The fizz of the beer numbed my lips. I played with savoring the sensation. I watched and smelled him cooking. Slow, slow. His slow, careful movements reminded me of Seb. Angus's body was larger than Seb's. But when night fell and we had eaten and began to make love, it was Seb's hand on the small of my back, pressing me to him and protecting the small bones in my back from the wood of the bungalow wall.

When I reached for Angus's hand and cupped it across my mouth, he didn't act surprised. He was probably high.

During nights with Angus, there were sometimes swells of disgust, though no feelings passed between us. Our coming together happened as if on its own, without pleasure or passion. We slipped into nakedness and the strange rhythm as if it were an extension of our meal. Angus smelled of musk and something very sweet. Animal flesh. I grazed the skin of his chest with my nose to find the source of the sweetness. It was everywhere. He pressed himself against me, into me with little interest. He never held me or clung to me, and this was good. He was always partly in the sea and thinking of other things, and I was, too.

Seb was the object of all my meditations. I learned I could make his face appear on the still surface of the sea at dusk. I thought about him so much that one day his whole body emerged, wandering among the palms behind my bungalow.

I knew I wasn't well in Chiang Rai—could read it in others' faces: Béa's, Aurelia's, Lek's, and Muay's. Muay had trembled as she gave me the news about my job. Teaching was okay. It might have kept my mind and thoughts in order. But at the university, too, they sensed something was wrong. In their way, through Muay, they asked me not to teach. Saving face—mine, mostly—they recommended I take a holiday; we would see about my job once I was "rested." So I meditated and asked the god powers I believed in from time to time what I should do. Home wasn't the answer. Neither was going to look for my birth mother in Paris—not yet. I needed empty space. But I feared every elsewhere would turn into here and I'd never be able to leave myself.

I brought one book with me to the island, thinking I'd read it over and over, like a Bible. I'd hoped it would be a manual for stoicism. It wasn't, but I read it anyway. The book was *Natural Questions*. It was falling apart because I kept returning to its pages and because the sun and salt got in its binding. "Death," Seneca wrote, "is the tribute and duty of mortals, the remedy for every suffering."

One night, by accident, I discovered Angus's library. Awake while he slept, wandering through his rooms, I found some hundred books in boxes. I didn't get the sense that Angus read much anymore, but he must have once. Why store them on the island? Had he nowhere else? In one of the books, there was a passage that singed me. It was about essences unable to flow in certain people: from these people into those they love and from those they love into them. Their ego is terrible. They are like a house "with the shutters eternally closed; the sunlight would like to shine on this house, too, and warm it up, but the house does not open . . . it is terrified by happiness." Inside the house, there is "wild and despairing activity . . . an endless rearranging . . ." No space can ever be the one in which we're meant to be.

When I grew tired of books, I read the sands.

In the sands are etched things of great importance, the past in the future. One need only know how to look and to translate. It was Seb who taught me. He gestured. I saw: sound waves pressed into the surface of the sands. Chladni figures everywhere. Tangible frequencies, physical sound. Oh, the sands were full of these present absences, and so full of sounds from all times that I stopped being able to read them, too much interference (like fuzz on the airwaves). I would retreat, at those moments, to the lazy indifference of Angus or to the relative silence of my book: "Enslavement to oneself is the most severe enslavement."

One day I looked toward the sea. Seb asked me, *Don't you want to know more about the shape of this place? How can you stand living on this bit of fringe, not knowing?* I asked him how many days it would take to circle the island by foot. He didn't know. We decided to find out. We knew we would have to sleep outside, but the rains had stopped and the sky was clear. In Chiang Rai, it would be the cool season. The semester would have started, first classes taught, students milling in their black-and-white uniforms. I thought of Aurelia, how she'd been dressed as a student the day we met. The sounds of the island were different at night. Seb and I could see the stars from the beaches and groves where we slept amid the constant tearing of tides and the insects tunneling earth and flesh.

It was on this exploratory adventure that I first chanced upon the *chao leh*, the Moken, the people of the sea, always casting their nets and pushing off in their boats. Their settlement was temporary, I discovered, for the *chao leh* were always moving. They traveled lightly, by boat, and touched down only during the heavy rains, when the sea was too rough to carry them. From the Moken I learned that the earth has veins and arteries. The *chao leh* could predict the moods of the sea, and they lived without leaving a scar on the land.

As the weeks and months passed, I saw them more and more, walking miles of coastline to be among them, sleeping in their camp at night. I spent a lot of time with them, fishing or drying fish in the sun, and learning their rituals. The rest of the time I spent with Seb, weaving paths through the island's forests.

I grew strange to myself. My clothing became tattered, faded by the salt breeze. Only one worry, persistent, like a delirium, kept me from dissolving entirely into the place. The worry was this: that the sand would forget me. No record, trace, or story of my having been.

Old habits are tenacious. The first thing I did when I met the Moken was to learn their names. We had no common language, so I placed a hand on my chest.

—*Name*, I said.

—Hantale.

—Hantale, I repeated. And her?

—Hantale.

—Her? I pointed to another woman across the beach.

—Hantale.

It's a generic surname, Angus told me, his usual airiness giving way to a British schoolboyishness, irritatingly pedagogical. I wondered again about him, about where the books had come from, but couldn't hold the sensation of curiosity.

Hantale was like a genus, I mused, binding individuals into a single family.

—It means "unafraid of the sea," Angus said offhandedly, sensing my irritation.

—Unafraid, I repeated. Unafraid.

It sounded like *unified.* . . .

—*What* does? I asked, suddenly unsure.

—What?

He was tying the strings of his linen pants. He looked up at me, concerned.

—Means unafraid?

—Hantale.

—Oh.

—All of them have it.

The joints that held our conversation together were wearing thin, the limbs of our speech too far apart. What is called the "thread" of conversation was unraveling. I could not keep up the pressure that lends order to thoughts. Mine seemed to stretch to the farthest reaches of space and farther still, pushing back the horizon so that sea and sky blended in an ever-present haze.

Because of this unraveling of words and thoughts, it became more comfortable to be among the Moken. At first, I was shy and would sit away from their company, just far enough so that I could listen to their speech and stare out to sea, watching them in their boats and as they dived and emerged from the depths. Then I didn't feel as much the growing spaces between words. It was like a loss of memory, sweet and terrifying. The women snacked on fish salted by the sun and spit out the bones. They would sometimes talk to me, though I understood nothing of what they said. Their smiles were easier to imitate, and the act of smiling planted in me a contentment

I hadn't known in many months. I was becoming other than myself, to my delight and terror.

Then Seb would return from time to time like a ritornello, bringing with him—or summoning from where they had scattered—memories and pieces of my old self.

Converting the Moken's monsoon-season settlements, I built myself a tentlike cabin. It had been a hut in their village, thatched and set on stilts. Now there were more woven palm branches, added with the help of a few women who understood, laughingly, that I wanted to live in the place where they would come ashore with their boats.

For long stretches, the Moken would travel from the island. Before pushing out to sea, they sacrificed a large turtle. As we ate the meat, I watched the children swimming with their plastic goggles. Even the tiniest mastered the water. I wanted to learn the Moken language, so I could know their myths and the reasons for their rituals. I felt the dread of abandonment each time they left, wondering if they would come back at all.

My clothes were shredded. I could see the color of my skin getting darker, my hair growing more like straw and the sands. I grew afraid—a sudden chill in the air—of becoming nothing other than the things around me.

Seb appeared.

There is a story . . . I began, so that he would stay. We were watching the orange sun sink beneath the waves. He pushed me on with his eyes, the way I wanted him to.

. . . of a woman in the jungle, an anthropologist, timid and shy. She is very organized, recording her findings every night on a Dictaphone and in notebooks. She begins to leave in the night. No one knows where she goes. She reappears covered in dirt, with a

secretive smile. Her speech changes; then she doesn't speak at all, her research abandoned. Then she's gone not just nights but days, too. She becomes like the land, indifferent to the rain. The villagers are frightened. When she has been gone for a week, a search party is sent. . . .

I looked at Seb to see if he was listening. He was picking at the sand. I went to pee behind a clump of bushes, building suspense. When I got back, he refused to look at me.

They never find her, I told him, *not even her body.*

The sun had gone down and shadows moved along the beach.

It will happen to you, he said coldly. *No one will look for you.* He didn't laugh.

Sometimes Seb turns cruel; his eyes darken and his mouth twists into a scowl. When I sense his storm moods coming, I retreat into the forest. If he follows me there, I go among the sea gypsies, where he will not venture. I grow afraid of him when he speaks about our child. The next time he grows reproachful, I will not be able to stand it. His spits his words: *You should've told me.* But other times he's nonchalant. I cry, and that's all he wants to see, that I am sorry. He turns away, glances over his shoulder, and says, *You might have asked me.*

I sometimes see the child.

She asks me if she can write her name on my legs. I hand her my pen, and she throws it in the sea. She takes fine rocks instead, or shells sharpened by the tides, and presses her little hands to my skin. She takes the flesh of my thighs and stretches it tight, so that my skin is paper; the blood her tools coax to its surface is ink.

We don't need to speak, she and I, for I know what she is

going to write. She has Seb's smile and nymphlike eyes. She is very beautiful, her perfect skin nut-colored from the sun. She is entirely my own. Of my making. Seb has gone into the forests, and she is with me, she with his gray eyes and hair the color of sand. I don't need to ask her what she will write. She will write her name on my body, over and over and over, her name with its pretty accent over the *a*.

She writes the letters of her name across my thighs and calves until I scream and tell her to stop for today. We'll continue tomorrow. I sit in the pools made by the tides, and the salt sets her childlike script on my skin. In time they will not scab and bleed, but scar amid the brownness of my skin so that there will be only her name in white, raised patches: siobhán siobhán siobhán siobhán siobhán siobhàn siobhán siobhán siobhán siobhán. She writes, and my skin breaks and forms again. She writes herself there, her name, into my skin. Pleasure of the salt pools when she has done, her writing fresh and the sea sealing her words into the surface of my body, the body I denied her.

Seb comes back from the forests in the heat of the day. But the three of us are never together, for that would mean we were a family, and this is not a place for families of the nuclear, explosive kind. Seb comes back from the forests and tells me I've killed her. I've angered her, and she has gone and drowned in the sea while I wasn't watching. He has had to fish her body from the shallows and bury her on the high ground, where the tides won't dig her out again. He is angry. His eyes are burning in a way that human eyes don't burn. He is out of place here, dressed in slacks and a button-down shirt. He must go to teach his class at the university. He will go. I can see the Moken boats in the distance. I am afraid of him, and of myself.

When he goes, I fall to the sands and weep, then lie in the shallows and hope that the sea will take me in its arms, returning to me all that's been lost.

FROM SIOBHÁN'S WHITE COUCH, I watch the pink and red geraniums in her window box, bald and withered, having survived last week's heat, but barely. Ella's green journal is on my lap. Siobhán sits on a low easy chair, professional and apprehensive, her lines of worry accentuated under the even light from the windows.

Opening the green journal, I run a finger along the place where its last page has been torn out. Most of the writing on the back inside cover is tiny, expanding the diminishing page— though Ella mentions a new journal, also green. Perhaps she was reluctant to let the old book go, to lose all that she'd been in its pages. Siobhán's address, most likely copied earlier, is in large, confident script: *11, rue Perrée #15, Paris 75003 FRANCE.* It's the flat where I am now, before a tray with small chocolates and espressos on red saucers with miniature spoons.

Siobhán wants to know where I am in my draft. It's mid-July. I should have been finished a month ago.

—I've written to where the journals end, I say, knowing the crucial part is still ahead of me.

Siobhán starts to say something and stops, seeing her address copied in the open journal.

—You see, she says, the journal was intended for me.

I ask her what she means.

Siobhán brings her espresso to her lips, pauses, sets it down without drinking, and stands. She goes to the antique cabinet by the window and takes out a shipping envelope, smaller than I'd imagined it, its Thai stamps faded. Sitting down, she draws from the package a sheet of paper. She looks away as she hands it to me. I recognize the paper. Its left edge is ragged.

For Siobhán, the letter begins, continuing diagonally down the page. The syntax—what I can read of it—is strange, like an ancient folktale. It leaves me with a sick and sad feeling. I hold the page to where it had been torn out years ago, as if the paper fibers might grow together again.

I imagine Siobhán receiving that package with its smell of windswept beaches. She knew as soon as she saw the Thai stamps who it was from. Her heart seized, reading the letter. Paging through the green journal, she asked herself why Ella had sent it. She kept all six journals close, their broken spines reminders of a burden she felt she deserved.

It makes sense for Siobhán to think the journals are Ella's revenge. Feeling condemned can be more comfortable than not knowing. But if Ella had an ideal reader, it would be a semblable, someone with no investment in her at the start but searching for something all the same. I'm preparing for a final leap into Ella. It's clear to me that Ella hadn't planned to send the journal. The gesture was spontaneous. Coming to the end of the book, one day on the beach, she rediscovered Siobhán's address, copied there after a painful conversation with her adoptive mother in July. (Ella bought two green journals when she was home, where it was easier to find the kind she liked.) The address gave her an idea—one she liked the more she imagined it.

A leap into Ella. More fully than before. Embody her long

enough to learn the truth. And once the mystery is solved, the letters set in type, will I be able to return: Elena?

The ink is running low, she writes, and presses harder. Ella has no money for postage and must steal it from Angus. She would have been too far gone by that point to ask. She writes the letter and mails it with the book. *And then?*

No fixed abode. Can't keep the old journal with me. It would disintegrate the way Seneca did. Binding weak. Can't care for anything with a weave this close to the sea. It took forever to finish because my little daughter kept throwing my pens to the waves. I had to steal others from Angus, who acts afraid of me. We are past the point of his being afraid *for* me, so he doesn't intervene. That's all I require. A full journal is the skin of a lost self, dead and dry, like discarded toenails or the paper scales of snakes that stick in the sand before blowing away. Her address glaring up from the page told me what to do. She'll have my husk of self, lost at last. Yes.

To find out how much money I'd need, I went to town. They don't approve of me there, can't fathom the creature I am. My Thai is halting from disuse, no song in it. Price of a padded envelope: two hundred baht. Postage to France is more, but the figure won't stick in my mind. Tourists have come to the island, making it riskier to sneak back into the lodgings I left many weeks ago. Touching that Angus hasn't rented my bungalow to someone else. He's leaving it for last.

Inside the bungalow, I found relics from my former life. The sight of my toothbrush warmed me from my toes. Pens scattered like pick-up sticks under the bed. No money.

After three nights of surveillance, I discovered where

Angus keeps the cash he earns from the bungalows. I learned other secrets, too, like that he takes one of the tourists to bed with him almost every night. He drinks, meditates, fucks, and swims alone in the dark sea. For three nights it was nearly the same. I took the money from his purple paisley sack. It was easy to take, morally I mean, since some of it had been mine. I was grateful to Angus, who gave me food before I knew how to spear fish and salt them in the sun, so I took only what I'd need.

How tidy, how neat that the civility of returning myself to the woman who made me lures me back into spaces left behind. Rooms and lives. Steps back in homage. Comforting discomfort of knowing she mourned me. It took losing a daughter—she would have been a daughter—to know. Yes, she will have the I that I was now that I'm not—unless I start a next one. Ha! A next one! Cover green like the last but fresh pages like clean white bedsheets.

Once I had the money, I sneaked back into my old bungalow and brushed my hair until I could tie it back. The sight of myself in a mirror made me laugh. I felt healthy and alive. Having a task will do that sometimes. I washed my face in the sink. The brownness collecting in the washbasin pleased me. Using the toilet was a delight. I rinsed my mouth and picked the scum from my teeth with a fingernail. I searched the backpack. Folded T-shirt at the bottom had the strangest scent, my old perfume. Memory pricked the ducts behind my eyes. I batted the feeling away like a mosquito and pulled on the T-shirt over my tattered bikini top. The cloth was heavy and hot. I'd throw it in the sea when I was done. I left on the sarong I wore among the Moken, though its edges were frayed and there was sand dust in its folds.

Then I lay on my stomach and tore out the last page of the green book. I couldn't make the letters neat, so I put the journal underneath and that worked better. Sensations stayed locked in letters. Pen tip made a place for the inexpressible. Listening to the waves for rhythm, I began:

> *For Siobhán,*
>
> *I write from blue calm, mangrove and beach grass. Important to investigate nature, the tastes of waters, sweet, strong, salt, and bitter. Distinctions of touch, weight, color, healthiness . . .*

Her letter reminds me of an object my mother made during her second episode of illness. I was a teenager at the time, and I saw in it only energy. Not knowing how to fear such things, I kept it, a little mound of stone and blue glass. I don't know where it is now. Probably destroyed with the rest.

> *. . . ink is running out, ink is unimportant, living the only record. Bodies grow into land. Ancient kin to Epimenides, I will live in a time I wasn't born. The Moken gods are not wrathful. They live in old sea turtles and trees. Not like my gods and ghosts. Word wounds in me. I send you a spell. If you read it, I will wake up in your future. The sand and sea do not notice, take no imprint. Need as basic as hunger: eyes for these words. For you at least to know better than I what I am.*

Footsteps outside. I thought someone had found me, a face to wear my impression. No. No one. Not Angus. Imagined. Not real. I began to worry about the soundness of my mind. I took this worry as proof of sanity.

My feet began to bleed on the road to town, where I hid from passing motorbikes, fearing it might be Angus, who would catch me and send me away from the island. The sea lay placid, parallel to my course for most of the way. The road hardened and made my soles bleed more. I staunched the wounds with hot sand.

At the shop that sent things to a post office on the mainland, I tried to remember what had become of my shoes. I couldn't. I approached the counter quickly, so the woman would see only my clean T-shirt and not notice the brown bits of blood on the floor. I wrote the address with care. After slipping the journal inside with the letter, I sealed the envelope with my dry tongue and paid. There was a little change.

Outside, I wished for the safe passage of the journal and dropped the bills and coins into a fountain in town, already buzzing with tourists, though it was still early in the season and early in the day.

38

ON THE ALABASTER COAST, two hours from Paris by train, the erosion of chalk cliffs make turquoise patches in the water. I will know that it is Normandy, of course, and not an island in the Andaman Sea, but I will feel close to her there, to what she lived, to the color of her sea.

The train is crowded. No one checks my ticket. After changing at Rouen, it is more peaceful. Fewer people. The air carries hints of grass and salt, and the roar of cities fades. Fields of wheat and green linen stretch to the sky, and finally it is quiet enough to hear her again: Ella.

I have booked four nights in a cottage by the sea, in the spare room of a woman who grows irises on her thatched roof and tends a garden teeming with roses and hydrangeas. She serves lavish breakfasts and tells me about the walking paths and tides, erratic and forceful in the region. Hot-colored roses in the morning fog remind me of the English countryside my mother loved. As a child, she spent her summers in Dover.

When the tide is out, I walk along the vast table of sands and slippery rocks. The cliffs are vertical drops of white that separate the village from the sea. Steep stone steps lead down to the beach, and, at high tide, right into the water. Down until the body is light, lifted by the waves.

But the sea in the morning is hardly there. The steps lead into a lunar landscape of tide-battered rocks and rippled sands and fields of seaweed like thick strands of hair. In the distance, men scavenge for shellfish or whatever the tide has left behind. The fog burns off slowly; then the sun filters into forest paths and lights the fields. The tide rushes in an hour later every day.

The jungle paths are so deep and lush, I can almost believe I am elsewhere, except then a clearing comes where noble Norman cows are grazing. The paths are damp and buzzing with insects. Each day, I alternate among forest, cliffs, and coast, carrying Ella's green journal and my notebook of possible endings. The innkeeper worries that the weather is too warm, but it is cooler here than in Thailand, so every degree moves me closer to Ella.

Encountering even one other walker takes me out of the spell I'm weaving, so I press deeper into the forests, away from the paths, and farther into the void of sands at low tide. At noon, most days, a blankness overtakes me. It's different from a loss of memory, just the cost of becoming absorbed in her. It means that something is working. I am out on the sands. The sun is high. There are no shadows. When I come to, I'm sitting in a tidal pool, wet through and very cold. The light is gold and slanting at hard angles.

This is intentional. I am in control. I walk her walk and swim with her body. Yes, I embody her. The ink runs out of my pen, and it is in such humble, subtle ways that one finds one's way into another skin. I can feel her thrill and devastation.

The waterline at low tide is far from the cliffs, and I wade in the shallow pools, my sandals slipping on the sharp rocks. Ella will race the tide. We must wait for it. We do. When it comes, it is very fast, but we see it and stay ahead, our lungs burning as we run, adrenaline charging through us. At the very end, we slip on the rocks, but there is still time. We pull ourselves up the stone steps, then dangle our feet in the sea to congratulate ourselves as the water swirls in little breakers below us. Then the water is green, and there is no more sun. The air turns yellow, the way it does before a storm. She dives. I hear her splash. I tell her to be careful. She bobs her head and laughs, her hair plastered to her shoulders, then ducks beneath the waves. The water turns greener in the changing light. Terrified, I call her name. She doesn't emerge.

The water is freezing, a shock to the whole body. Salt stings my eyes as I grope wildly, cutting myself on the jagged edges of rocks. I dive lower, then charge up for air. The surface gets choppier. Currents threaten to dash us against the cliffs. I can't breathe and am afraid, and I must tell myself the cold isn't real, none of this is real—a flaw of this body I must use to discover you.

Then, suddenly, it is morning, and the innkeeper hums as she sets out coffee, fruit, and croissants with salted butter. She goes out to the garden to feed the roses. Birds are singing. My bag is packed beside me, ready for my train. There are scratches on my arms, and I smell of unfamiliar lavender soap.

39

O F THE 572 ISLANDS IN THE ANDAMAN SEA, which was hers? I am empty of Ella, bereft, confused. No ending I have written so far will do. My body knows there will never be a body.

Siobhán left yesterday for London to learn the letterpress process. Aidan is in town for work. I wait for him in the gallery, which is cool and smells faintly—I think—of jasmine.

The Ormeau is the house by the rice fields. The light is the same, and the wall of glass.

When I close my eyes, the rice fields appear.

Climbing the spiral stairs, I sit in the loft, swinging my legs over the space. Under me, the press waits, spiderlike, its tiny letters scrambled in drawers. I might ask them if Ella has to die.

Cross-legged, knees flush with the ledge, I try to meditate the way Pra New taught Ella to do. Wind in the trees and shouts from the park outside play over breaths in and out, Ella's, mine.

Aidan arrives. He stares up at the loft, shocked the way he was when he first met me. His surprise lasts only a moment, but the effect of his look stays; he has mistaken me for my mother.

—Fancy a spritz? It's summer, after all, he says, recovering.

His neat white hair and collared pink shirt give me a shock of recognition, too. Having borrowed his physique, his style, I feel I know him in a different key.

Aidan is here to make sure that I'm okay, that Siobhán and the project haven't damaged me. He is avuncular, like Anthony, whom I miss.

Ella is on the beach with her phantoms.

As we leave the gallery, I catch sight of my mother's sculpture through the glass front, egglike, dappled in sun. I forgot to touch it before leaving. We find an outdoor table at a café across the park, and Aidan orders spritzes.

—Oh! he says, as if just remembering. Our mother's first chapbook was printed on a letterpress machine. In Ireland. Before she was married. There's some sense to this after all—if sentiment qualifies as sense. . . .

I see an elderly woman with skin as fine as paper and sharp blue eyes like her children's. But Aidan's comment grates at me. Any mention of the press is a reminder that Siobhán thinks my writing will be its own end. The artist's book reduces me to human material, a living canvas or sentient palette knife—when the point is to find Ella. I'm left alone to care for her.

—Here I am off track. We were speaking of endings, Aidan says.

—No, I say, correcting him. Of Ella. Of her whereabouts.

He frowns, leaning back in his chair.

—I never liked the idea of your rewriting the journals, he says. It's not fair to you.

It's surprising to hear this. I was sure Siobhán put him up to this meeting.

—The situation is terrible to start, Aidan says. But it's one thing to set yourself a problem, quite another to involve another person. Just don't knock your head against a wall. You know what's likely. Use your instinct. If Siobhán doesn't like it, believe me, she'll tell you.

Our drinks arrive. Aidan sips his through a straw. His resemblance to Siobhán is striking: the same eyes, the same sharp features.

—What's troubling is that Siobhán doesn't tell me everything, I say. I don't even know the details of why she gave Ella up. Couldn't she have kept her, or if she didn't want the child . . .

Crossing his legs, Aidan starts to tell me about the little clan he joined when he followed Siobhán to London: three women, all closer than sisters. Ella's adoptive mother was American, six years older than Siobhán, four years older than my mother. She was married to another American—they were in London temporarily—and trying desperately to have a child.

—More than anything, she wanted a little girl, he says. She learned she was infertile right around the time Siobhán became pregnant. I didn't know anything about it until it was over. I've no idea how the decision was made. It's such a sensitive issue. Even then it was. Twenty-one years old and she didn't tell *anyone* what she was going to do—except your mother. She said she was traveling with Ida. Next time I saw her, Ella was in America, and Siobhán was starting architecture school in Paris. She confided in me only when the adoption turned sour. She didn't expect to be cut out absolutely, to have no part in the little girl's life. I've always thought she'd have been better off not knowing where Ella went. Brutal of me, but there it is.

—Did she consider just . . . terminating the pregnancy?

—It's not something we've discussed. I don't know. But we were raised very Catholic, and there's a strong sense in our family of what you can and can't do. My mother knows, for instance, why I'm not married, but it's not something we talk about. Listen, I've said more than I should, but Siobhán doesn't always express what she feels. You're precious to her, though, you and what you've done. She trusts you. I can see why. You see things clearly, like your mother.

My breath catches. Aidan sees this. There's warmth in his gaze, a solicitude that makes me wonder about their friendship, what they talked about, how they cared for each other.

—You knew her well? I ask, so that he'll keep talking.

—Years ago, but yes. There's much in you that's like her. Though you seem a touch sadder.

—She was happy?

—Her energy, my *God,* Aidan says, shaking his head.

I find myself eager to talk about her, to describe how she would get excited over things that weren't there. I tell Aidan about her episodes and her time in recovery. I tell him, too, what I can't tell Siobhán, about the vow I made after my missing months, after her death, to attach myself to certainties. I became a scholar. It fills me with terror not to *know,* to invent, to create.

Aidan fixes me with a stare that seems so much like Siobhán's, determined and calm.

—Ida was the freest person I've ever known, he says. She did *see* things others didn't. She'd ask whether arms were made of serpent tails or fish scales and make a note in her sketchbook. She was having a laugh, of course, but at other times I had the impression she was really checking herself. She made ordinary things beautiful, and bizarre. Being around her filled out the world.

There's familiarity in what he says, and I find myself smiling at her memory, as if she were here with us.

—I didn't know things got so bad for Ida, he says, but it's rare to encounter a person like your mother. Please don't let what happened to her make you afraid. She had something so vital about her. Don't ever be afraid of that.

40

ITHOUT MAPS, THE MOKEN KNOW the way to the water's
deepest parts, where even a tidal wave would merely
bobble the surface, raising it no more than the height of four
hands. Their boats buoy as they might in the wake of a passing
speedboat. Do they think of the girl with dry lips and dirty hands,
her face browned by the island light, writing in her worn book and
sticking her feet in the sea?

Home, for Ella, is oneness with things. The pull of any concrete place dissolves in the salt-swollen depths, where other worlds
expand like sunken ships or like the bodies of the drowned. She
touches her scars from the little Siobhán. Ella will be wise, fully
fused with the world.

No. Too easy. Start again:

Ella is on the beach. Can you see her? Tattered sarong, fabric of
a T-shirt worn thin and soft, her skin rough, hair bleached by sun.

The Moken have been at sea for weeks. But she has lost track of
time. When they are on land, the fishermen wake early, and Ella,
too, so she can watch them cast off in their boats, slicing through
the glass sea toward the dark part of the sky. Ella's hut, made with

the help of the Moken women, sits at the edge of their rainy-season settlement. But now they have gone.

Closing her book, she walks down the beach, wishing, the way I did once, that she were elsewhere. In the sameness of days, this one seems sadder and more lucid than the rest, her imagination is at its limits to imagine a road home, dissolved like the white wakes of airplanes.

I know what she feels. I remember how spaces emptied themselves of color, how houses, streets, cities, and countries lost distinction. My body closed. Space lost its quality.

Here, in this room with wide windows, I can see to the dome of the Invalides and beyond when the day is clear. But today the fog is close, clouds slinking in through the open windows.

In her journals, Ella describes a *property of the human body that renders it susceptible to the reciprocal action of those which environ it.* There is a force, then, that destroys this magnetism among bodies. Maybe it's sadness. It destroys our sensitivity to space. Left should be green, and right should be the color of persimmons.

The morning in the Andaman is fine and fair. Only the mind prints textures on the waves, stirring storms in perfect skies. Imagination fears to lose itself. How far can a self expand without shattering? She walks to where the sea meets the sky, water moving over her knees, her thighs, giving her goose bumps—not because it is cold, but because she is thrilled, terrified.

It is said that in the seconds before drowning, a tremendous calm comes over the body, which becomes like one about to sleep or blend into things, a world of objects. The autonomic nervous system tries—without the will, whose intentions (who knows?) might have sabotaged survival—to keep the mouth above water.

Medical dictionaries describe how the larynx spasms to seal the windpipe, so that water fills the stomach first. When consciousness goes, the spasm relaxes, and the lungs pull in. The old instinct. Ella's mouth is open, her lips parted. Her body, her limbs, her hair extend across a deafening silence, vatic and infinite.

The fog lifts over the city, a camera lens twisting into focus.

Imagination at its limit, wanting words that aren't the property of others—hewn and tilled by others. No words in any language not already owned. *Toti se inserens mundo.*

Z's voice is metallic and makes me think of cables running under the Atlantic.

—I killed her, I say.

—Who? he asks, his voice cracking (my call has woken him up).

—Ella.

—So you're done, he says, without surprise. You're coming home.

The cobblestones, slick and shiny, reflect the sky. Street name on a blue-and-white sign: rue de l'Abreuvoir. It slopes from Montmartre's little vineyard. A man with a dachshund stops short. What must he see? A woman laughing, running, her hair loose and wet from the rain.

When I came to Paris for the first time, it was with my mother. She showed me what was beautiful even in ugly things. We practiced finding the "interesting" on sidewalks, in chaos, or in what had been discarded—things that matched in unexpected ways. The pun of the universe is pattern. I remember her laugh. I still hear it some mornings before I wake. At an art show, I find a small print with a blue-and-white design. On the back is a quote from Baudelaire, which I copy out the way Ella would have done: *Le merveilleux nous enveloppe et nous abreuve comme l'atmosphère; mais nous ne le voyons pas.* The marvelous floods us like an atmosphere. We don't see it, but it's there.

There is a dinner at Siobhán's in honor of a young sculptor. Her show is the last to go in the Ormeau before Siobhán closes the gallery for our printing.

—*Je m'abreuve de tout ça!* the sculptor is saying, laughing with pleasure, unable to stop.

She is short and charming, full of energy.

—What does it mean? Aidan asks, because everyone is laughing.

—It's like . . . I'm drunk or swimming from so being glad, she says.

For the first time, I hear my mother's laughter in the sound of my own.

41

A PASSERBY GLANCES THROUGH the gallery's glass front. Inside are two women in baggy clothes, the ages of mother and daughter, hunched over a press. Drop cloths cover the floor.

Siobhán's silver hair has grown out to frame her face. She fastens it back, pushing wisps into place with the back of her hand. Her eyes seem darker. She wears loose cotton pants and a man's plaid shirt rolled up at the sleeves.

On our first days of printing, she speaks mostly in anecdotes, perhaps to ward off more serious talk. The press, an antique, is rumored to have passed through the atelier of Ambroise-Firmin Didot. She tells me about the Didot family and their inventions across the eighteenth and nineteenth centuries, their printings of Virgil, Horace, Don Quixote, and Thucydides.

Siobhán is a careful compositor. She doesn't seem to read as she sets the type, but I can't dissociate from the text. Unnecessary words offend, and it is agony to set them.

Pages appear. Their pile grows. Siobhán tries dampening the paper. She says it opens the fibers for clarity, luminosity of impression. In the Middle Ages, she tells me, paper was made from the skins of stillborn calves, stretched and cleaned of animal hair, rubbed with pumice, and treated with lime to become absorbent.

My neck grows stiff from standing over the press, muscles

tensed in concentration. Evenings, I return to the flat with aching arms and back. Even my hamstrings are sore.

I apprentice myself to Siobhán's work ethic, laying letters in the bed, aligning the parts of the press before each printing. I come to understand her renown as an architect. Methodical and calm, she does not accept even the smallest of errors. If a print comes out smudged, or even the slightest bit uneven, we print again. Everything diminishes around us, Siobhán, the machine, and me, with Ella's absence pressing into the skin of every page.

It is early September and still very hot. The gallery door stands open to invite the breeze. Siobhán's face glows with sweat as she sets the type. She is nearing the end of a page.

—We'll be done in a week.

My words hang in the air until Siobhán finishes the plate.

—If that, she says, missing nothing.

She goes to the back room and returns with a flyer. *Loose Boat* is reproduced above the text:

Artist's Book/Livre d'Artiste
Ormeau Gallery/Gallérie Ormeau
Vernissage le 30 septembre de 19h à 22h

The vernissage is almost a month away and feels too sudden. Lek's photographs will arrive to accompany the artist's book. We hope that he will come, too, but his wife is pregnant, and he wants to be sure she can travel before confirming. He would prefer not to leave her.

Dread in my stomach at the thought of the project ending, of returning to Philadelphia.

We take turns again at the press. We'll finish for the day when it's time to reink.

Siobhán pulls out a printed page. Catching sight of her own name repeated over and over, she draws in breath. Ella is hallucinating among the *chao leh*. Finally, she asks:

—There was no child. You made her up?

I nod, and we print for several minutes over the sounds of birds, children, and traffic.

—For the Thai police, there was no doubt what happened to Ella, Siobhán says quietly. It was her adoptive mother who refused to list her among the missing. From Krabi, we hired boats to every island from which the journal could have come. We saw so much wreckage. Everyone was looking for someone.

I take out the page, checking it over mechanically. She continues:

—I stayed on to rebuild houses. It was my job to design and build. It was something I could *do*. Then the news came from the detective that Ella had been seen in Isan.

—Do you think it was really her? I ask, responding to something in Siobhán's tone.

—The woman fit her description, but if it was Ella, why would she use a different name?

I mount fresh paper. The question is rhetorical, but I answer anyway:

—There are cases of people forgetting who they are, dissociating, inventing a persona.

—As soon as I read the green journal, Siobhán says distractedly, I knew that whatever happened to her—whatever she *did*—had to be connected to it.

It's clear now why the only chance of finding Ella lay in the journals. It was always clear, though how could Siobhán have insisted? Ella's disturbance was too dramatic to be unrelated to her disappearing; coincidences of that order are too unlikely. Ella's adoptive mother fought the Thai police for listing Ella among the dead, and what I've found is more unsettling. Siobhán doesn't seem surprised. At some level (this might be what she's trying to tell me), she suspected, and feels an odd relief, reading the confirmation of her worst fears in my story.

It's my turn to print. I botch the copy. Siobhán takes it from the machine and tells me not to worry. We put things away, wipe down the press, then sit together in the doorway of the gallery, on its low step.

—If you knew, why put me through all the searching? I ask, too exhausted to be angry.

—I *didn't,* Siobhán says, as surprised as if I'd struck her. I *still* don't. What you've written is a fiction, one in which I can live, but it's not the same as certainty.

—Only a body could give us that, I say, and regret it, the crudeness of it.

Siobhán looks at me evenly. When she speaks, she seems sunk in on herself.

—I became an architect because I wanted to design space, give it order. Painting was the opposite—*feeling* anchored to material. It made ordinary things volatile. I saw it this way. Ida disagreed.

It makes me smile to think of how my mother hated order, of how, when I was five, we made the kitchen wall our canvas, to my father's horror.

—In Ella's case, Siobhán says, I wanted to give order to some part of what happened. It was too painful thinking she might turn up at any moment. And . . . you helped me see her.

—What was I then, a *vessel*? I ask, feeling a noble anger, a spirited sarcasm in my voice.

Siobhán frowns, drawing away from me.

—The project was your design as much as mine, she says.

The idea's force sends a shudder through me. Siobhán's gaze is calm, her chin tipped up slightly. She looks the way she did a year ago, except for a trembling in her lower lip, so slight that it would be easy to miss. My mind rushes back over our early meetings, her air of authority that so impressed me. Was it *hers,* or had I invested her with a conviction I badly needed? After six years of disorientation, only the journals made me feel I was writing myself—and someone else—alive. It was as if Ella found herself a body, adopting my memories just long enough to write over them with her own. I don't believe this, but it accounts for my connection to Ella.

—This has been hard for me, I say, sorry for my outburst, for my anger.

Siobhán nods as if she knows.

—During the time I can't remember, people say I acted like myself. Except I had to be told things, personal details you don't forget. The hardest part, though, was afterward—whole *months,* December to June, nothing. It's as if the time never happened.

When I look up, Siobhán's lips are parted in shock.

—Working on the journals was strange, I say. They felt more real than my own life.

Beside me, Siobhán draws in breath. She understands, but I say it anyway:

—I started thinking once memory slips how fallible it *all* might be. . . .

She looks at me a long time. Then her arm circles me, comforting, and we sit like that, awkwardly, until the streetlamps flicker on in the dusk.

—I want to show you something, she says.

We cross the park, and in the elevator of her building, our images multiplied by mirrors, she squeezes my arm, nervous. What can she have, still, to show me? There is the slim, tender hope that whatever it is will change the end I've written for Ella.

She leads me past her flat to a low door at the end of the corridor. A small key opens it. We duck up a set of stairs into sharp smells of wood and dust. A bare bulb suspended from the ceiling gives off little light. Beyond a single window, remarkably clean, the evening sky is a violent blue. The walls of the small room are lined with paintings, all different sizes, all turned to the wall like timid children, their canvases fixed to their slim wooden backs. The only furniture is an armoire with a missing door, inside of which are shelves of figurines, shadowy in the dim.

Siobhán switches on a lamp, and dust flies up from its pleated shade. She picks through the paintings, peeling them one by one from the wall. The heterogeny of objects—suitcases, easels, records, and sketchbooks—makes Siobhán's flat downstairs, with its white couches, designer lighting, and evenly spaced Oriental rugs, seem like a fantasy from a different life.

The lamplight strikes the figurines in the armoire, revealing their curves: humorous, expressive, and deeply familiar. It takes effort to look away when Siobhán calls out, having found what she was looking for.

She positions the life-size painting so that I can see. Within its straw, orange, and butter shades, there is a woman's face and body, patterned by rectangular brushstrokes. I notice her curving belly and bright eyes, challenging. Eyes that could open your soul with their sharpness. I know her immediately. Moving closer to it, I touch the painted scarf, her black hair.

—She was pregnant with you.

I study the curve of the belly, Siobhán's name in a corner of the canvas.

—It's the last painting I made, she says. Ida asked me to.

I turn from the painting to the figurines, all wooden. The limbs are long, like dancers.

—They're hers.

Siobhán nods. Setting the painting against the wall, facing us, she goes to open the other side of the armoire, taking a large envelope from a high shelf. I sit with her on the dusty carpet under the lamp as she sorts the photographs, selecting which ones to show me, and spreads them in front of us. Black and white. My mother: black hair, big boots, and a large jacket. She's looking out to vineyards and hills, her face in profile. I've seen many pictures of her—even at this age—but my emotion is still fierce. There is so much of her in the image, something so alive and strong that my stomach twists with longing. Next is a series of her and Siobhán together, making faces, flowers behind their ears, a tenderness and uncertainty in Siobhán's gaze that isn't there now. Siobhán's hair is long and messy, freckles on her nose and cheeks. In another of the pictures, my mother, smiling, is pressing her ear to Siobhán's round stomach. They must have taken the photos themselves. The angles are too close. In a last photograph, my mother is lying supine on a low wall, sticking out her stomach to match the curve of a hill in the distance. Remembering her love of patterns, her body humor, I laugh.

—Where was this? I ask, because all around them is countryside, fields and stone walls.

—Near Beaune, a farmhouse that belonged to an older couple. I let a room there.

The painting faces us, propped against the wall.

—I left London suddenly. I didn't want anyone to know, Siobhán says.

She looks at the painting wearily.

—In some ways, my life has been a success. I've been able to do what I do because I don't get weighed down. I made only one mistake. For a time, I thought it would lead to my greatest happiness. Ella was an error. An affair with someone unworthy.

Siobhán shakes her head.

—Much as I rebelled against my parents, much as I believed in the right to choose, I wanted the child. I don't know why. Ida said I should trust my instinct. I found a farmhouse in France and hid out there until I gave birth. Those were the happiest months of my life.

Siobhán's voice breaks.

—The plan was for Ida to join me. The day she showed up, she told me her news, news of you, due five months after Ella. I'd had a feeling. What I hadn't guessed was that your father had accepted a job in the United States, a good academic job.

I nod. It's the job he still has.

—Ida was meant to join him in September, but she stayed with me until Ella was born. We had four months together, summer into fall.

Siobhán pauses, her voice full of emotion.

—She always knew she'd go but was lagging. We would walk in the vineyards, help in the gardens, and make things. We went to markets. We talked. She kept saying she was too happy in Burgundy to really sculpt, but I still have what she made there. She never came for them.

Siobhán gestures to the figurines in the armoire.

—The sculpture in the gallery, I ask, that, too?

—No. She sent that from London. After she left.

Siobhán gathers up the photos, her hands nervous.

—She wasn't conventional, but she was loyal to your father.

Siobhán looks down quickly, unable to hide a look of pain.

—You know the rest, she says, her voice controlled. Ella went to a friend, who, desperate and thrilled, cut me out of their lives. I did other things. I tried to forget, until, decades later, the two people I'd loved most in the world were lost in the same month. You are neither of them, yet you remind me . . . and you came to get in touch. It made me feel Ella was alive.

So little of this was visible to me. I think how difficult our first meeting must have been for Siobhán, seeing the grown child who had drawn my mother to a different life. From the top photograph in the pile, my mother stares up at me, very alive. I have never seen her so happy.

Siobhán, following my gaze, shakes her head.

—Our lives, she says, Ella's, yours, *everything* would have been different if she'd stayed. I wanted her to. You and Ella would have grown up like sisters.

Siobhán smiles at the ground; then she sighs.

—It wasn't only up to me, she says, standing to replace the envelope of photographs, then closing the door to the armoire.

42

TWO WEEKS PASS. WE FINISH PRINTING. In place of Ella's journals on the writing table I've stacked some of my old books: Bazin, Bergson, and an English translation of a Marker screenplay. I open the screenplay, my eyes lighting on phrases the way they used to with the journals: "I'd have your death / on the tip of my memory." Or: "One day my image would / begin to blur, you'd realize / the scraps / of words, / scraps of life filling your memory, / were shifting out of focus." I flip the page: "A real fairy tale, one of them / falls asleep / and never changes."

Suddenly, I no longer feel like watching the old films or reading the old books. So I walk.

I bring nothing with me on these walks, drifting farther each day from what is familiar. I cross the Périphérique and wander up the canal de Saint-Denis, sometimes as far as the basilica, where I took shelter once during a cloudburst. Doubles of my mother no longer appear, but Ella's words won't leave me. I read somewhere that by killing, you become what you've destroyed.

After the markets and hawkers by the porte de Clignancourt, the canal peels northward from the city until there are no more shops, just cranes and warehouses. Smells are wet asphalt and exhaust from the boulevards. The sky is overcast, yellow with unbroken storms. Across the water, a cement manufacturer—CEMEX emblazoned on the building—raises its silo towers to the clotted sky. By the canal, there are no other pedestrians, only a few scraggly trees.

Ahead, there's a flash of orange—the color of the inside of a nectarine, or of the stiff blossoms of a bird-of-paradise. The flash was smaller even than the stripe of a scarf in dark hair. On a stucco wall a moth lands, pressing its wings together, a somber creature to match the dun-colored buildings and the canal made sluggish by plastic bags and bottles. Then the creature, too large to be a moth, opens its wings of orange, rimmed and spotted with black and violet.

Often, I'm disoriented as I navigate back to the city. When there is sun, I work out which way is south from its position in the sky. Other times, it takes a while to find a landmark. Hunger and thirst don't bother me on these walks, but I eat ravenously when I return. Or else I stop at a bookshop close to home, where the owner is a woman wearing glasses with bright red frames. She is very learned, and she recommends books. Then, reading them in cafés or parks, I recognize human gestures: glances, manners of asking, negotiating, courting, consoling. I pick out a notebook of my own to house this noticing.

Some evenings, I go out with Zoë or Jérémie, or both. They get on well. I meet their friends: artists, photographers, writers. Dinners with Siobhán are full of laughter now, and we've gone together twice to the cinema. Still, for hours each morning, I walk with no purpose or plan. There is a world in color I can't inhabit now that the journals have ended. Or, rather, there are different lives in me now, different threads of lives, and my own is less important. I want to remain in the fiction, delaying my return to the gray.

One afternoon, after a particularly long walk, I lay my head down for a moment on the writing table, my notebook open beside me. A familiar voice wakes me.

—The door was open, it says.

It takes a moment to attach the voice to the body, gesturing to the door propped open in the heat of Indian summer. Z in the flesh. Seeing him feels like a long exhale.

He makes a show of looking around the room, even checking under the bed. I shake my head. No, no, I haven't hidden a lover. We laugh. He finds my waist and brings me next to him.

—I smell like the airplane, he says quietly.

My voice muffled, my cheek grazing the buttons of his shirt, I say:

—You smell like you.

We hold this pose, my cheek against his body, which does smell slightly of airplane and feels strange to me. His lips graze my forehead. He breaks away, moving to the kitchen bar. He pours himself water, asking with his eyebrows if I want a glass.

After almost a year—ten months since our trip to the Loire—I notice things about him that are different, physical details that don't match my memories: gray at his temples, purple half-moons under his eyes. He looks tired.

—Writing? he observes, leaning over the notebook.

I smile, still groggy, not quite believing he is here.

—You look tired, I say.

—You look amazing.

He moves swiftly to catch me in the center of the room.

His kiss finds my cheek.

—You look good but tired, I say.

We are magnets with the same charge, gently pushing each

other around the space. He retreats to the far window. He won't sit down. His large suitcase is still in the doorway.

—How are you here? I ask, knowing how demanding his work is.

He sits down on the bed, grins, and makes a show of reclining.

—Technically, I'm in Brussels. The next round of client meetings *should* be in person but can also be by video call. I have to be back for a presentation on the first, but . . . until then I can work from anywhere.

Ten days. I realize with pleasure that I want Z to stay.

—I'll go if it's not a good time for you, he says.

He sits up, looking at me.

I move next to him on the bed and put a hand on the thigh of his khakis. The gesture feels odd, unlike me. We are nervous around each other.

—You'll be here for the vernissage, I say. There'll be photographs by a Thai artist Ella knew in Chiang Rai. We found descriptions of his work in her journals. Siobhán contacted him through the gallery—

I break off because Z is staring at me.

—What? I ask.

—Nothing.

Ashamed, I think of how Z's anecdotes are always tailored to me. He speaks only of what might interest me, in compliance with some personal code of ethics— burdening others with facts irrelevant to them is out of tune with self-reliance. It gives me the illusion that I know Z completely, and that I'm the focus of his thoughts and days.

—When is it? he asks, stretching out again, propping himself on an elbow.

—The thirtieth, in the evening.

—Do you want me to come?

—Of course.

—Then I'm there. I'll book a night train and leave straight from the varnish thing.

—Vernissage.

—Simple, he says, dusting his hands together.

He pulls me down next to him on the bed, folding me into place in the crook of his arm.

HIS VISIT WEARS AWAY AT BOTH OF US. We've been living on top of each other for a week, working and thinking in the same space, so close that we hardly see each other anymore.

Z gets up early. There are croissants on the breakfast bar, coffee brewed, and his work things by the far window, the corner he has colonized because he likes the chair and the view. When I wake, he comes to sit on the bed to say good morning.

—This is nice, I say—about this routine, about everything we do—until the phrase accretes the automatism of a mantra. *This is good.*

My walks stop. We work in different corners of the room, sometimes making love in the daytime or strolling through the neighborhood or taking the Métro to walk along the quais. Z's mother likes the Botticelli frescoes in the Louvre, so we go look at them. Evenings we talk, and the phrase—*this is good*—beats its refrain under everything we say.

This is nice. Agreement. Accord.

On my way to the gallery, alone, the city is my own again.

Light, people, and façades of buildings come alive and gather my attention. And yet having Z here is good. Very good.

Lately he has grown preoccupied, things untalked about thickening between us. And I wonder more about his life when he's not with me: the atmosphere of his office, bars he likes, weekend drives to parts of New England he's coming to love, people he talks to, cares for.

—Are you seeing someone in Boston? I ask casually, though I know it will trouble an evening that is beginning well.

We've opened a bottle of rosé just as dusk is settling, earlier now, over the city.

—Is that where we are now? Z asks, sarcastic.

I stare, intrigued by his flash of anger, real emotion. Z is always so careful around me.

—You're not under contract, I say, wanting it again, the flash, the real Z.

—I wouldn't do that to you, he says, all control. I'm here for you no matter what.

—But you don't *owe* me anything, I say.

The months I didn't ask him to visit hang between us, unspoken of. I watch his Adam's apple as he swallows, an opportunity opening and closing in the same instant.

—Jesus, Elena, I hope you find God—or, fuck it, the *Buddha* in all your empty space. That's all you fucking want.

He looks out the window. I can't see his face.

—I'm sorry, he says. It's just—I remember things you don't. . . .

He is ready to remind me of promises we made during months only he remembers. He doesn't say more, but his familiar stories are evoked anyway, having left their impressions. I take a sip of rosé, which tastes watery. In conversations over the last months,

I had only Z's voice (rarely a pixelated image, since he prefers the phone). Now I stare at lids low across large dark eyes that refuse to look at me full on.

—I don't get why you left, he says, still angry, why you gave up on your work, your father, everything—*me*—to try to make sense of some other girl's life. I've tried. I don't get it.

He wants a reason.

I think of Siobhán and my mother, of the pictures from Beaune. How to explain that the journals felt important, offering something I needed, or needed to learn?

—I thought I would find Ella, I say, cringing at how ridiculous it sounds.

—No, you didn't, Z says coldly. You were never going to find someone missing for six years by reading her diary. And didn't you say yourself she was *insane*?

The word is too blunt, too harsh.

—I'm sorry, Z says hurriedly.

—I *understand* her.

—I don't, Z says, bitterness returning to his voice.

—She just felt things too much. After a point, she couldn't tell what was coming from her and what from outside her. It could happen to anyone.

—Oh, Z says, his eyes widening. Like your mom.

He comes over, takes my glass, and cups his hands around my elbows, the way he used to.

—Ella's story is not yours, he says. It's a fallacy to think she can help you. By the same token, her death shouldn't scare you.

I want to tell him again that the best things aren't logical. We just need logic so we can talk to one another. But Ella's story *hasn't* unlocked anything. I've learned that my mother was in love, charismatic, adored—and almost nothing about my own life.

—All I have from those months is what you tell me, I say.

He understands my fear, that these months of dissociation link me to her (also to Ella).

—There is *nothing*, not even a smell or a light. I was tired of not knowing. I thought that by helping someone else, I could at least stop thinking about it. Then, through Ella, I could *feel* things. I had dreams—

—Dreams like the one in the Loire? Z asks sharply.

His concern sends chills through me. He brushes the hair back from my face.

—You should try not to worry so much about the missing months, he says reasonably. Maybe your mind will give them back to you when you're ready for them.

We sit down on the edge of the bed and a trembling begins in my arms. Z notices. I force my mind back over the hole in memory. It's like licking my lips. Evening in December, train from New York, where I was living, Union Station, then metro, walking with the bulky portfolio—my photographs to show my mother—I'd come home a week early. The cold and the dark, lit houses, it's all there, vivid and clear. Then lying in a field with Z in hot sun, asking him what day it was and how we got there. His cautious regard, his surprise: *You're back.*

I press harder, forcing the locks of forgetting, knocking at my mother's studio. It was a converted barnlike space beside the house, probably once used as a garage; an old car smell layered itself among the woods, resins, and clays. I remember seeing the dim lights across the yard through her small, high windows. She was working on a collage of wood, metal, and glass; we'd talked about it over the phone. Tightness in my chest as I reached for the door—then Z and that vivid green field. When it became clear how little I remembered, he told me what happened; he cried. I want scenes from that time to stretch into focus, glitch, and then clear. But there is only the field of bright grass and yellow flowers I still don't know how to name. Z the same as ever: I saw "you" again in your eyes. You asked when it was, where you were. You were you.

My first days of memory were as painful as any I can remember. The tragedy came on fresh each day. I'd wake to its reality, shame compounded by the memory of having done the same the day before. I'd look for her, then realize. My body was the same, except thinner, cheeks gaunt, hair longer than I usually wore it. The hair on my eyebrows had grown in. Was it a different self, living those months? My nails were well groomed, short. There was the eerie pressure of time having passed without me. Now I feel cheated, as if writing an end to Ella's story didn't yield the insight it promised. In some recess of my mind, there is a hidden image, a scene, witnessed and forgotten, that will bring everything back. I want that image and what will follow: cliffs eroding at hyperspeed, everything tumbling into view.

The room with Z in it seems to breathe in and out, inflating and disappearing. The air is sticky and hot. Z is saying something I barely hear. The image is there, almost graspable, but out of reach with Z holding me on the bed like something breakable. I need air. I'm still assuring Z I'm okay and telling him not to follow me when I hear the door shut behind me and see the dizzying steps carpeted in red. I run down two at a time, swinging around each landing, then out into the humid night, through streets where ivy tugs down in thick strands along stone walls lit by the moon. I sit in a cobblestone street under a window box of geraniums, my head between my knees. My breath comes fast, in sobs. Z has narrated so many times the events of that night that I've stopped wondering about it. I can almost see it in the darkness: the studio, sheets of glass she hadn't yet cut. They say she died without pain. There was a leak, probably from one of the canisters she used for metallurgy. The studio blurs out, and I see the greenhouse it has become, where my father grows peppers, tomatoes, and red dahlias because she liked their yellow centers. I want to feel what it was like for her, every thought, impulse, sensation. Did she know? Was there fear, panic, pain, or just terrible sweetness at passing into things, becoming material, no longer responsible, or capable of building or wrecking or hurting or pleasing? A different image darts up: her wall of chisels and hammers, air heavy with debris like fog, pieces of sculptures, dust of breakage, carnage of glass and granite, then flames licking up to swallow the drop cloths. Z has told me nothing of this. It must be my own. My memory.

My thoughts fly, trying to piece it together. Had it been not merely her wish to destroy her sculptures but also her act? Is that what I'd seen? A chemical accident in the studio: too vague. Weak fables leave a nervous scrambling, a scratching of the truth they've boarded over.

When her episodes first came on, it wasn't a problem of *not* her, but *more* her, something vigorous in which I delighted, a too muchness I craved and courted: a mood, a capricious charge in the atmosphere. There was a delighted longing in me each time she sailed off—terror, too, because it wasn't what I was supposed to feel. The world she saw was chimerical, more alive than our own. When she was returned to us after weeks away, she was frail, medicated. Not her.

Z has told me the story of my missing months enough times over the years that I can picture certain parts: my hospital room with fluorescent lights and flowers that made it junglelike—a botanical garden. My father, not noticing, brought clippings of the first daffodils. When I came home, we would sit on the porch, listening to the breeze and the sounds of birds. Z would tuck me in at night, not staying. When the cherry blossoms bloomed, I started watching films over and over again because it was the only way I could feel—to see whole lives tucked into hours. I took the parts out of my camera. There were therapists, neurologists, and recommendations to swim and walk, to be outside every day. I want to remember more. My forgetting is the source of all loss.

—Elena! Z's voice rings out from the shadows.

He sits beside me, breathing hard.

—Why did you run like that? he asks.

—I need you to tell me everything, I say, my voice raw. Was my mother ill before she died? What am I not seeing?

Z sighs, shifts so that we can see each other, badly, in the darkness.

—Nothing full-blown, he says. Your dad played it down. We didn't want to worry you. Every doctor who treated you advised him not to tell you unless you asked. But you're wondering if it was really an accident.

I look at him steadily.

—There's no certainty we're keeping from you, Elena. Everything I've told you is true—at least as I remember it. But we don't know. We're probably never going to.

—That's impossible, I say, fighting down panic, feeling again the tenuousness of the story I'd written for Ella, *as* Ella.

—Can you just be okay with not knowing? Z asks, pressing his lips together.

The moon is large and light, crossed by thin clouds. I think again of the image—the second one—of fire and debris in the studio.

—What happened to her sculptures? I ask. Did she destroy them?

Z sits up, looks at me carefully.

—No.

I let the image fade, a false memory, but Z is still looking at me strangely.

—Why do you ask?

I tell him about the image. I must be inventing things. I've gotten good at it.

—It's not made up, he says, his voice hoarse. It was you.

His face is all shadows. What he's saying makes no sense.

—You were scratched up badly, but no burns. You got out before the fire. You cut up your own things, too, prints, negatives. You didn't know what you'd done. Three months after she died.

I go cold with horror. I remember thinking that if I kept my photographs, I'd go the way she did. If I wrecked them, I'd escape. If I wrecked everything, she might escape, too. It's hard to breathe.

—I was like her? I ask, my mouth dry, my father's concern taking on new urgency.

—No, Z says quickly. You knew it was what she wanted. Then June came. You were yourself. It was over.

Z pulls me to him, and we stay pressed together, my tears wetting his face and hair.

After a few minutes, I stand and pull Z up after me, leading him through the narrow streets and down a flight of stone steps.

We're both very hungry. At a brasserie on the rue Caulaincourt, we sit staring at each other until the waiter asks us what we'll have. Seeing oysters on ice, Z orders a dozen. We can do little but tell stupid jokes. We're a little stunned, yes, but we can really laugh the way we couldn't before, when things between us were so heavy.

Eventually, he admits that there is someone in Boston. He hates himself for lying.

—I didn't want to ruin things between us. What we have is more important than anything. But you grew distant. We never saw each other. I didn't know what was happening or where we stood. I tried to be there for you, but I felt like I was crowding you.

Z cups his chin in his hands and looks at me. In his face is something like acceptance, submission to something bigger than himself—an expression I never knew how to see.

Affection wells up. I don't know what to say.

43

HER WORDS WILL COVER THE WALLS. Inhabiting her a last time, I chose a hopeful passage, Ella wondering where the world and she would be in ten years, twenty years. Nothing stays the same when you're alive, she wrote. Perspective pushes out with the years like the rings in ancient trees; old ways of thinking don't disappear, but hug the center and seem smaller as the trunk grows wide. Aurelia, at thirty, was ancient, too, she wrote. But Ella would be nearly that old if she were alive. I try to imagine her my age, hair darkened from living in cold cities, pupils too wide in low light, hungry to take it all in, not to miss anything. If she needs a body, I'll give her mine, to experience things from time to time. I'm calling on her, too, now, a last time. Because the dead with their fixed perspective are good for composing epilogues. It's because the future is all there in the past, encoded. I believe this. But the future is also how you write the past, so I still have some say. It's not too late for me. I'm living.

In the loft, I turn on the projector; it awakens, humming, warming under my hand. I wait for Ella's words to appear in light across the space. Zoë helped make the slides, but it was my idea— to give her some say, she who is fixed now, the heroine tucked too neatly into my slim book, like a guest of Procrustes. Below me in the gallery, the tops of heads are glossy under the lights as people circulate among the photographs and gather in clusters to talk.

Z is standing in front of *Loose Boat,* his black hair wavy under the gallery lights. He'll leave soon to catch his train. Ella's script appears, playing over Z's dark blazer and the photograph in its frame. Her words are hard to see at first, broken over people and images, but with effort I can make them out. They're more familiar than my own.

In the journals, Ella quoted Isherwood, not naming him: a camera with its shutter open, quite passive, recording, not thinking. I've become this, too. I've become her and the writer she cited. We are all one another, borrowed words and images, webbed together in bands of light.

Soon Siobhán will present the artist's book. The heads below will turn to look at the pages. They might notice the way the ink has been absorbed by the paper, evenly. They might glance at the press next to the spiral stairs. The book won't pass into the mind until it has burrowed into the eyes and hands, more *thing* than idea, sculpture as much as book.

Siobhán cleaves the crowd like an arrow to greet Zoë and the short, charming sculptor who loves to laugh. She guides them to *Loose Boat,* where Z leans in to hear what she has to say. She shows the photograph, her body moving with new grace. She is back to wearing suits, but her usual gray blazer is paired with jeans. She seems younger somehow, hair swept loosely to one side, fuller lipstick giving her an air that is almost voluptuous. She isn't the same woman, tight-lipped and exacting, who delivered her proposition so matter-of-factly over a year ago.

Siobhán doesn't see me here, above her sight line. She hasn't noticed the projector image. Her hand flies up to beckon Lek, who sidesteps other conversations to make his way toward her, curling his hair around his ear. He checks his impulse to *wai,* though she would have found this charming. He nods in response to Siobhán, then holds up his cigarettes and moves through the open door, asking a pair of smokers outside for a light. He appears through the glass front, chin down, gray smoke dissolving into the blue night.

He is sturdier than I'd imagined. The Lek in the book is waif-like, barely attached to earth, with long limbs and melancholy features. It was jarring to meet him, days ago, when he arrived, and I spent much of our outing just staring at him. In person, he struck me as both serious and jovial, a joke at the edges of his lips and a playful-mournful gaze, directed always outside himself.

On Lek's first day in Paris, we walked along the quais from Saint-Michel to the pont de l'Alma. The city showed itself differently with him there; he wanted to know the histories of buildings and to check if the city was really made of light. He made us laugh. He said his wife had been to Paris before, when she was a child, and that she would join us for the opening. He put his hand across his belly to show us she was pregnant.

Siobhán laughed.

In the gallery, I scan the lower floor, trying to identify Lek's wife. But there are no Thai women, none that I can see. A woman's voice floats toward me from the base of the stairs.

—You live in London? Aidan asks.

He is the only one in my line of sight.

—We go back to Chiang Rai every year. We love it, the voice is saying. I'm sorry about your niece. I knew her very well. We laughed a lot together.

Béa comes into view as she places a hand on Aidan's arm:

sharp, delicate features, thin lips pursed in observation. She is as Ella described her, but the effect of her presence is different. The world around me flickers a moment, as if it weren't really there.

I look around the gallery: a game of matching people to versions of themselves that may have existed in a different place, in a different time, for someone else.

Siobhán sees me on the ledge and motions. Climbing down the spiral stairs, I join her in front of *Loose Boat*. Silence spreads through the gallery. Faces turn. Siobhán is speaking. Next to me, Lek blushes. Siobhán is holding the book in her hands, indicating the letterpress. People laugh, responding to her words. But in her voice, I hear only emotion, a frequency to which only I am tuned.

As planned, I read a short passage, an account of *Loose Boat*. People clap. Lek jokes that he likes the description better than his photograph. Small currents of energy from the crowd make the space feel very full of everything, full of life.

Z approaches with a copy of the artist's book. He tells me it's *cogent*, which from him is high praise. He says he wishes he didn't have to go, but he has to catch his train. We take his suitcase from the back room, and I walk with him to the boulevard, where the car he called is waiting.

—I'm glad you came, I say.

—It's strange, he says. I'm *proud* of you. You feel different.

Every day, there are more moments from my missing time, isolated flashes—lane markers at the local pool, the grass of the front lawn, the yellow shirt Z liked to wear in those days. No longer my proxy memory, Z is Z. Himself. He puts his arms around me and we stay like that until the driver gets out of the car to take his suitcase. Then he is gone, his taillights disappearing, absorbed into the other lights of the boulevard. It feels like the tide rushing out.

Back at the Ormeau, a small band is playing, and faces are warmed by the liquor and lights. In a corner of the gallery, Béa is talking to a woman with short dark hair. Muay's build. I walk toward them, full of excitement. Then the woman turns, revealing a face that isn't Thai.

I retreat to the table with hors d'oeuvres. It is next to another table, where copies of the book are fanned out. A woman is reading one, her dress lit by the beam of the projector. Watching her read is uncomfortable, as if someone were touching my skin at a sensitive spot, like the stomach, except it is not only *my* stomach—also Ella's, our bodies together. The woman looks to be about Siobhán's age, also my mother's age, and she moves in a way that reminds me of someone, elegant and anxious at the same time.

Scanning the room for an instant, I let myself see them all here: a young man leaning against the back wall, copper hair and linen trousers, dusty sandals and a satchel, gray eyes narrowing at the room. He has cheekbones prominent enough to brighten an otherwise suffering face. He gazes up to the loft, where Ella is now sitting, next to the projector, swinging her legs over the space. Her sarong is sand-worn and bleached. Her T-shirt is almost transparent. Traces of blood on her cracked heels. Long, tangled hair the color of straw. Her face is the face in the picture Siobhán showed me so long ago. They who are absent are probably not how I imagine them at all.

—Elena, Béa says, placing a hand on my arm. This must be strange for you. I'm Béatrice.

—It's great to meet the people Ella cared about, I tell her, though she is right about the strangeness (I know her, and I don't). Are you still in touch with many of them?

—No, apart from Lek. I left Chiang Rai the year after Ella disappeared.

—Do you know what happened to Sebastian? I ask, still searching for information.

It has become a habit.

Béa sighs.

—Not really. To be honest, his reaction to the news about Ella turned me off him. He refused to talk about it at all. And they were so close—everyone thought he was in love with her.

—I thought it was the opposite, I say, perplexed, then suddenly anxious.

The book is there, on the table, full of lies. What if Ella's unrequited love wasn't at all what the journals describe, or I imagined it wrong, or invented it entirely? Béa only shrugs.

—You could never tell where they stood from one day to the next. When he heard she was missing, he went into his house, pulled in all the shutters, and wouldn't talk to anyone.

She shakes her head.

—He refused to socialize with us at all. I went to check on him. There was a student of his he'd started seeing, a pretty Thai girl. We didn't get to really talk. When I went over a few weeks later, with the detective and Siobhán, the neighbors said he had moved to Japan.

—And Aurelia? I ask, absorbing this, trying to imagine how the others reacted.

Béa purses her lips, and a smile breaks across them. She motions to the far end of the room, where Lek is sliding his arm around a blond woman in a cotton dress. The woman turns to whisper something in Lek's ear. She is resting one hand across a large belly.

—Lek was in love with her for years, Béa explains, then finally it happened.

I study Aurelia. She is startlingly pretty, as Ella described her: hair so blond, it looks white. Yet she seems at peace, one hand across her stomach. She is softer. Perhaps she has discovered something, just by living on.

—I have a daughter now, Béa is saying. She plays with their children when we're in Chiang Rai. They have a house in the hills—a bed-and-breakfast.

Alarmed, I stare again at the artist's book.

—Don't worry, Béa says, guessing my concern. She's stronger now. She's open about it. Lek did a shoot of her during her first pregnancy—this will be her third child—it was really sensual, beautiful.

Aidan appears beside us with Siobhán. He points to one of the large framed photographs on the gallery wall, one of fishermen netting their catch, and announces that he and his partner have purchased the print for their flat.

—What about Anthony? I ask Béa, looking at Aidan.

—He never came back, she says. He left all his things in the village. I called him many times, and then one day his mobile number had been given away to someone else.

To put everyone at ease, Béa raises a glass, congratulating Aidan on his purchase.

—What will you do now? she asks me. What are your plans now that the book is done?

Siobhán looks on with interest. I have the sense I've misplaced something. A vague fear, constantly with me, isn't anymore. My own notebooks come to mind, inside of which are stories, other lives. I'll need a job. My British passport (through my mother) makes this possible. Maybe one day the old films and theories will feel urgent, the way the stories feel now. If they do, I'll go back. Siobhán says I can stay in the flat until I find a job.

I laugh, to cover the trembling under it all.

Ella stares out from me a moment, taking in the crowd. She's feeling something stronger than pain—a longing for our living, for the possibility of withstanding what destroys, rocked by moods that pass like monsoon storms, for the knowledge that no matter how long fear sits heavy on your soul, there is always the infinitesimal chance that it will pass, and imagination will run wild in the world again. That's the difference between the dead and the living: the possibility of the impossible, the going on, the not knowing, the inability to epilogue.

Siobhán puts her arm around my shoulders and pulls me close, encouraging. Ella must feel, through me, that Siobhán is hugging her, too.

44

A PATH WINDS THROUGH CLIFFS. Steep stone steps descend into the sea. In the forests by the coast, we track each other under a copper sky split by tawny hues. A light rain begins to fall, rust-colored in the twilight.

I am two. I have descended the stone steps, making no splash. Ella beckons from the water. Her face is blurred, as in a photograph out of focus. Mists steal in across the horizon.

Ella reads to me from the last journal, the lost one. Its pages are underwater. *At the edge of the world, in the salt sea, all channels open.* She ducks under the surface, laughing.

My mother is watching us from the steps. She is drawing something in red chalk on the stones. At first, I think it's a script of ideograms I cannot read. I look more closely and see that it's the image, over and over, of a swimmer, a little body. Her orange scarf billows out against the rust-colored sky.

The air is humid around us, and my hands are not my own. They are tanner, gripping a book that doesn't dissolve in the sea. I've never understood her so well, the whim that sent us beyond ourselves, beyond what we wanted, into something greater. This part is indistinct, but I go over and over it, remembering, until it is clear: My mother, with a quickness that is hers alone, pulls me from the other body, leaving me alone, struggling to hoist myself up via the steps with my shaking arms, stinging with scratches. I crouch on the steps, clinging to them, coughing water, struggling to breathe. The warm mists are gone; the cold is bitter and shrill. My towel and sandals are gone. I walk to the inn along stone and mud paths, between the cliffs, through the village, empty in the spreading darkness. My breath still comes in short gasps. The innkeeper is home when I arrive and rushes to me, alarmed. She says over and over again that I am lucky in view of how fast the tide comes in, in view of the cold front and the storm. She towels me off and draws me a bath so that I'll stop shaking, gives me lavender soap to use and makes verbena tea in a red pot when I am dry and can breathe again. I sleep soundly, without dreams.

AWAKE. THE DAY IS CLEAR. Wide windows let in the early-autumn air that carries hints of things complex, cold, to come. I stand for a moment, breathing the place, savoring the ripeness of the morning. Beyond the dome of the Invalides, the peaks of the Pyrenees rise up, then the sea stretches on to Malta and Cyprus, then over Iran and Afghanistan, India, Thailand, and Indonesia. My gaze floats over the Pacific and across the Americas.

There's a writer somewhere who says that a journal kept by an artist must be banal, compensatory—grounding in the turmoil—full of lists, recipes, appointments, all the particulars that keep a self alive. Ella didn't bother. She looked into the depths and drowned. What else could she have done? Outside the window, a white trace cuts across the blue.

WALKING ALONE. THE CITY OPENS. Leaves scatter across the place des Abbesses with its carousel, painted horses frozen in space, deserted by tourists. Sky the blue of potter's glaze is crossed by tracks of airplanes.

Colors vibrate an instant and are still.

Stones are grown over with vines, like young ruins in the city of the dead. The cemetery stretches beneath the bridge that leads to place de Clichy. Ghosts breathe into spaces sewn by shadows. Under a tree with orange leaves, a woman sits and sketches.

The cover of the artist's book is rough, like the surface of the tombstones or like the skins of elephants. One hundred and fifty copies pressed and bound. The day after the vernissage, I packed all six journals into a briefcase—so light!—and took them to Siobhán.

The cemetery moves like a film in full color and keeps moving. Ella dead, and we keep moving, she in us, her words dilating space like an aperture as I stumble over roots up quiet streets into the world. Streets beyond the cemetery go up and up and I can feel the way time moves in me as I climb, shaping space with my limbs, letting a world rush in, when for so many years I kept it out. Something loosened, opened, and I may never understand, but I go on, climbing the hill to its peak, the sky shaking with color, the city glittering out of thin cloud into color and form, peopled by trajectories, movements through space to the speed of time. Higher still to the steps flowing down from the mouth of the church. In a body, you feel this breaking without dying, this entrance of light, of color, of sound.

ACKNOWLEDGMENTS

WITHOUT ERIKA GOLDMAN'S EDITORIAL GUIDANCE, the book would not have found the shape it now has. Her energy, talent, and stimulating conversations helped focus my vision of the work, and I admire her larger dedication to publishing literature that takes risks. Everyone at or connected to Bellevue Literary Press—Molly Mikolowski, Laura Hart, Joe Gannon, Carol Edwards, Elana Rosenthal—has been delightful to work with. I appreciate their precision and creativity. Thank you to Michael Coffey and Douglas Atkinson, who read and believed in this book, and who each had a special role in helping it find its way into the world. I'd also like to thank my agent, Marya Spence, for her enthusiasm in championing this novel and for being the first to call it an existential detective story.

The Iowa Writers' Workshop and Columbia's School of the Arts provided convivial, peaceful environments in which to write, due, in large part, to the work of Connie Brothers, Deb West, and Jan Zenisek. I'd like to acknowledge the generosity of the Whited Fellowship from the Iowa Writers' Workshop, which gave me valuable time to revise the manuscript. Thank you also to Howard and Patricia Kerr, whose funded fellowship enabled me to attend the Workshop and whose company and conversation I enjoyed so much in Iowa City.

For their insight and encouragement, and for pushing me beyond where the possible seemed to end, I thank Lan Samantha Chang, Paul Harding, Charles D'Ambrosio (especially for the "you are here" sign), Margot Livesey, Rebecca Makkai, Wayne Koestenbaum, and Stacey d'Erasmo. To my peers, many now friends, from whom I learned so much, thank you—especially Raluca Albu, Mia Bailey, Sasha Khmelnik, Claire Lombardo, Paul Maisano, Regina Porter, Will Shih, Nyuol Lueth Tong, and DeShawn Winslow.

I'm grateful to Mui Poopoksakul for expertly vetting my language games at the last minute, and, for other reasons, to the international Beckett community, fierce-witted, wise-hearted people, all. I'd like to acknowledge and thank Tinnakorn Nukul, whose arresting photography inspired *Loose Boat,* and also the Center for Writers and Translators and the Department of Comparative Literature and Creative Writing at the American University of Paris—I'm thrilled to have found such a lively literary and intellectual community.

To my writer friends who read the manuscript multiple times at various stages and talked matters through with me at length, I'm so grateful: Albert Alla, Susan Barbour, Kate Brittain, and Tasha Ong. And to friends who read extensively, commented, or offered conversation, inspiration, and encouragement, thank you, especially Molly Crockett, Lauren Elkin, Nina-Marie Gardner, Violeta Gil, Eliza Gregory, Dan Gunn, Jane Han, Cary Hollinshead-Strick, Rafael Herrero, Delphine Jacq, Matt Jones, Rachel Kapelke-Dale, Alexandra Kleeman, Corinne LaBalme, Ferdia Lennon, Harriet Alida Lye, Spencer Matheson, Mark Mayer, Reine Arcache Melvin, Chris Newens, Helen Cusack O'Keeffe, Lex Paulson, Rosa Rankin-Gee, Jonathan Schiffman, and Erik Zwicker. I'm grateful for your perspective, intelligence, and humor. My love and thanks go also to Jack "Giant" Mahaffey (for sharing his love of Cormac McCarthy), to Mindy (for her stories and her verve), and to all the Dennises.

I've dedicated this book to my mother and father and to my sister, Laura, and would like to thank them here also—for being unflagging in their belief and support, which they put into action in so many ways over so many years. And thank you, Emmanuel, my traveling companion, for sharing the journey and for pointing out magic in surprising places.

ABOUT THE AUTHOR

BORN IN PHILADELPHIA, AMANDA DENNIS studied modern languages at Princeton and Cambridge Universities before earning her PhD from the University of California, Berkeley and her MFA from the Iowa Writers' Workshop, where she was awarded a Whited Fellowship in creative writing. An avid traveler, she has lived in six countries, including Thailand, where she spent a year as a Princeton in Asia fellow. She has written about literature for the *Los Angeles Review of Books* and *Guernica*, and she is assistant professor of comparative literature and creative writing at the American University of Paris, where she is researching the influence of 20th century French philosophy on the work of Samuel Beckett. *Her Here* is her first novel.

BELLEVUE LITERARY PRESS is devoted to publishing
literary fiction and nonfiction at the intersection of
the arts and sciences because we believe that science and the
humanities are natural companions for understanding the human
experience. We feature exceptional literature that explores the nature
of perception and the underpinnings of the social contract. With each
book we publish, our goal is to foster a rich, interdisciplinary dialogue
that will forge new tools for thinking and engaging with the world.

To support our press and its mission, and for our full catalogue of
published titles, please visit us at blpress.org.

BELLEVUE LITERARY PRESS
New York